MAGICALIA

Race of Wonders

JENNIFER BELL

**WALKER
BOOKS**

1

Until a monster swallowed her PE kit, Bitsy's evening had been going to plan.

She'd finished all her homework, tidied her room and defeated her best friend, Kosh, at *Mario Kart*. *Twice*. After dinner, the two of them had blown up an inflatable mattress so he could stay over this weekend while his parents were away and join Bitsy and her dad on a holiday to Paris on Monday. There was only one thing left to do before they could call it a night.

"Recording in three, two..." Bitsy tapped a button on her laptop, adjusted her headphones, and leaned closer to the wireless microphone on her desk. "Hello and welcome to *Poddingham*, the local news podcast for Oddingham village. It's Friday the twenty-ninth of March. I'm your host, Bitsy Wilder, and this week I'm joined by our sports correspondent—"

"—Koshan Ranasinghe!" Kosh declared his Sri Lankan surname like a football commentator announcing a goal. Sitting beside her, he had a tatty Oddingham FC beanie pulled over his floppy black hair and was wearing his usual slouchy T-shirt-and-tracksuit-bottoms combo. "Some of you might also know me as the boy who delivers your newspapers and *accidentally* rides a bike through your flowerbeds. Shout out to Mrs Harris on Bridge Lane for always being so chill about it!"

Bitsy covered the microphone with the sleeve of her cardigan. "Mrs Harris is *not* chill about it, by the way. I saw her yelling at your mum yesterday."

"You did?" Kosh paused. "Maybe edit that bit out."

Shaking her frizzy blonde curls, Bitsy ploughed on. "Coming up, Kosh has the lowdown on last night's football match between Oddingham and Bletchy Town. First, though, the headlines." She flipped open her trusty reporter's notebook and tried to ignore a heavy feeling of disappointment as she read, "*Tarmac trouble*: residents concerned as potholes worsen on Church Street. *Wood you believe it?*: sighting of rare woodpecker thrills local birdwatchers. And *Gotta ketchup-all*: Oddingham gardener grows tomato shaped like Pikachu."

"*Gotta ketchup-all?*" Kosh laughed. "That's got to be one of your best puns yet."

Bitsy gave him a weak smile. As much as she enjoyed devising witty headlines, she wished there was more interesting news in Oddingham. She'd never understood why her dad had relocated from London to such a boring village in the middle of nowhere, but if she was ever going to become a professional journalist, she had to start by reporting the experiences of the community she lived in. Even if that meant talking about lookalike vegetables.

She gazed at the pinboard above her desk, cluttered with newspaper clippings of the articles her mum had written. Matilda Wilder had passed away in a car accident when Bitsy was five, but Bitsy's dad, Eric, talked about her all the time – how she'd been an investigative reporter for the BBC and had adventured around the globe, sniffing out important stories that exposed corruption and fought injustice. Matilda had recorded her investigations in reporter's notebooks too. Someday, Bitsy was determined to follow in her footsteps.

Glancing back at her notebook, Bitsy was about to begin her report on potholes when a rumbling *boom* reverberated around the house.

"What was that?" Kosh asked. "It sounded like thunder … but *inside* the house."

Bitsy slid off her headphones. She could hear voices

talking downstairs – her dad and someone Bitsy couldn't place. Something about her dad's tone made Bitsy's heart race.

Stuffing her notebook into her jeans pocket, she rushed to open her bedroom door. A strange shadow was climbing the stairs. It looked like the outline of a large animal with long whiskers and a bulbous head. *"Dad?"* she called uncertainly. He had a goofy sense of humour; perhaps he was playing a practical joke. "Dad, are you——?"

But her question wedged in her throat as a hamster the size of a bathtub heaved itself to the top of the stairs, wheezing heavily. Amethyst-purple fur covered the beast's entire body, except for a bald patch above its nose where a jagged black rhinoceros' horn protruded. The beast's violet eyes glittered as it spotted the wicker laundry basket on Bitsy's landing. Scurrying forward, it snared the basket in its claws, opened its mouth – revealing four overgrown incisors – and tossed the contents, PE kit and all, to the back of its throat.

"What in the world is *that*?!" Kosh choked, jumping out of his chair.

Bitsy stumbled back. For a split second, she thought she might be hallucinating – after all, a purple hamstoceros couldn't possibly be real – but that didn't explain how Kosh could see the monster too. "I don't know!" she spluttered, diving behind her bedroom door. "Hide!"

Kosh dashed across the floor and flattened himself against the wall beside Bitsy. "Do you think it's friendly? What if it wants to eat us?!"

The wobbly pitch of his voice matched the jumpy feeling in Bitsy's stomach. She peeked through a gap in the door. The hamstoceros was sitting on its hind legs, gobbling the contents of her dad's bookcase. Its diet seemed to consist of absolutely everything... "We need to sneak downstairs and find my dad – he could be in trouble," she whispered, desperately hoping he was OK. As the hamstoceros tramped into her dad's bedroom at the other end of the landing, she steadied her nerves and snuck out from behind the door. "Come on, this is our chance."

They tiptoed towards the stairs. Like most houses in Oddingham, Bitsy's was old and the floorboards were notoriously creaky. Her knees trembled as she crept forward, trying to remember the quiet parts of the landing. Kosh trod carefully in her footsteps, holding his arms out for balance. At the top of the stairs, Bitsy grabbed the banister and lowered her slipper onto the uppermost step...

But as she shifted her weight forward, the door to her dad's bedroom clattered and the hamstoceros waddled out, chewing on one of her dad's work ties. Its cheeks had swollen to the size of beach balls and were now stuffed with so many oddly shaped lumps, the hamstoceros could barely fit its head through the doorframe.

Bitsy froze as the monster caught sight of them. It hastily slurped down the rest of her dad's tie and lowered its horn like it was taking a bow.

Kosh hesitated. "What is—?"

"Yeeee!" With a high-pitched squeal, the hamstoceros charged.

"Not friendly!" Kosh wailed, pushing Bitsy forward. "Go!"

They scrambled down the stairs two at a time as the hamstoceros rammed into the wall behind them. As if struck by an earthquake, the staircase shook in all directions. Plaster crumbled from the ceiling, and a couple of pictures fell off the wall and smashed onto the steps. Coughing dust out of her lungs, Bitsy landed on the ground floor and raced along the hallway. Voices were coming from the lounge.

"Give the book to me!" a woman snarled.

"You can't have it," Bitsy's dad said fiercely. "It doesn't belong to you."

With a burst of speed, Bitsy bolted through the door ahead of Kosh and skidded to a stop in the middle of the carpet.

A tall, raven-haired woman with pale skin was pacing by the TV. Bitsy had never seen her before, but with her shaved undercut, dark eyeliner, combat trousers and heavy biker boots, she cut a striking figure.

"Bitsy!" Eric Wilder blinked at her from behind his steel-framed spectacles. There were tea stains on his jumper and an empty mug rolling back and forth by his feet. "I'm, uh, just dealing with a surprise visitor. Take Kosh back upstairs and—"

But before he could finish, the hamstoceros barrelled through the door behind them, roaring furiously. Clumps of shredded wallpaper dangled from its horn and dust caked its whiskers like it had faceplanted in icing sugar. It surveyed the room and fixed Bitsy and Kosh with a malevolent glare as if to say, *Prepare to join your dirty laundry.*

Eric stiffened. "On second thoughts, both of you get behind me. Now!"

Bitsy grabbed Kosh's arm and they dropped behind the closest sofa. "What's going on, Dad?" she asked breathlessly. "What *is* that thing?"

"It's called a *magicore*," Eric said, backing steadily away from the hamstoceros. "They're powerful beasts conjured from emotional energy. That particular species is conjured from greed."

A beast conjured from greed? The concept pinballed around Bitsy's head, making her dizzy. "I don't understand. What's it doing here? And who's *she*?"

11

The raven-haired woman studied Bitsy with a wry smile. She wore studded leather gloves and a dagger-shaped bronze earring in one ear. Eric glowered at her, pain flickering across his face like it sometimes did when he spoke about Bitsy's mum. "I'll explain later. Just stay down, both of you."

A cold feeling spread through Bitsy's chest like she'd just been stabbed with an icicle. How did her dad know all this? Had he been keeping secrets from her? It didn't make sense.

The raven-haired woman stomped over to the hamstoceros. "Well?" she asked sharply, surveying the monster's bloated cheeks. "Did you find the book?"

As if it had understood the woman's question, the hamstoceros snorted. It wiggled its cheeks like it was gargling with mouthwash and, with a loud clatter, vomited up an assortment of her dad's possessions, including two pairs of shoes, a dozen astronomy textbooks, a long black telescope and a fleecy tartan dressing gown with a hole in the sleeve. Finally, it spewed up a week's worth of Wilder dirty laundry.

The raven-haired woman scrunched her nose as she kicked through the drool-covered pile. "It's not here. Keep hunting."

The hamstoceros huffed and, with its cheeks now shrunk to the size of watermelons, plodded towards a glass cabinet that stood against one wall. Bitsy tensed. The cabinet contained a collection of her mum's journalism awards, plus several souvenirs from her mum's travels.

She sprang to her feet as the hamstoceros smashed through the front of the cabinet, reached inside and began devouring trinkets. "Dad, *do something*!"

Eric's expression tightened. He looked back and forth between Bitsy and the hamstoceros like he was wrestling with a decision. Finally, he pulled a fountain pen from his trouser pocket and aimed it threateningly at the raven-haired woman. "You have until the count of three to take your magicore and leave. One..."

"What's he going to do with *that*?" Kosh whispered as Bitsy crouched back down. "Squirt ink in her face?"

Bitsy shook her head. She'd never seen the fountain pen before.

"Two..."

The woman flared her nostrils. "I don't have time for this. If you won't give me the book, I'll have to take the next best thing." She signalled to the hamstoceros. "Prepare for extraction."

The hamstoceros' fur bristled. It promptly abandoned the statuette it had been about to eat and bared its teeth at Eric.

Eric's fingers tightened around his pen. Bitsy noticed the barrel glowing blue under his touch.

"Three!"

A cloud of twinkling copper particles burst from the pen with a soft crackle. They whirled through the air like a murmuration of starlings and formed a wavy sausage the width of Bitsy's thigh. The sausage wriggled, and the particles blew away...

...to reveal a flying, silver caterpillar. Beneath its transparent skin, its body appeared to be made of dense fog that flickered with electrical sparks.

Kosh's mouth fell open. "Tell me you see..."

"I see it," Bitsy said, squeezing his arm. Her pulse was racing. Had her dad just conjured a – what had he called it? – *magicore*?

The caterpillar had a round face with a tiny black mouth, neon-blue eyes and a pair of squidgy antennae. As it whipped through the air, it kept changing direction like it wasn't sure which way to go.

Bitsy's dad smiled at the caterpillar like it was an old friend. "Quasar, over here. I need your help."

The caterpillar zoomed to Eric's side and nuzzled against his ribs, causing a fine layer of Eric's sandy-blond hair to stand on end from a static build-up. Was Quasar the magicore's name? Eric was an astrophysicist and had once told Bitsy that a quasar was a brightly shining nucleus in space...

"Protect Bitsy and Kosh at all costs," Eric told Quasar

firmly. He jabbed a finger at the hamstoceros. "And extinguish that magicore!"

On command, Quasar whirled around to face the hamstoceros. It wiggled its bottom and shot towards its opponent like a giant silver bullet. The hamstoceros growled and lowered its horn. Just as it prepared to charge, Quasar hurled a bolt of electricity at its feet.

A loud clap pierced the air, making Bitsy flinch. The hamstoceros squealed and rocketed to the ceiling in a cloud of smoke. Shrieking in outrage, it rushed at Quasar, slashing with its claws. Broken furniture went flying as the two magicores grappled with each other, tearing around the room in a purple and silver blur.

In the tussle, the hamstoceros got its foot tangled in the electrical cord of a table lamp. The lamp went flinging through the air and struck Eric hard on the side of the head.

"Dad!" Bitsy cried, jumping up.

"Bitsy…?" he slurred, wobbling forward. "Stay—"

But then his pupils rolled back in his head and he collapsed onto the floor like a sack of potatoes. Although Bitsy could see his chest moving, the rest of his body was motionless.

"Look out!" Kosh yanked on Bitsy's leg and she ducked just in time as a flaming table leg came frisbeeing over their heads and smashed into the wall behind.

She protected her face with her arms as fiery debris rained over them. "We have to help my dad!"

But her voice was drowned out by another rumble of thunder. Lightning flared across the ceiling. The floor vibrated.

Then all at once, the room fell quiet.

Bitsy listened carefully for sounds of movement but there was nothing.

"Is it over?" Kosh asked, lifting his head out from under his arms.

Gripping the sofa tightly, Bitsy pulled herself to her feet.

The room looked like a bomb had hit it. Scorch marks peppered the walls, ripped cushions and broken furniture lay strewn across the floor, and sparks jumped from a crack in the TV. A splintered heap of wood rested in the middle of the carpet where a coffee table had once been.

But the damage wasn't what troubled her. As Bitsy surveyed the room, a bubble of panic rose to the back of her throat.

The raven-haired lady, the hamstoceros, Quasar and her dad…

They had all vanished.

2

"This is impossible," Kosh said, emerging shakily from behind the sofa. "They can't have just disappeared into thin air."

Adrenaline was still coursing through Bitsy's veins as she staggered into the centre of the room. "Then where did they go? They didn't escape into the garden because the patio doors were locked, and the only other exit was via the hallway behind us." She paused as she pictured her dad sprawled on the carpet. "Also, my dad was unconscious. He couldn't have moved anywhere." Her insides churned with worry. She had to find him.

"In that case, the goth lady must have taken him somewhere," Kosh concluded. "It's the only explanation. The question is: why?"

A feeling of dread crept over Bitsy as she remembered something the raven-haired woman had said. "She was looking for a book. She warned my dad that if he didn't give it to her, she'd be forced to take the next best thing. I think… I think she meant *my dad*. When she told her hamstoceros to prepare for extraction, she must have been referring to him! Kosh, he's been kidnapped!"

It suddenly felt like the room was spinning. Bitsy had no idea where her dad was or what was happening to him. But that woman looked dangerous. She grabbed Kosh's arm to steady herself, feeling woozy.

"It's going to be all right," he said, squeezing her shoulders. "Listen to me. Wherever she's taken him, we'll find him together."

Bitsy nodded, but her head was swimming. *Conjuring… Magicores…* How was she going to rescue her dad when she didn't even understand what was going on?

Kosh pulled his mobile phone out of his pocket and tapped the screen.

"We can't call emergency services," Bitsy said, shaking her head. "If we tell them Dad's been snatched by a lady with a hamstoceros, they'll just think we're pranking them. No one in the village is going to believe us, either. And your parents are away."

"I'm not dialling 999 or my parents," Kosh said,

holding his phone to his ear. "I'm calling your dad. If he's got his mobile with him, we can track his location."

Hope blossomed in Bitsy's chest, although it wilted a moment later when the voice of Buzz Lightyear rang out from the sofa.

"To infinity … and beyond!"

Her dad's ringtone. She rummaged under the cushions and found his Samsung lodged in a crevice at the back. Her spirits plummeted further as she swiped at the screen and saw that the device had a biometric lock. She couldn't even search it for information. "Any other ideas?"

Before Kosh could offer a suggestion, something buzzed under the broken coffee table. It sounded like an enormous bee.

Bitsy stepped closer. The rubble was vibrating. She poked her foot inside the heap and glimpsed a patch of silver. "It's Quasar!" she realized.

Together, they tossed away the splintered wreckage, freeing Quasar from beneath. The caterpillar's antennae had been flattened and there was a dazed look in its blue eyes. It hummed on and off like a defective generator as it levitated unsteadily into the air.

"Whoa…" Kosh murmured, his eyes wide.

Goosebumps rippled along the backs of Bitsy's arms as she watched electricity light up Quasar's foggy innards.

The air around Quasar smelled fresh and metallic like rainwater. She still didn't understand how Quasar could exist; everything about them seemed impossible.

Kosh signalled to a dark gash in Quasar's side. "Looks like it was injured in the fight. How are we going to help it? We can't exactly call a vet."

"I don't know," Bitsy admitted worriedly. She gently lifted a hand towards Quasar's glassy skin. Her scalp tingled as her fingertips made contact, and she felt her hair go static like her dad's had earlier.

Quasar turned to look directly at her. With no obvious nose, all of the magicore's expression came from its eyes, mouth and antennae. Its lips parted and its cheeks twitched, almost as if it was trying to smile...

And then it spat in Bitsy's face.

A small projectile hit her on the bridge of her nose and bounced to the floor. "Ouch!" She rubbed the spot where it had struck. "What was that for?"

"Bitsy, look!" Kosh reached down and picked up her dad's fountain pen. "Quasar must have been keeping this in its mouth."

Bitsy didn't understand how Quasar had got hold of the pen. The last time she'd seen it, it had been clutched in her dad's hand. She took the pen from Kosh and wiped it clean on the bottom of her cardigan. The barrel was made from smooth brown stone, marbled with lightning-bolt seams of copper. As she turned it over in her hand, the stone glowed where her skin had touched it: red, yellow, purple, green, white and blue. She remembered it had reacted to her dad's touch, too, except it had only changed to blue. "Perhaps it's heat sensitive?" she guessed, passing it back to Kosh.

The barrel shimmered the same six colours when he held it. "It looked like your dad used it to conjure Quasar. Sort of like Quasar came *out* of the pen."

He returned the pen to Bitsy and she tried aiming it in front of her like she'd seen her dad do. She tightened her grip around it, but no flecks of twinkling dust appeared. She experimented by twisting the top of the pen and pressing the nib against the back of her hand, but nothing happened.

"Something's wrong," Kosh said, pointing at Quasar. The magicore was shaking. The fog inside its body had darkened and its electrical sparks sputtered like a dying car engine.

Bitsy stuffed her dad's pen into her pocket and tried to cradle Quasar in her hands. "What should we do?!"

"It's made of electricity, so maybe we should connect it to a live wire?" Kosh flapped his arms. "Or, I don't know, feed it batteries?"

Quasar bobbed forward and wobbled to a stop in front of the glass cabinet containing Matilda Wilder's awards and souvenirs. Its antennae strained as it attempted to point to something on the bottom shelf.

Bitsy glanced between the cabinet and Quasar, realizing the magicore was trying to tell them something. "What is it, Quasar?"

But she was too late. The final sparks inside Quasar fizzled out and the magicore burst into copper dust. The particles twinkled as they fell through the air, disappearing before they reached the floor.

Kosh's jaw slackened. "How did…? What even…?"

A lump rose to the back of Bitsy's throat as she realized Quasar was gone. She might have only known the caterpillar for a few minutes, but she had seen how friendly it was with her dad, like a family pet.

She dropped to her knees in front of the cabinet, determined to understand what Quasar had been trying to communicate. "Quasar used the last of its energy to direct us over here. There's got to be something important it wanted us to see."

She examined the bottom shelf of the cabinet. Behind a couple of toppled photo frames, a wooden flute was mounted on a silver tripod. Her dad had told her that her mum had purchased the instrument on a trip to Austria, although Bitsy had never been sure why. Her mum couldn't play the flute. She stretched her hand towards it, but when she went to pull it out, it wouldn't budge.

"Found anything?" Kosh asked.

"There's a flute down here, only it's stuck." Bitsy tried wiggling the tripod and the flute in different directions, but it felt like they were glued together to the base of the cabinet. As she repositioned her fingers for a better grip, she pressed several of the flute's keys … and heard a soft *click*.

The floor vibrated. Bitsy scrabbled back as a crack appeared down the cabinet's centre, splitting it in half. The two sides slid soundlessly away to reveal a small, brick-lined space no bigger than a cloakroom. Inside was an ornate chest of drawers, inlaid with ebony and mother-of-pearl.

"A secret room…" Kosh gawped as he stepped inside. "It's like something out of James Bond."

Bitsy pushed herself to her feet, struggling to understand how she didn't already know about this. She pictured the layout of the ground floor of her house. Behind this wall were the kitchen and the hallway, only … there had to be this hidden space between.

As she shuffled over the threshold, the cabinet closed behind her and a ceiling light flickered on. Bitsy spotted a lever on the back of the cabinet and gave it a tug. The cabinet silently rolled apart again. "Well, we know how to get out," she muttered. "But what is this place? Why would my dad have it here?"

"I don't know, but Quasar wanted us to find it for a reason." Kosh opened the drawers in the chest. The first was empty, but the second contained three puzzling objects.

"Are those *leaves*?" Bitsy lifted out a small, toothed comb made of silver birch wood. It was covered in flaky white bark and had new leaves sprouting along its spine, as if the wood was still alive. "How can this be growing? There's no light or water in here."

Kosh inspected another item – an intricately twisted wooden key attached to a long gold chain. It was made of rough, lumpy plant roots covered in emerging shoots and was shaped into a capital letter E. "This is still growing, too. E for Eric – this must belong to your dad."

Bitsy wondered what the key opened. It was too large for any regular keyhole.

The final item was a brown, teardrop-shaped pendant hanging from a length of black cord. Bitsy's heart fluttered when she saw it. "This was my mum's! I've seen her wearing it in old photos." She picked it up and noticed the pendant glowing in different colours under her touch. "It must be made from the same stone as my dad's pen. Maybe my mum used it to conjure magicores, too…" Her chest stung, realizing her mum had secrets she didn't know about.

Tucking the pendant into her pocket, Bitsy returned the wooden items to the drawer and continued searching.

The remaining drawers were empty, apart from one at the bottom. Stored inside was a large, old, leather-bound book with discoloured pages. Bitsy removed it from the drawer and placed it on top of the chest. Its brown cover was damaged with scorch marks and water stains, and there were three slashes down the spine that looked worryingly like claw marks. Similar to the comb and key, tiny green shoots poked out of the book's headband, as if a living plant had trussed together its pages. Embossed in gold letters on the front cover was a single word: *MAGICALIA*.

"The woman who kidnapped Dad was looking for a book," Bitsy said, glancing nervously at Kosh. "This could be it."

Eager to learn more, she hooked her fingers under the cover and heard the pages crackle as she lifted it up. The endpapers were printed with a detailed world map drawn in muted shades of green and blue. Written in ornate script at the top were the words CARTA MAGICORA and a date, 1676. Bitsy had seen antique maps in museums before, but this one was different. Scattered across the oceans and lands were paintings of strange beasts labelled with tiny red text.

"Magicores," Kosh said, marvelling. He squinted to examine a key in the top left corner of the map. "It has their *species name* and *source emotion* written below them. Didn't your dad say that magicores are conjured from emotional energy? That might be what a source emotion is – the emotion a species is conjured from."

There were so many different species; Bitsy didn't know which to study first. In one scan she saw an enormous, flaming-hooved *grudgernaut* conjured from anger; a ghostly *flabberghast* conjured from surprise, and an impish *proxiwig* conjured from impatience. She pointed to a silver caterpillar floating above Brazil. "This looks just like Quasar – a *waywurm* conjured from confusion."

A line appeared between Kosh's eyebrows. "Quasar did give off really confused vibes. It was zipping around erratically like it was permanently disorientated, and its body was made of fog, which is exactly what your brain feels like when you get confused."

"You're right," Bitsy agreed. "Maybe magicores are similar to their source emotions in some ways? The hamstoceros was a bit like greed – grasping and powerful with an uncontrollable desire to take whatever it wanted."

Kosh tapped the date at the top of the map. "If this was drawn in 1676, then magicores have been around for about three hundred and fifty years. So, how do we not know about them?"

"My dad might be able to answer that," Bitsy said hollowly. Knowing he had hidden something this momentous from her was a bitter pill to swallow.

Although she was itching to ask him about everything, she couldn't help but feel deflated that he'd never revealed any of it before. What else hadn't he told her?

But the questions would have to come later. First, she had to get him back.

She flicked past the map, to the very beginning of *Magicalia*. A paragraph of printed text filled the first page:

NOTE TO READER

Magicalia is the name for the kingdom of organisms known as magicores. Although these extraordinary creatures share some of the same powers, each species has its own unique gift. These are grouped into six types and indicated by the magicore's eye colour.

Armourer *magicores are red-eyed and have a remarkable physical gift*

Clairvoyant *magicores are white-eyed and can influence the minds of others*

Elemental *magicores are blue-eyed and have the ability to control a particular force, energy or element*

Metamorph *magicores are yellow-eyed and are talented at transformations*

Weaver *magicores are green-eyed and can craft remarkable objects*

Hunter *magicores are purple-eyed and skilled in seeking particular things*

Readers are cautioned to conjure magicores at their own risk. The publisher shall not be liable for any injury, loss of limb or death arising from any information contained in this book.

Bitsy glanced worriedly at Kosh before turning the page. A shining, gold-leafed capital *A* sat at the top of the next sheet. Written below was a list of magicores, organized alphabetically by their source emotion:

agitation
HUFFLUFF
[Armourer, gamma-level]

The huffluff is an extremely fidgety magicore with a flat, rectangular body that goes limp when the huffluff is frightened. Its eyes, ears, nose and mouth are located on its smooth, rose-pink underside, while its back is covered in a layer of wiry grey hair. The huffluff is a graceful flyer, even whilst carrying extraordinary weight on its back. Due to its restless nature, it never stays in one place for too long.

28

amazement
LORPLE
[Hunter, beta-level]

The nocturnal lorple is a furry beast weighing between thirteen and twenty pounds. It is quiet and slow-moving, with long arms and legs. The lorple has the largest eyes of any species of magicore, and its vision can penetrate materials as dense as lead. Like all hunter species, it is excellent at tracking and has a particular gift for hunting knowledge. Wild lorples have been known to gather on hilltops with beautiful vistas.

amusement
HIX
[Clairvoyant, alpha-level]

The hix is a mischievous and fun-loving magicore, known for its remarkably ticklish hair which can grow up to two feet long. It can weigh anywhere between six and thirteen pounds and is around a handspan wide. It has a spherical body and moves by rolling around at high speed. Once a hix has made someone laugh, it has the power to temporarily persuade them of anything. Its fur varies in colour from sunset orange to shades of red and gold.

29

"It's like an encyclopaedia of magicore species," Bitsy realized. "I wonder what the different levels represent?"

Kosh scratched under his beanie. "Maybe they've got to do with how powerful each species is or how difficult they are to conjure? We should look up 'greed' to find out more about the hamstoceros. It might tell us something about your dad's kidnapper."

Right at that moment, *Magicalia* rustled. A wodge of pages flipped over as if a breeze had lifted them, although Bitsy didn't feel any shift in the air.

"OK…" Kosh murmured. "Am I imagining it or did *Magicalia* just move by itself?"

Bitsy's skin prickled as she looked down and saw that the encyclopaedia now lay open on the entry for "greed". "I think you might be right," she admitted, nervously. "Look what's written here – it's as if the book heard what we were saying."

Feeling equal parts alarmed and amazed, she turned her attention to the text.

greed
GROBBLE
[Hunter, gamma-level]

Weighing anywhere between sixteen and thirty stone, grobbles resemble giant rodents with stout bodies,

round ears and long whiskers. Their thick fur is highly insulating and the horn above their nose is strong enough to pierce steel. They have a special gift for hunting gold and can detect deposits of the element from up to one mile away. Unique amongst hunter-type magicores, grobbles gather information by eating the objects around them. They have the strongest constitution of any species of magicore and have been known to store twice their own body weight in their extraordinarily stretchy cheek pouches.

Bitsy couldn't believe what she'd just read. The grobble, *née* hamstoceros, had been eating objects in her house in order to *gather information*. It was certainly one way of learning new things, although she didn't much fancy munching her way around her chemistry classroom in order to get a better understanding of the structure of an atom. She ran her finger across the page, rereading the entry. "If grobbles have a special gift for hunting gold, then maybe this *is* the book Dad's kidnapper wanted. There's gold leaf on some of the pages; she might have been using the grobble to detect it."

She fetched her notebook from her pocket. If she was going to rescue her dad, she needed to know more about the woman who had kidnapped him: who she was, what she wanted and where she had taken him.

As she started scribbling ideas, Kosh reached into the bottom drawer. "Hey, look. There's something else in here."

He pulled out a small brown envelope addressed to Eric Wilder, which had already been torn open along the top. Bitsy put her notebook down, took the envelope from Kosh and slid out a sheet of thick paper from inside. Typed upon it was a short letter with a design at the top showing a galleon within a ring of silver stars:

The European Conservatoire of Conjuring
Chancellor's Desk
3 January 2024

Dear Mr Wilder,

It is my duty to inform you, as per the terms of the 1889 Statute of Conjuring, that any person aged twelve years or over, with at least one conjuring parent, is required to undergo a cosmodynamics test at their nearest conservatoire of conjuring.

My records indicate that your daughter, Miss Elizabeth Wilder, will turn twelve years old on the

26th of July. Therefore, with your permission, I would like to invite her to attend a cosmodynamics test on the 27th of July. This test will decide whether Elizabeth has an aptitude for conjuring magicores. If the test is positive, she will be invited to enrol at the conservatoire to study conjuring in the summer term.

I have written to Elizabeth's cosmodian, Miss G. Greynettle of 7 Andromeda Mews, to inform her of our invitation.

Please feel free to contact me should you wish to discuss this matter further.

Yours sincerely,
Chancellor Edith Hershel

Bitsy's hands trembled as she finished reading. "Kosh, this is about *me*. I've been invited to be tested at some sort of school to see if I can conjure magicores like my dad."

"Is that what *conservatoire* means?" he asked, reading over her shoulder. "School?"

She nodded, her gaze fixed on the letter. The last thing she'd been expecting was for any of this to connect to her. Why hadn't her dad said anything? "The letter's dated January. My dad received this nearly three months ago..."

"Maybe he wanted to tell you, but something happened and he couldn't?" Kosh suggested. His eyebrows knitted as he scanned the final paragraph. "Do you know who this other person is? *Miss G. Greynettle?*"

Bitsy shook her head. *Cosmodian* sounded like a professional title, but she had never seen the word before.

Kosh took out his mobile phone and googled the address. By a stroke of luck, there was only one result. "Andromeda Mews is in Kensington, West London."

"That's only a few hours away on public transport," Bitsy realized. "We've got to go check it out. It's our only lead."

"All right, but it's too late to get a train to London now," Kosh said, noting the time. "We'll have to leave first thing in the morning."

Bitsy's stomach tightened. She didn't want to wait until tomorrow to continue their investigation. She wanted to start looking for her dad now. She looked Kosh in the eyes. "Fine, let's go tomorrow. But are you sure you want to come with me? It might be dangerous."

Kosh gave a determined frown. "I told you, wherever that woman's taken your dad, we'll find him together. He's like family to me, too; I'm not about to let you rescue him without me." He added quickly, "Besides, it can't be more dangerous than school dinners and I eat those every day."

Bitsy laughed. Somehow, even in the most daunting of situations, Kosh could always lift her spirits.

She returned her notebook to her pocket, collected *Magicalia* and the Chancellor's letter, and left the secret room. Pausing by the pile of grobble vomit in the lounge, Bitsy picked up her dad's dressing gown. He had been wearing it earlier that morning as he made her breakfast. She pictured him in the kitchen, pouring her a glass of orange juice with one hand while stuffing a slice of bread into the toaster with the other. Despite the gown being covered in grobble-slobber, Bitsy clutched it tightly to her chest. It still smelled like him, of pencil shavings and aftershave.

Hold on, Dad. We're coming.

3

It was early morning, but the parade of designer cafés and high-end boutiques on Kensington High Street was already buzzing with activity. Staff were busy laying tables or vacuuming floors while locals sauntered by, walking their dogs. The air hummed with the drone of traffic and the clang of distant building works.

As Bitsy and Kosh walked past shop windows, Bitsy tried to push down her frustration at all the unanswered questions whirring through her head. She and Kosh had spent the train journey searching through *Magicalia* and asking it questions – where was her dad? Who is Miss G. Greynettle? What does *cosmodian* mean? But the book had remained still. Either it was no longer listening to them or it didn't have the answers they needed.

Kosh glanced at his phone and then pointed towards a row of leafy chestnut trees in the distance. "That's the edge of Kensington Gardens. We need to take a right opposite there to get to Andromeda Mews. It's twelve minutes' walk away."

The journey so far had been relatively straightforward: a bus from Oddingham to the local train station, a high-speed train to London and then an underground train to High Street Kensington. Bitsy had taken her dad's wallet and paid for everything using his debit card, which in the circumstances, she didn't think he'd mind. She pushed her hand inside her satchel to reassure herself that *Magicalia* was still there beside her dad's fountain pen and her mum's teardrop pendant. The letter from Chancellor Hershel she'd tucked in her coat pocket next to her notebook, while the wooden comb and key were hidden in the secret room back home. "Assuming we find Miss G. Greynettle at this address, I don't think we should tell her about *Magicalia* or the other items we've discovered," Bitsy said. "At least, not until we know we can trust her."

"Copy that," Kosh replied.

As Bitsy's fingers grazed her dad's fountain pen, she worried whether he might need it, wherever he was. She hoped not.

They turned off the main road and continued along a few side streets until they came to a cobbled lane flanked by modest terraced houses. It looked unassuming and quiet – not the kind of place you'd expect anyone involved with magicores to be living.

"It's this one." Kosh stopped outside a small, shabby-looking building with cracked pebble-dashed walls. Several of the roof tiles were missing and a broken section of drainpipe had been repaired with string and tape. The white front door had a brass knocker shaped like a shield with a lily in the centre.

As Bitsy approached the door, she took a deep breath and tried to focus. This was their first real opportunity to learn why her dad had been kidnapped and how they might rescue him. She reached up and banged the knocker. After a few seconds, a shadow moved behind the glass.

"One moment!" called a chirpy voice.

Bitsy heard several clicks and scrapes that sounded like multiple locks being undone. There was a creak and then the door opened onto a stocky, olive-skinned woman in a pinafore dress and long-sleeved blouse.

"Yes?" she asked, smiling. She had twinkly hazel eyes and an abundance of silver waves that were fixed in a wobbly pile on top of her head with what appeared to be a chopstick. Deep wrinkles extended around her mouth and eyes.

Bitsy blinked. "Are you Miss G. Greynettle?"

"That's right." Miss Greynettle arched an eyebrow. "And who might you two be?"

Trying to hold her nerve, Bitsy fetched the letter from Chancellor Hershel. "My name's Bitsy and this is my friend, Kosh. We got your address from this letter. It says you're my … *cosmodian*?"

Miss Greynettle's mouth shrank to a small "o". "Elizabeth Wilder? Does your father know you're here?"

"No," Bitsy said, relieved that Miss Greynettle at least knew who she was. "That's why we've come. He's been kidnapped and we need your help."

"*Kidnapped?*" Miss Greynettle swayed. "You'd better come inside. Quickly."

She ushered them into a draughty hall with threadbare carpets and shut the door behind them. The air inside smelled clean and fresh, like cotton sheets. "Your father didn't say you use the name Bitsy," she muttered, signalling for them both to remove their shoes. "You can call me Giverna."

As Bitsy kicked off her trainers, she spotted a rucksack stuffed with medicine vials, brown bottles and bandages at the foot of the stairs. "What *is* a cosmodian?" she asked, wondering if Giverna might be some type of doctor.

"Your father still hasn't told you?" Giverna tutted as she placed their trainers on a rack by the door. "A cosmodian is a conjuring mentor. Young conjurors-in-training are

39

called *initiates*. They hone their skills at conservatoires like the one where you were invited to attend a cosmodynamics test."

She spoke so breezily that it was as if she was talking about something completely normal. Bitsy had to shake off her shock in order to concentrate.

"A negative test result indicates the participant is cosmotypical and unable to conjure magicores, but a positive test result indicates the participant is cosmodynamic and can become an initiate," Giverna explained. "If successful, every initiate has a cosmodian with whom they can talk about their training. Your parents asked me when you were born, should your cosmodynamics test be positive, if I would be your cosmodian. I was one of their tutors at the European Conservatoire, but I retired a few months ago."

Bitsy shared an incredulous glance with Kosh as Giverna led them along a narrow corridor, towards the back of the house. She'd always known her parents had met at school, only she'd assumed it was the type of school where you studied maths and English, not magicores and conjuring.

They entered a bright room with floor-to-ceiling windows along one side that overlooked a well-tended vegetable garden. A network of tarnished copper pipes scaled the walls, passing through cupboards and feeding into various beakers, flasks and test tubes before channelling into a wide porcelain sink. Given the presence of a fridge and cooking stove, Bitsy couldn't tell if Giverna used the room as a kitchen or a laboratory. In the middle of the ceiling, a dusty stained-glass chandelier cast muted rainbow splinters onto a wooden dining table below. Giverna pulled out a couple of chairs on one side. "First things first, have either of you had breakfast? I can make you some toast."

Bitsy had tried to eat earlier but her stomach felt like a cement mixer. "Thanks, but I'm good," she said, pulling out her notebook as she took a seat.

"I would love some toast," Kosh replied, happily. Although he'd already munched a large bowl of cereal and an apple before they'd left, Bitsy was pleased. Kosh's mood was directly linked to his stomach and she did not want a hangry partner on this rescue mission.

"Excellent. You can't solve problems on an empty stomach." Giverna slotted two slices of bread into a toaster and collected three glass mugs out of a cupboard. Like the other cookware on display, the mugs looked like they might have come from a laboratory. They had twisted glass stems and strange markings up the side, like on a measuring flask. "I'll make some chamomile tea, too."

Bitsy skimmed the questions in her notebook, wondering which to ask first. "Do you know why

Dad has never told me anything about magicores or conjuring before?"

A sad look crossed Giverna's face as she carried a kettle to the sink. "After your mother passed away, your father turned his back on the conjuring world. He moved to your village to try to forget it all. When I received my copy of that letter, he told me he didn't want you to take a cosmodynamics test and that would be the end of it."

So that's why we moved to Oddingham... Bitsy fell back in her chair. She wished her dad could have told her this himself.

"You said he'd been kidnapped?" Giverna prompted, turning on the tap and holding the kettle underneath.

"By a woman with a grobble," Kosh explained. "It happened yesterday evening."

"A *grobble*?" Giverna recoiled. "What did the woman look like?"

Bitsy turned back a few pages to consult her notes. "Tall with pale skin and dark hair. She had a dagger-shaped earring in one ear."

The kettle wobbled in Giverna's hand, sending water sloshing into the sink. A scowl deepened on her brow. "Melasina Spires," she growled. "The leader of the Hunter Guild."

"What's the Hunter Guild?" Bitsy asked. She instantly didn't like the sound of it.

"To answer that, I need to tell you a story. It's one that initiates usually hear on their first day of training." Giverna returned the kettle to the side and switched it on. She reached into the pocket of her dress and pulled out a white cotton handkerchief printed with tiny multicoloured polka dots. As she spread it flat on the table in front of Bitsy and Kosh, the polka dots started *moving*.

Bitsy leaned closer, staring. At first, the polka dots whizzed around chaotically, bumping into each other like static-charged polystyrene balls. But then they moved with purpose, shifting into a pattern of coloured pixels.

"This is a thinkerchief," Giverna explained, keeping one hand on one corner of the fabric. "They're made by thimbulls – weaver-type magicores conjured from sympathy. Conjurors use them to display what *they're* thinking."

As Giverna spoke, the pixels on the thinkerchief resolved into the image of a shaggy-haired yak with six horns sprouting from its temple. Threads of white yarn were looped between its horns like the string of a cat's cradle. It seemed to be spinning another small white handkerchief.

A thimbull, Bitsy guessed, scribbling notes. It looked both cuddly and terrifying. The pixels shifted and the thimbull was replaced by a fireball streaking through a dark night sky.

"Long ago," Giverna went on, "a meteorite landed on a remote island in the Atlantic Ocean. It was found in 1656 by the six surviving crew members of a shipwrecked vessel. Exposure to powerful cosmic matter at the landing site affected the crew on a cellular level, turning them cosmodynamic. They named the meteorite *farthingstone* and discovered that they could use it to conjure powerful beasts to do their bidding. Magicores."

The image on the thinkerchief changed. It showed the bottom of a sandy crater where six men with straggly hair and ragged, old-fashioned clothes were gathered around a mammoth boulder of metallic rock. One wore a once fine coat and bicorne hat; one carried a bag of navigational equipment and another wore a sleeveless shirt and knife through his belt.

"The crew were from all over the world and had different beliefs and values. Gradually, they learned that each of them was able to conjure a different type of magicore, according to their personality. The ship's creative carpenter could conjure weaver-types; the kindly surgeon could conjure clairvoyant-types; the brave gunner could conjure armourer-types and so on. After the crew escaped the island, they brought the farthingstone to England, where they split the meteorite into six pieces. They each wanted to use magicores for a different purpose, so they founded six different guilds of conjurors. They pledged to keep secret what they had learned, and to work together in an alliance to use their gifts to benefit humanity from the shadows, hidden from the rest of the world."

Bitsy's heart raced as Giverna's story swirled through her head, like whispers from the past. The old map at the beginning of *Magicalia* made sense now, although Bitsy still couldn't believe this had really happened hundreds of years ago and yet nobody knew about it. She leaned closer as the pictures on the thinkerchief altered to show six coats of arms. They were shaped like shields with different objects inside each one.

"These represent the different guilds?" Kosh guessed.

"That's right. Bitsy's father is a member of the Elemental Guild." Giverna pointed to a blue shield with a telescope in the centre. "Elementals are curious, bookish and experimental. They use their magicores to make progress in science and technology, exploring new fields of discovery and learning more about the universe. Eric used to work in one of the Elemental Guild's laboratories when Bitsy was small."

Bitsy's forehead tightened. She didn't remember that, but she did recognize her dad in Giverna's description. He was always reading and asking questions; he loved travelling to new places and his experimental cooking was infamous.

Giverna tapped a green shield featuring a harp. "Bitsy's mother belonged to the Weaver Guild – the creatives of the conjuring world. Weavers work as writers, musicians, artists and craftspeople, using their magicores to help weave extraordinary structures or objects, like the thinkerchief. Matilda had a particularly close bond with her mudtail, a weaver-type species that crafts items from organic materials such as paper and wood."

Wood... Bitsy glanced meaningfully at Kosh, thinking of the key and comb they'd found in the secret room. Wondering if her mum's mudtail had woven them, she suddenly wanted to examine them again. Perhaps *Magicalia* had been woven by her mum's mudtail, too? That might explain why the book seemed to understand what they were saying...

"Which coat of arms represents the Hunter Guild?" Kosh asked nervously.

Giverna's expression soured as she tapped a purple shield with a crown inside. "The Hunter Guild was founded by the ship's greedy and arrogant captain. As time passed, he grew hungry for power and tried to steal a dangerous artifact from the Alliance. As a result, the Hunter Guild was expelled from the Alliance and became an organization of outlaws. For hundreds of years, hunters have attacked us, stolen from us and spied on us. When the Alliance was nearly destroyed by dark forces, the Hunter Guild refused to come to our aid. They are cold-blooded, deceitful and ruthless."

A vice tightened around Bitsy's chest as she realized her dad was being held captive by a bunch of thugs. Whatever they wanted with *Magicalia*, it couldn't be good.

The toast popped up with a clang. As Giverna went to collect it, she let go of her thinkerchief and the fabric went blank.

"The woman that took my dad – Melasina Spires – she asked him for a book," Bitsy ventured, hoping Giverna might be able to shed some light on the matter.

Concern flickered through Giverna's hazel eyes. Bitsy noticed her hands tremble as she placed the toast on a plate and spread it with butter and jam. "And how did he respond?"

"He wouldn't give her anything," Kosh replied. "He told her to leave, then he conjured a waywurm and there was a big fight. He got knocked unconscious in the battle."

Bitsy watched Giverna's face carefully. She had the distinct impression that Giverna knew more than she was letting on. Unfortunately, Bitsy couldn't press Giverna without revealing that they had found *Magicalia*, and Bitsy wasn't sure they could trust her with that information yet.

"It's imperative we find your father as quickly as we can," Giverna said, sliding the plate of toast in front of Kosh. "Melasina will probably want to interrogate him

47

about this book, and he might not be able to stay silent for long. If he's been hurt, he might need urgent medical attention."

Bitsy swallowed, hoping he was going to be all right. She wondered if he'd woken up already. "Do you have any idea where Melasina is holding him?"

Giverna touched her thinkerchief and the image of a vast, festering swamp appeared. A collection of military style buildings was half-buried in the bog. "The last I heard, the Hunter Guild was operating out of a series of secret underground barracks. I know there's been a recent spate of conservatoire thefts attributed to hunters. Maybe those incidents are connected to your father's kidnapping, but I need to talk to the Alliance. They'll have more information than me."

The vice loosened a little around Bitsy's ribs. It felt good to have a plan of action. She smiled hopefully at Kosh, who was already munching on his jam-smeared toast.

"I'll contact them now. It won't take a moment." Giverna tugged the chopstick out of her updo, letting her long silver waves fall to her shoulders. Then she aimed it at Kosh's toast.

Kosh curled an arm protectively around his plate, still chewing. "What-er-yoo-doing?"

It was only then that Bitsy noticed flashes of copper reflecting in the chopstick. As it glowed white under

Giverna's fingers, she realized it had to be made of the same stone as her dad's fountain pen and her mum's teardrop pendant.

Giverna winked. "Conjurors have magicore-means of getting everything done. Watch and learn."

SPRINGLE

4

With a slight crackle, a flurry of twinkling copper dust spurted out of the end of Giverna's chopstick and whirled into the air.

"Your chopstick's made of farthingstone, isn't it?" Bitsy said, connecting the dots. So was her dad's pen. That was how he'd used it to conjure Quasar.

"You need to be touching farthingstone in order to conjure a magicore," Giverna explained as the dust spiralled into the middle of the table. "The material is very rare. Each conjuror has only one piece, usually disguised as jewellery or a small object."

A magicore no bigger than a teacup took shape within the dust. It resembled a tortoise with seaweed-green skin. A mass of fuzzy white hair covered its shell and a few cottony strands swayed from the middle of its head. It had a smiley face and a short tail that stuck up at right angles like the tether of a helium balloon.

Giverna tickled the magicore under its chin and it gargled like a baby. "This is my springle, Crumbs. He's a clairvoyant-type conjured from joy."

Crumbs' eyes were solid white, like fresh morning snow. Gazing up at Bitsy and Kosh, he wiggled his tail.

Kosh grinned. "How did you just do that?"

Giverna scooped Crumbs into her hand and he started plodding up her arm. "Did Eric ever talk to you about the science of energy?"

"A little," Kosh answered, glancing around the kitchen. "I know there are lots of different types of energy that exist in the world. A kettle is powered by electrical energy; a lightbulb gives off light energy and things that move have kinetic energy."

In fairness, Bitsy often cut her dad off whenever he started droning on about anything scientific in front of her friends. She was super proud of him for being an astrophysicist, but it could be a little embarrassing when he gave a lecture over the dinner table. "He told us that energy cannot be created or destroyed – it can only be transformed from one form to another."

"That's absolutely right," Giverna commented. "There are different types of energy in our bodies too, including chemical energy in the food we eat, electrical energy in our brains and heat energy in our muscles. When a cosmodynamic person touches farthingstone, they are able to *transform* these energies into *magicore* energy." She pointed her chin at Crumbs, who by now had clambered onto her shoulder and was burrowing under her long silver hair. "We don't know where in the universe magicore energy comes from, but on Earth, it exists as magicores."

Bitsy's skin tingled as she considered the magnitude of what Giverna was saying. If magicore energy was responsible for all the impossible things they'd witnessed, then its discovery could change the world. And yet ... nobody knew about it.

Kosh's eyebrows jumped under his beanie. "Does it hurt when you conjure a magicore?"

"No, but conjurors can feel tired, weak or hungry afterwards," Giverna said. "Conjuring uses up some of the energy in a conjuror's body, so there are only so many times we can conjure before we need to rest. Magicore species with more powerful abilities require more energy to conjure. There are five different energy levels – alpha is the lowest, then you have beta, gamma, delta and finally, omega."

"What level are waywurms?" Bitsy asked, thinking of Quasar. "That's what Dad conjured."

"They are delta-level – the highest energy level a person can conjure on their own." Giverna looked thoughtful. "It takes time to recover from conjuring a delta-level magicore. I expect your father will be unconscious for longer than is usual."

Bitsy recalled the torn expression on her dad's face right before he'd taken out his fountain pen. He must have been weighing up the risks and deciding which species to conjure. She turned to a new page in her notes. "So, if delta-level magicores are the highest level you can conjure on your own, how are omega-level magicores conjured?"

"They can only be conjured by three or more people, working together to channel their combined energies through a special device. But that device was lost hundreds of years ago." Giverna's fringe parted as Crumbs crawled out of her hair and settled on top of her head like a strange fascinator. "Conjuring omega-level magicores requires more energy than any single person has in their body. If anyone tried, the effort would kill them."

As Giverna went over to the kettle and filled the three glass mugs with boiling water, Bitsy took a deep breath. She was beginning to understand why her father might not have wanted her to attend a cosmodynamics test. The conjuring world was obviously a very dangerous place.

"But Eric told us that magicores are conjured from

emotional energy," Kosh recalled. "So, what do people's feelings have to do with it?"

Steam rose in front of Giverna's face as she carried the glass mugs over. She pushed one towards each of them. Bitsy hadn't asked for chamomile tea, but not wanting to be rude, she took a sip. It tasted sweet and soothing.

"Have you ever noticed that your body reacts in different ways when you feel different emotions?" Giverna said. "Your skin can prickle, your eyesight can sharpen and your muscles can tense. Even your temperature can change. Every emotion generates a unique combination of energies within our bodies. It is these mixtures, when transformed by farthingstone, that allow us to conjure different species of magicores."

Bitsy recalled her heart racing and her hearing sharpening earlier, when she felt scared of the grobble. Giverna was right.

"Of course, emotions vary across different languages and cultures," Giverna continued. "That's partly why conjurors summon their emotions through *memories*. Every magicore we conjure is linked to a moment from our past. Take Crumbs, for example."

At the sound of his name, Crumbs extended his neck and peered around the room. He fixed his gaze on Bitsy and Kosh, padded to the edge of Giverna's head … and jumped off.

Bitsy thrust her arms out to catch him, but she needn't have bothered.

Crumbs was floating like a bubble. He bobbed through the air towards her, his mouth hanging open in delight. Bitsy couldn't help giggling as he swooped closer and started nosing through her hair and clothes. She wondered what his unique gift was. Clairvoyant-type magicores, she remembered, had the power to influence the minds of others.

"Whenever I want to conjure Crumbs, I hold my chopstick and recall a specific memory from my sixth birthday," Giverna shared. "I was standing in the kitchen, watching my mother carry over a huge yellow birthday cake. The room was dark and the glow from the birthday candles illuminated the faces of all my family and friends. I felt like the luckiest girl in the world – everyone there, just to celebrate me!" She laughed as she described the scene. "The overwhelming feeling of that memory is *joy* – Crumbs' source emotion."

"Is that where Crumbs' name comes from, too?" Kosh guessed, as Crumbs circled his head. The springle closed his eyes, enjoying the wind through his dandelion-fluff hair.

Giverna nodded. "To command a magicore, you must give it a name connected to the memory you used to conjure it."

Bitsy's wrist ached from scrawling so many notes. "It sounds like you can conjure Crumbs whenever you want, but what happens when a magicore dies?" She glanced forlornly at Kosh, thinking of Quasar.

"When a magicore uses up all its energy, it bursts into farthingdust. We call it being *extinguished*." Giverna sipped her tea. "But magicores are like candles; they can be relit. Once Crumbs has expended all his energy, he will go *poof* too. But I can use the memory of my sixth birthday to conjure him again."

So, Quasar hadn't gone for good... Bitsy's heart lifted, realizing she might yet see the silver caterpillar again. She jotted a few more sentences into her notebook. *Farthingdust.* That was what that twinkly stuff was called.

"Now, let's see about rescuing your father. Crumbs?" Giverna beckoned the springle over and he came whizzing towards her, burbling excitedly. "Not only can springles levitate small objects around them, but their fur allows two people to communicate telepathically."

Telepathic communication. Bitsy had read about that in comic books. It was when people could hear each other's thoughts.

Giverna teased away a piece of Crumbs' fluff and stuffed it in her ear. "There's already a sample of Crumbs' fur stored in a special switchboard at the European

Conservatoire. I just have to wait for a representative from the Alliance to collect it."

Crumbs shook his shell and his missing patch of fluff regrew instantly. As Giverna secured her hair back up with her chopstick, Bitsy saw the farthingstone glow white. "Why does farthingstone change colour like that when you touch it?" she asked.

"It only changes colour because I'm cosmodynamic," Giverna remarked. "If I were cosmotypical, it wouldn't react to my touch at all."

Bitsy went still. Her dad's fountain pen had changed colour when both she and Kosh had touched it, which meant they *both* had to be cosmodynamic. She glanced at her best friend, feeling heat rush to the surface of her cheeks.

Kosh swallowed. "Err, so, why are some people cosmodynamic and others aren't?"

"The gift is genetic," Giverna replied. "It usually runs in families, although it can skip a generation or two. If you go far enough back, all cosmodynamic people are descendants of the six men who discovered farthingstone. A cosmodynamics test is just an official ceremony where a person touches a piece of farthingstone. The glow-colour indicates the types of magicores a person can conjure – yellow for metamorphs, white for clairvoyants, green for weavers, red for armourers, purple for hunters and blue for elementals. Initiates are able to conjure all six types, but this decreases as they get older. By the time an initiate graduates from a conservatoire at the age of sixteen, they're able to conjure only one type of magicore. At that point, they're invited to join a guild. Most people share an affinity with one of the six magicore types based on their personality."

"So, you're a member of the Clairvoyant Guild?" Bitsy said.

"That's right." Giverna reached for her thinkerchief and the six coats of arms reappeared. She indicated to a white shield with a lily in the centre. Bitsy recognized the design from Giverna's door knocker. "Clairvoyants are healers. We use our magicores to treat the sick and wounded wherever there is most need. Usually that's after a natural disaster like a hurricane or a landslide, or a human accident like a chemical explosion. You might never see us, but we are always there, helping in secret. Our guild is also responsible for making people forget when they've seen a magicore – a skill that has helped keep the conjuring world hidden for hundreds of—"

All of a sudden, Giverna fell silent. Staring into the middle distance, the lines on her forehead deepened, her expression serious. Crumbs nudged Giverna's cheek with his nose, but she didn't respond.

"Is she ... talking to someone *telepathically*?" Kosh guessed.

Bitsy watched the muscles twitching on Giverna's face. It seemed astonishing that she could be having a conversation inside her head with someone who was miles away. "I think she might be. Someone at the conservatoire must have picked up the other piece of Crumbs' fur." She leaned into Kosh's ear. "I think she knows more about *Magicalia* than she's telling us, by the way."

Kosh side-eyed Giverna. "Yeah, I got that sense too. I still like her, though. She's got a plan to help us find your dad and she made me toast."

"That shouldn't be your criteria for trusting someone," Bitsy argued, although she had to admit, she had also warmed to Giverna. Crumbs floated down onto the table and rolled onto his back. Bitsy tickled his belly with her finger and he kicked his legs, deliriously.

Giverna was lost in telepathic conversation for at least ten minutes before she pulled Crumbs' fluff out of her ear and the light returned to her eyes. She shook off a serious expression. "Good news!" she announced. "There's to be an emergency meeting at the conservatoire tomorrow morning to discuss how to free Eric. The Alliance have agreed to assemble a rescue team."

Bitsy felt a swell of relief, although tomorrow morning seemed frustratingly far away. "Can't the Alliance meet today?"

"They need more time to locate the Hunter Guild's

barracks before they can formulate a plan," Giverna explained. "They're working with their magicores now to try to find them. In the meantime, perhaps you would both like to stay with me tonight? I'll admit there's not much space here – you'll have to sleep on the couch in the front room – but I think Eric would prefer you to be here than home alone."

Bitsy considered Giverna's offer. Honestly, she was more concerned with finding her dad than with where she was going to sleep. Still, spending more time with Giverna might give her and Kosh the opportunity to investigate deeper. She looked at Kosh, who shrugged like he wasn't bothered either way. "All right, yes. Thanks, Giverna, that would be great."

Giverna beamed. "Do you want to nip back home and fetch your overnight things?"

"We can't exactly 'nip' back," Kosh commented. "It's a three-hour journey."

"Not if you travel by magicore-means." Giverna stretched a hand towards Bitsy's notebook. "May I?"

Bitsy tore off a sheet of paper and Giverna scribbled something on it.

"Go onto the balcony upstairs and read this aloud," Giverna instructed, passing the sheet back to Bitsy. "Trust me, you'll be blown away."

5

Giverna's balcony felt like a secret wilderness hidden in the city. It jutted out from the middle of her grey-tiled roof, concealed from view by tall iron railings overgrown with ivy. Sweet-smelling jasmine rambled over the walls and copper pipes fed up through the balcony floor, supplying water to the plants with the odd hiss and splutter. Medicinal herbs, fruits and vegetables grew in pots around the edge – although many of the vessels had cracked or overturned and there was soil scattered everywhere.

"Must have been a storm," Kosh muttered, stepping over a broken terracotta pot. "Can you believe that we're *both* cosmodynamic? Do you think my parents are conjurors like yours? Or maybe my grandparents in Sri

Lanka? Or *their* parents? Giverna said the gift can skip generations."

Bitsy shook her head, still struggling to absorb everything. She wondered if her dad already knew that she was cosmodynamic; he could have tested her with his pen when she was a baby.

"What did Giverna write on that paper?" Kosh asked.

"Umm…" Bitsy scanned Giverna's handwriting. "This can't be right. It sounds like a joke."

She passed the sheet to Kosh, who took one look and burst out laughing. *"Armoured rider, I'm in need. Prithy lend a noble steed.* What is it meant to be – Shakespeare?"

But as soon as he'd finished speaking, a mysterious breeze swept around the balcony, rustling the ivy and whipping up the fallen soil. Bitsy's pulse quickened as a shadow drew overhead.

"What in the—?!" Kosh exclaimed, looking up.

Bitsy tipped her head back to see the feathered underbelly of a magicore the size of a truck hurtling towards them. With its two tiny arms, muscular tail and plumes of dazzling blue, it looked like a cross between a kangaroo and a peacock … only a hundred times bigger.

They dived to the edge of the balcony as the magicore landed with a thud in the middle. Giverna's house shook. Dust crumbled from the roof tiles and a few more potted plants toppled over and cracked open.

The magicore had a narrow head with a long, scarlet beak and two eyes that shone like rubies. Fitted to its back was a metal saddle occupied by a young man with windswept brown hair. His uniform was emblazoned with a red coat of arms featuring a sword.

"Mornin' folks," the rider said, tipping his cap. He had a thick South London accent. "Where can I take yer?"

The magicore shook its feathers, lifted its chin and made a powerful bleating noise. As Kosh and Bitsy edged back, the rider laughed.

"You two never ridden an ozoz before?" he guessed. "There's nothing to be scared of, honest. The Armourer Guild operates a network of ozoz riders in most cities around the world. It's the fastest way for conjurors to travel inland. Now, where am I taking you?"

Bitsy craned her neck to examine the ozoz's face. The creature had a poised, assured expression like it was ready for anything. "We want to go to…" But she found herself so absorbed by the ozoz's ruby eyes that she couldn't remember her address. She looked at Kosh for help.

"Number 3, Mercury Crescent, Oddingham," he finished for her.

The rider beamed. "All right then, take your seats." He pulled a lever next to his knee and a slatted metal ladder unfurled from the saddle with a chair on either side.

The seats reminded Bitsy of the flimsy swinging

chairs she'd ridden at fairgrounds. She glanced nervously at Kosh who grinned at her. "YOLO, right?" he said.

They climbed into a seat each and fastened their safety bars. Bitsy slid her satchel into her lap to keep it safe. The ozoz took a deep breath, its rib cage expanding, nudging them forward. Bitsy noticed glowing threads snaking between the different parts of the saddle, as if it had been stitched together with pure light.

"Hold on tight. The journey shouldn't take more than five minutes." The rider tugged on the ozoz's reins and the creature did an about-turn, making the entire balcony judder. As its tail smashed through a few more pots, Bitsy wondered how Giverna explained all the noise to her neighbours.

Her chair wobbled as the ozoz bent its knees, its leg muscles straining. She suddenly wondered how it was going to fly. Despite the feathers on its head and body, it didn't appear to have any wings. "What's an ozoz's source emotion?" she asked the rider, hoping the answer might give her a clue.

"Con-fi-deeeeeeeence!" he shouted as the ozoz leaped into the air.

Bitsy's stomach lurched as they rocketed skywards, her seat shaking violently.

"Wahhhhhh!" Kosh screamed, gripping his safety bar.

Wind roared in Bitsy's ears as Giverna's chamomile

tea threatened to make a reappearance at the back of her throat. Daring to look down, she saw London getting smaller beneath her. Roads shrank to the size of matchsticks and cars appeared like coloured dots. The late morning sun burst through the clouds, illuminating vast patches of the great city like spotlights. "We're so high!" she yelled.

Kosh held on to his beanie with one hand. "It's incredible!"

Moisture settled on Bitsy's cheeks and eyelashes as they soared through a cloud. Slowly, their trajectory began to level out. "How can nobody see us?" she called up to the rider. "Are we moving too fast?"

The rider looked surprised. "Magicores are able to cast illusions called shades that make them invisible to the human eye. The three of us are hidden by stealth technology in the saddle. It was supplied by the Weaver Guild."

That explained the threads of light – the saddle must have been woven by a magicore. Bitsy held her safety bar tighter and leaned forward, peering over the edge. She had never seen such an amazing view.

"Does that mean there could be magicores all around us, and we couldn't see them?" Kosh asked, loudly.

"Technically yes," the rider called back, "but a conjuror can only ever have one magicore at a time, and there aren't more than a few thousand conjurors in every guild, so it's unlikely. Of course, there are still *wild* magicores in the world – those who endure after their conjuror has died. They have black eyes, but they're very rare."

Bitsy was itching to write everything down, but she worried she'd drop her notebook and lose it for ever if she tried to reach it now. She brushed a few wet curls out of her eyes, squinting into the sun. "What does the Armourer Guild do apart from transport?" she asked.

"Security and logistics," the rider answered. "Armourers are forceful, fiery and strong. Most of our magicores are good in combat, too, so you wouldn't want to cross us." He added with a wink, "I prefer riding, though. Nothing quite compares to ozoz-jumping."

Kosh frowned. "What do you mean *jumping*?"

It was then that Bitsy felt them slowing down.

"Every journey is a single jump," the rider said. "Most ozoz have enough energy to travel a hundred miles in a shift. They need a hard surface to take off from, which is why they're mainly used for shorter journeys and inland journeys."

Bitsy gulped as it dawned on her that if they had been travelling upwards all this time…

…they had to come down.

A gust ruffled the ozoz's feathers as Bitsy's bottom

lifted slowly off her seat. She clasped her satchel, feeling gravity take hold of her body.

Before she knew it, she was screaming. "Ahhhhhhh!"

Her insides twisted as they fell. Kosh wailed and held on to the sides of his seat, his dark hair billowing around his face.

Their chairs vibrated as they picked up speed. The ozoz extended its legs and used its tail for balance, steering them lower.

A patchwork landscape appeared below – sloping green fields bordered by winding country roads and clusters of dark buildings. Bitsy recognized the layout of Oddingham with its triangular village green and small parade of shops.

"Place your arms across your chest!" the rider instructed, reaching for another lever on the ozoz's saddle.

Bitsy did as she was told, performing her best *Wakanda Forever* impression. The ozoz spread its toes, revealing webbed flaps that helped steady their descent. Oddingham drew closer. Bitsy stared as the chimney of her house got bigger and bigger...

The rider pulled his lever. "Thank you for travelling by ozoz. Please make sure you have all your belongings with you before you drop."

"Drop! What do you—?" But before Bitsy could finish her question, her seat fell out from under her.

She shrieked as her satchel flew above her head, before whacking her on the shoulder a moment later as she landed in a bouncy pile of grass cuttings.

Oomph. Kosh bashed Bitsy on the knee as he tumbled into the grass beside her. There was a thud as the ozoz landed a few metres away, making the ground shake.

Trying to catch her breath, Bitsy looked around and found she was in her back garden. She glanced worriedly at her next door neighbours' windows, but no one was watching.

"Until next time," the rider said, tipping his hat. He tugged on the ozoz's reins and it did an about-turn.

A gust of wind socked Bitsy and Kosh in the face as the ozoz took off again, streaking skywards. Bitsy brushed a few blades of grass off her cheeks. "Well, that was—"

"Absolutely amazing," Kosh said, repositioning his beanie. "And at the same time, completely terrifying."

Bitsy laughed as she got to her feet and offered him a hand up. "Come on. Let's get our things."

It didn't take long to gather their overnight stuff, partly because they'd already packed for Paris on Monday. Bitsy added extra underwear and a waterproof jacket to her suitcase, plus additional pencils and a spare notebook in case she finished all the paper in her current one. As she zipped her bag shut, she imagined what their holiday might have been like if all this hadn't happened. They'd been planning to go up the Eiffel Tower, picnic by the River Seine and visit the Parc des Princes football stadium where Kosh's favourite French team, Paris Saint-Germain, played. Instead, her dad was possibly still unconscious, locked away in secret barracks, awaiting interrogation from the leader of a gang of dangerous criminals. With every hour that passed without his safe return, her heart felt heavier.

Once Kosh had finished his packing, they carried their bags downstairs and wheeled them along the hallway. As they approached the door to the lounge, a rumble of thunder sounded in the kitchen, followed by a loud *bang* and the scratch of claws against lino.

Bitsy froze. She'd heard that same thunder twice yesterday evening – once when it had interrupted her Poddingham recording and then again, right before her dad had been kidnapped. She glanced worriedly at Kosh, who abandoned his suitcase and signalled to the lounge.

"Stay low," he whispered.

Bitsy held her breath as Kosh turned the handle on the lounge door, careful not to make a squeak. He pulled it open and they both crept inside.

The previous owners of Bitsy's house had installed a hatch between the kitchen and the lounge, presumably so they could pass through plates of food rather than having to walk from room to room. Through the hatch, Bitsy could see shadows moving in the kitchen. She tensed as a young man in black clothing appeared from behind one of the kitchen cupboards. He was tall and slight with golden-brown skin and a shock of curly dark hair. He wore a mass of beaded bracelets on his left wrist and an expensive-looking camera hung around his neck.

"Come on, come on," he muttered, scowling. "It's got to be hidden here somewhere…"

As he rummaged through a cutlery drawer, a dark grey leathery-skinned magicore padded over the work surface. It was the size of a small dog, with floppy ears, a shiny nose and multiple tails sprouting from its rear end. The tails looked like they were made of plasticine because they kept morphing into different shapes: arrows, zigzags, circles and snowflakes. Bitsy gasped as she saw that the magicore's eyes were a deep purple.

"He's a hunter," she hissed, ducking down behind their damaged sofa. Her stomach wobbled as everything Giverna had said about the Hunter Guild came flooding back.

"What if Melasina sent him to look for *Magicalia*?" Kosh realized, throwing panicked gestures at Bitsy's satchel. "We need to hide."

They turned for the door, but the hunter and his magicore were already on the move. Heavy panting echoed in the hallway, along with the shuffle of footsteps.

Thinking quickly, Bitsy crawled to her mum's display cabinet and pressed the keys on the flute. The two halves of the cabinet parted silently, allowing her and Kosh to slip inside the secret room. Bitsy got to her feet and pulled the inner lever, sending the cabinet sliding back into place.

"Do you think they saw us?" Kosh asked, breathlessly.

Bitsy held her ear to the back of the cabinet. She could hear the hunter moving around the lounge. "I don't know…"

She looked around the secret room, thinking of how they might defend themselves if the hunter tried to break inside. She opened a drawer in the chest and lifted out the wooden key and comb that she suspected her mum's mudtail had woven. "Maybe we can use these to protect ourselves? They must do *something* unusual."

Kosh looked doubtful, but he took the comb anyway. "Let's experiment."

Bitsy examined the key, turning it over in her hands. She considered all the things that had locks: diaries, jewellery boxes, suitcases, windows… But then, it probably didn't open something ordinary.

"Well, unless we intend to beat them at a hairdressing competition, this is useless," Kosh concluded drily.

Bitsy turned to see he had removed his beanie and his floppy black hair was now coiffured into an Elvis-style quiff. She covered her mouth to stop herself laughing. It looked ridiculous. "How did that…?"

By way of an answer, Kosh swept the comb through his tresses and his hairstyle changed. This time, he was rocking a spiky punk look. Without discussion, he placed the comb back in the drawer and pushed his fingers into his hair, messing it up. Then he grumpily tugged on his beanie. "What about the key?"

"My guess is … it probably opens something made by a magicore, too," Bitsy said, handing it to him.

Kosh twisted the key in mid-air, pretending to unlock something. "It feels too fragile to turn a heavy lock." He held it against the wall and tried the same thing.

This time, the key sank *into* the wall, as if the bricks were made of dough.

They both staggered back as hundreds of tiny, pale roots burst through the cement in the brickwork and snaked across the wall, forming a doorway. The bricks in the centre vaporized revealing a gnarled wooden staircase descending into pitch black. The crooked, bark-covered treads looked like ancient tree roots.

Kosh gawped at the key. "How did…?"

"I don't know," Bitsy said, fumbling for her phone. "Keep it safe."

As Kosh pulled the gold chain over his head and tucked the key under his hoodie, Bitsy turned on her torch. "Come on, we've got to see where this leads."

6

Slowly and carefully, Kosh followed Bitsy down the stairs. They'd only descended a few steps when the doorway of roots knitted closed behind them and everything went dark.

"Who turned out the lights?" Kosh hissed.

Bitsy waved her phone around, but the torch beam faded after only a few metres. She rubbed the bulb to check it wasn't covered in dirt. "My torch isn't working very well. Can you try yours?"

A few seconds later, a light flashed over her shoulder as Kosh switched on the torch on his phone. But the same thing happened. The beam could only penetrate a short distance into the darkness. Although Bitsy could see Kosh, her eyes strained to make out any shapes beyond him. It was like they were surrounded by thick, black fog.

Kosh returned up the steps and tried pushing the wooden key into the wall behind them. Nothing happened. "Apparently we can't get out the same way we came in," he said. "What is this place?"

Bitsy could hear strange echoes rumbling all around them, giving the impression that they were inside a huge cave. She sniffed and caught the scent of freshly turned soil hanging in the air. "It must have been made by magicore-means." She looked anxiously back the way they'd come. "At least the hunter can't follow us down here without a key. Stay vigilant."

They continued steadily, holding their phones low to the ground so they could see where to step. When Bitsy cast her beam over the edge of the stairs, she saw nothing but darkness. Worried about what might be beneath them, she stuck cautiously to the centre of the path.

The stairs sloped down and levelled off onto a narrow platform constructed from more tangled tree roots. A few steps across, Bitsy bumped her head.

"Ouch!" She rubbed the sore spot and aimed her phone above her. In the weak torchlight, she could see the bottom of another platform. "There must be a whole network of pathways in here. It's like a maze." With a shiver, she realized that if they got lost, no one would come to help them. They'd be stuck in there for ever...

"Can you see that?" Kosh pointed to a faintly glowing symbol in the distance. It looked like a line of clam shells.

There was something familiar about its shape, but Bitsy couldn't quite put her finger on it. "It could be a way out," she decided, ducking under the low-hanging root. "Let's head towards it."

They clambered over a mound of rough, scratchy roots before turning a corner. Their track twisted under and around, spiralling down and rising over ramps. Every so often, Bitsy would glimpse another path crossing above them, and get some idea of how vast the web of roots was.

Eventually, they came to a steep incline where the roots were worn smooth. They swung their legs over the side and Kosh slid down first. But as his torch beam strobed ahead of him, Bitsy saw he was heading for a sheer drop.

"Kosh, no!" She pocketed her phone and scrambled after him, pushing with her hands to go faster. "You're going to fall off!"

He scratched at the roots with his fingernails. "There's nothing to hold on to!"

"*Me!* Grab hold of me!" Bitsy stretched her foot towards him, but as Kosh's fingers clasped her ankle, she realized the major flaw in her plan: she was still falling.

She flailed her arms, trying to catch hold of something. A hard, snarling root bashed against her hip and she managed to grasp it. "I've got you!" She locked her fingers

75

together and braced herself as Kosh's weight yanked on her leg.

Fire burned through her arms, but she tried to ignore the pain. She gritted her teeth, her muscles trembling. "I. Can't. Hold. Yo—!"

But just as her fingers slipped apart, Kosh's weight vanished.

"It's OK!" he yelled as Bitsy plummeted.

Screaming, she fell into Kosh's arms and he dragged her onto a platform on one side. A dim light flashed in her face as he found his phone.

"Thanks," she said, panting.

"You, too." Kosh shone his torch ahead of them. They were standing on a wide ledge, halfway up a huge circular shaft. The walls were composed of interlacing roots, reminding Bitsy of the plaited structure of her wicker laundry basket. Dotted at different heights all around were more glowing symbols. In the dense fog, they seemed suspended like stars in the night sky.

She studied a symbol on the opposite side of the shaft. It was shaped like a suspension bridge with two towers. "That looks just like Tower Bridge in London…"

"And that's the Eiffel Tower in Paris!" Kosh pointed to a glowing, three-tiered pylon with lattice walls. "Maybe all the symbols represent famous landmarks?"

Landmarks… Bitsy jolted as it occurred to her what

the shells reminded her of. "The symbol we followed to get here was shaped just like the Sydney Opera House in Australia! I saw a photo of it in one of my mum's articles. Kosh, I think you're right."

They walked carefully around the chamber, examining the other symbols. There were all sorts of bridges, buildings, sculptures and monuments. Bitsy pointed out the ones she recognized. "That's the Colosseum in Rome, and over there is one of the temples in Chichén Itzá in Mexico."

"How do you know so many of them?" Kosh asked.

As Bitsy considered her reply, she realized something. "My mum reported from a lot of these cities. I've even seen photos of her standing by the landmarks."

Continuing along the pathway, a symbol appeared in the gloom ahead of them: an Art-Deco skyscraper with a pointed top. "Even I recognize that one," Kosh said. "It's the Empire State Building in New York."

Up close, Bitsy saw the symbol was made out of thin, luminescent roots. An arched frame grew around them like a doorway. She glanced nervously at Kosh before giving the symbol an experimental shove…

The roots creaked as the symbol gave way under her touch. It *was* a door.

As it swung open, sunlight blinded her and she staggered back. Wind blew out, smelling of exhaust fumes and fried food. Horns blared and voices shouted in the distance. When her eyes adjusted to the brightness, she saw a deserted alleyway flanked by tall concrete buildings. Traffic lights flashed at the far end of the street, where a yellow cab was driving along a busy road.

"That can't be *New York*," Kosh uttered.

Bitsy's mind whirled, struggling to understand how this was possible. She reached through the doorway and wiggled her fingers. She could see the shadow of her hand on the pavement below and feel a breeze against her skin. "I think … it *is*."

A few people in warm coats sauntered past at the end of the alleyway, carrying shopping bags. Bitsy quickly pulled the door shut before they spotted her, returning her and Kosh to darkness.

"This is *wild*!" he said. "The other symbols must be doors, too; the landmarks probably represent the cities they lead to."

Bitsy gazed in awe at the sky of glowing shapes. "Maybe my mum used this root-network to travel around the world when she was reporting? Her mudtail could even have woven it; everything looks like it has grown into shape." Her skin tingled, considering there was a whole place her mum had created, one she was just beginning to discover.

"We didn't enter this place through a door with a

symbol on, though," Kosh noted, pulling the wooden key out from under his hoodie. He held the key against a section of root wall and tried turning it clockwise. Nothing happened. "I bet this key opens a doorway to the root-network no matter where you are. Then, once you're inside, you have to choose the right exit."

Bitsy did a double take. "Talking of the right exit...!" She pointed to another symbol, a few levels below them: a small building with a steepled clock tower. The spire had a distinctive crooked shape that Bitsy would recognize anywhere.

Kosh's face brightened. "Oddingham Church! Let's go."

Ladders of coiled tree roots scaled the chamber walls, granting access to the other pathways. Navigating through the gloom, they descended to the correct level and hurried to the Oddingham door.

It opened onto a concealed area of bushes near the back of Oddingham Church. There didn't seem to be anyone around, but Bitsy and Kosh remained alert as they stepped into the afternoon sun. Bitsy pushed the door shut behind them and it dissolved like ash in the wind.

"Do you think it's safe for us to return home?" Bitsy asked. "The hunter and his magicore could still be there."

Kosh shrugged. "Only one way to find out."

They approached Bitsy's house from the side, slinking

through a neighbour's garden in order to stay hidden. Bitsy examined the downstairs windows for signs of movement but couldn't see anything.

She was about to creep around to the back of the house when she spotted a sheet of paper attached with a dagger to her front door.

Panic rose inside Bitsy's chest and before she knew it, she was running.

"No, wait—!" Kosh called.

Bitsy hurtled towards the door and tore the sheet down. The Hunter Guild's coat of arms was printed at the top of the page. Below it was a chilling handwritten message:

If you ever want to see your father alive again,
find Arkwright's Gyrowheel.
Speak of this to no one.
I will be watching.

Melasina Spires

7

The following morning, Melasina Spires' threat echoed through Bitsy's head like a ghostly taunt.

If you ever want to see your father alive again…

She shuddered and gripped the seat in front of her as their bus rattled around another corner. "What choice do we have?" she asked Kosh, who was sitting beside her. "The ransom note says *speak of this to no one*. If we discuss anything with Giverna, Melasina might kill my dad."

The top deck of the bus was busy and Giverna had taken the only other empty seat, four rows in front of them. The cold morning air had fogged up the windows and a few children were drawing faces on the glass.

"But how would Melasina Spires find out?" Kosh asked, keeping his voice low.

Bitsy eyed the other passengers warily. "She said she'd be *watching*. Giverna said hunters are trained spies; who knows what magicore-means they might have of snooping on us."

"Right. I hadn't thought of that." Kosh slid his neck deeper inside his hoodie, like he was trying to disappear. "OK, so we keep the ransom note a secret. But what about Melasina's other demand?"

After Bitsy had ripped the ransom note from her front door, the two of them had ventured back inside Bitsy's house to find the hunter gone. There was no trace of him or his magicore, and the cabinet concealing the secret room didn't look as if it had been moved. Still, it hadn't been wise to linger. They'd grabbed their bags and hailed an ozoz back to Giverna's.

"I don't think we have any option but to do what Melasina wants," Bitsy admitted, miserably. "Dad's life is on the line." She fetched her notebook from her pocket and turned to the last page, where she'd copied the ransom note word for word. "If we can find *Arkwright's Gyrowheel* – whatever it is – we can keep my dad safe."

"*Arkwright's Gyrowheel* sounds like something scientific," Kosh said, his index finger gliding across his phone screen. "There's no record of it in Google. I wonder why Melasina needs us to find it for her? She's the leader of a powerful gang of literal 'hunters'; it makes no sense."

Bitsy tapped her pencil against the page. That wasn't the only curious thing about Melasina's message. Bitsy thought that Melasina wanted *Magicalia*, so why had her interest now switched to Arkwright's Gyrowheel?

They rocked forward as the bus pulled in at a stop. A few passengers bundled towards the stairs, freeing the row of seats in front. Giverna got up and started to move closer, when a couple of teenagers barged past her.

"Mind out, grandma," one of them sneered.

Giverna shrugged them off and slid into the seat in front of Bitsy and Kosh, mumbling something that included the words *rude* and *ungrateful*.

"Are you OK?" Bitsy asked, glaring at the teenagers as they disappeared down the stairs.

"I bet cosmotypicals would be a lot nicer if they knew I might be saving their life one day," Giverna grumbled. She was dressed in a flowery woollen coat with her medical supplies bag slung over her shoulder. Her long silver hair was twirled into a helter-skelter-shaped bun and fixed in place with her chopstick. "We've not far to go now. It would have been faster to take an ozoz, of course, but there's no magicore transport allowed near a conservatoire entrance. Helps to keep it hidden."

"Where exactly *is* the European Conservatoire of Conjuring?" Bitsy asked. "There wasn't a proper address on the Chancellor's letter."

"Nobody knows the exact address except the Chancellor," Giverna replied. "Discounting Antarctica, there is a conservatoire on every continent. Their locations are top secret but they can be accessed via a number of different entrances in most major cities. The London entrance for the European Conservatoire is on Kean Street, in the West End."

Bitsy presumed the building had been built using magicore-means, just like the root-network. That had to be how it had multiple entrances all over the world.

"Don't the local residents notice there's an entrance to a conjuring school on their doorstep?" Kosh asked.

"Every few years, the conservatoire takes on a new disguise," Giverna explained. "At the moment it's a rather exclusive martial arts training centre."

Bitsy gazed out of the window as they trundled past Hyde Park, where a Lycra-clad group were practising their morning yoga. The city felt so modern and vibrant that it was sometimes easy to forget that it had been founded by the Romans two millennia ago. She supposed in such an old place, it was easy to keep secrets.

"When we get to the conservatoire entrance, stay close to me," Giverna advised. "It's a Sunday, so it'll be busy."

Kosh snorted. "School on a weekend? That sounds awful."

"The conservatoire isn't a normal school. It's only

open evenings, weekends and school holidays, and initiates can attend any workshops and demonstrations that interest them, completing tasks to earn badges. The only rules are concerning safety and secrecy."

The conservatoire sounded interesting but Bitsy bit back her questions. She had to focus on finding Arkwright's Gyrowheel and saving her dad's life.

"During the week, conservatoires are used for Alliance business," Giverna continued. "Every guild has a headquarters, but conservatoires are cross-guild spaces. That's why this meeting is taking place there."

Coloured lights flashed in the windows as they passed through Piccadilly Circus. The sprawling junction was busy with tourists milling to and fro under giant video screens that displayed adverts for fast-food chains and sportswear brands. Bitsy remembered weaving through the crowds there last December with her dad, after he'd taken her to London to see the Christmas lights. The thought of never seeing him again made her heart ache. She couldn't lose him, too.

After getting stuck in roadworks on the Strand, they alighted twenty minutes later at a bus stop in the West End. Giverna guided them along the pavement, past several theatres and bistros, and onto a narrow side road flanked by high-rise buildings.

Kean Street.

At first, the only activity Bitsy saw was a van being unloaded at the back of a restaurant and a group of construction workers leaning against a wall, drinking tea. But as the road bent round, the air filled with conversation and the slam of car doors.

A silver Toyota pulled up to the kerb and a gangly boy with orange freckles jumped out. Over a striped T-shirt, he wore a pair of black dungarees with multiple pockets. They looked like work overalls because they were covered in stains. Colourful badges of various designs were sewn onto the straps.

"Catch you later, bro!" he called, closing the door.

The driver-side window slid down, revealing a much older boy with just as many freckles. "Good luck with the combat workshop! Remember: look for weaknesses in your opponent's magicore."

The younger boy nodded before running off into a crowd of other children. They all looked Bitsy's age or older and wore the same black dungarees with badged straps.

"Over there." Kosh signalled to a grey stone doorway between two rows of steel shutters. "That must be the entrance."

Two men with moustaches were standing outside, marshalling a queue of initiates. One was tall and skinny, dressed in cherry-red dungarees with the Armourer

Guild's coat of arms on the front pocket. The other man, who was much shorter and rounder, had on mustard-yellow dungarees adorned with a coat of arms featuring a gold coin. He was holding an enormous candy-pink helium balloon like he was about to go to a children's birthday party.

Ignoring the queue, Giverna marched Bitsy and Kosh straight towards the door. The initiates were talking in small groups as they passed and Bitsy caught snippets of conversation.

"OK, I got a good one," one teenager sniggered. "Would you rather share a bath with a lubberwharl or ride a rollercoaster with a thornsprout?"

Laughter rippled through his group.

"Can you imagine how painful it would be sitting next to a thornsprout on a rollercoaster?" someone asked. "Every time you turned a corner, you'd get thrown against it – ouch!"

Someone else giggled. "Yeah, but lubberwharls *stink*. If you shared a bath with one, you'd smell like fart for weeks. Miss Wu conjured a lubberwharl in the demonstration hall two weeks ago, and everyone in the audience had to wear nose pegs!"

Listening to them talk, Bitsy imagined what it might have been like for her mum and dad to study conjuring there. She wondered what badges they'd earned and who their favourite teachers were. She had so many questions for her dad when he returned.

As they approached the door, Bitsy saw that the pink helium balloon was covered in a layer of fine hair. What she'd presumed was stretchy rubber was actually veiny skin.

It was a *magicore*.

The neck of the balloon appeared to be the beginning of the creature's long, thin tail and at the top of the balloon were two triangular flaps which Bitsy guessed might be small ears.

Kosh tilted his head, squinting. "Is that…?"

"A bundler," Giverna said. "A metamorph magicore conjured from boredom. The species' unique gift is that they can increase the size of their personal shade, rendering nearby objects, people and areas completely invisible. In an emergency, it's their job to hide the conservatoire entrance." She raised a hand to greet each of the men by the door. "Lars, Hasim, good to see you both."

The men tipped their heads.

"Morning, Miss Greynettle," said the taller one Giverna had addressed as Hasim. "We were told to expect you and two guests."

Lars, the man in the yellow dungarees, considered Bitsy and Kosh carefully. "They'll need to wear conjuring overalls inside. A wild rumbleplume got loose in the atrium earlier, and it's caused all sorts of havoc. Best to wear something fireproof when one of those is around."

Hasim reached into a box behind him and grabbed two pairs of loose black dungarees, identical to those the initiates in the queue were wearing. "You can borrow these from lost property. Just make sure you return them on your way out."

He handed one pair to Bitsy and the other to Kosh. Although the material was thick and heavy, it felt incredibly slippery against Bitsy's fingers. She spotted a label on the inside that read: *Thimbull-woven garment. Fireproof, waterproof and non-conductive. Wash at 30.*

"I'm not sure I want to know what a rumbleplume is," Kosh muttered to Bitsy, taking off his coat and stepping resignedly into his overalls.

"Me neither," Bitsy agreed. She tugged on her overalls and pulled the straps up over the shoulders of her cardigan. They were baggy enough to fit over her clothes. "We might be able to find out more about Arkwright's Gyrowheel inside the conservatoire. Keep your eyes open."

Before they went inside, Giverna paused to admire the heavy stone doorway. "Conservatoire entrances are magi-woven. Once we pass through this, everything you hear will be in your own language."

As Bitsy stepped over the threshold, she felt a subtle

change in the air. Her vision darkened for a split second, almost like she'd blinked…

…and then she was walking across the marble floor of a vast circular hall. She drew her breath as she looked up. Dozens of balconies with gleaming brass railings climbed the walls to a domed glass ceiling high above. Bitsy had been inside football stadiums with Kosh, but she'd never seen anything on the same scale as this.

"No way," Kosh breathed, craning his neck.

Every balcony had at least twenty doors leading off from it, and each level was accessed by spiral staircases made of more shiny brass. Initiates hurried between doors, chatting and pointing, but Bitsy was too far away to hear what they were saying. As she marvelled at the architecture, she slowly realized that each building level was *rotating*. Some balconies were turning clockwise, others anticlockwise. It felt like standing in the middle of a kaleidoscope.

"This space is known as the atrium," Giverna said, looking around. "It's the most important area in any conservatoire, at the heart of the building. All other rooms lead off from it."

Something swooped over their heads, and they all instinctively ducked. When Bitsy looked up, she saw a girl with pigtails riding what appeared to be a flying carpet.

"Maja Olsen, this is your last warning!" shouted a

red-faced man, his blue overalls billowing as he ran. "No huffluff flying outside the practice theatre!"

Giverna hastily ushered Bitsy and Kosh away. They headed towards a large wooden desk in the middle of the floor. A rusty iron chain dangled from the centre of the glass ceiling, right over the desk. Fixed to the end was an empty bracket that looked like it might have once held a lamp. A woman with a neat strawberry-blonde bob and calm eyes stood behind the desk. Over a pinstripe shirt, she wore the same mustard-yellow overalls as Lars. By process of deduction, Bitsy figured that the coat of arms on her pocket, a yellow shield with a gold coin, belonged to the Metamorph Guild.

"Chancellor Hershel," Giverna said, smiling wearily. "This is Bitsy and Kosh, whom I told you about."

The Chancellor pushed a pair of spectacles up her nose as she leaned over the desk to study Bitsy and Kosh. Bitsy noticed the frames turning yellow under the Chancellor's touch and realized with a jolt that they must be made of farthingstone.

"It's a pleasure to meet you both," Chancellor Hershel said. She enunciated her words clearly, like someone who makes safety announcements on public transport. "You can wait here with me while Giverna attends the meeting."

"Don't worry, I'll tell you everything that happens," Giverna insisted, placing a hand on Bitsy's shoulder.

Bitsy nodded. Then Giverna straightened her coat and strode purposefully towards one of the spiral staircases. She climbed the stairs and disappeared into a door on the second level, which was slowly turning clockwise.

"I've worked with Giverna for many years," the Chancellor told Bitsy and Kosh. "She is a hard-working conjuror. She will do her best to help your father, of that you can be sure."

Bitsy was confident that the Chancellor was right, but the Alliance's rescue plan would make no difference if Melasina killed her dad. She fiddled anxiously with the pockets of her overalls, feeling the ransom note's threat hanging over her like a poisonous cloud.

The Chancellor must have noticed Bitsy's glum expression because she added, "Waiting can be frustrating. Why don't I give you a tour to help pass the time?"

She escorted them slowly around the edge of the atrium. Between the doors were various cabinets displaying shiny awards. There were trophies for magicore racing, shields for conjuring battles and medals celebrating achievements such as *LONGEST MOLLOWUP TUNNEL* and *MOST ACCURATE GROBLIN CLONE*.

"Initiates come to us at age twelve, study for four years and graduate when they are sixteen. In that time, our tutors teach them everything they need to know about conjuring and working with magicores for them to become valuable members of the Alliance."

A broad-shouldered woman in riding boots and red overalls marched past, herding a group of young initiates.

"Do you have tutors from all the guilds here?" Kosh asked.

"All except the Hunter Guild," the Chancellor stated.

Bitsy recalled Giverna describing how guilds claimed initiates after they had graduated. "What do you do when an initiate discovers they can only conjure hunter magicores? Does someone from the Hunter Guild come here to claim them?"

The Chancellor shifted uncomfortably. "It is forbidden for a member of the Hunter Guild to set foot inside a conservatoire. In those instances, our rules dictate that the initiate is immediately banished and must not be contacted by anyone. The Hunter Guild has its methods of contacting an initiate afterwards."

"*Banished?*" Bitsy's forehead twitched. That didn't seem fair. Any of the initiates they'd seen might become a hunter and, without doing anything wrong, they'd find themselves ostracized from their friends and family.

"It is how we keep everyone safe," the Chancellor explained, her tone firm. "Hunters are rebellious, arrogant and strong-willed, even at a young age. The Hunter Guild has been spying on the Alliance for hundreds of years; it would be too risky to trust them."

She marched ahead, clearly not willing to discuss the Hunter Guild any further, and slowed beside a series of dark oil paintings decorating the walls. As Bitsy and Kosh drew closer, it became clear that they were all portraits. In each one, a finely dressed man or woman in conjuring overalls was posing in a chair with the atrium in the background.

"My predecessor," the Chancellor said, pointing to what looked like the most modern portrait. It depicted a woman with a stubby nose and tightly curled black hair. "Chancellor Pleiades was an elemental. She added new laboratories to the conservatoire and increased the number of initiate-led research projects."

They walked to the next portrait, showing a wild-eyed gentleman in emerald-green overalls. At the bottom of the frame were the words: *Chancellor Alfred Haumea, 1976–1991.* Judging by the dates of the portraits on either side, they'd been hung in chronological order.

"Chancellor Haumea was an eminent weaver. He improved the creative spaces in the conservatoire and left behind a legacy of exciting competitions between the guilds."

"What will *your* legacy be?" Kosh asked.

The corners of the Chancellor's mouth twitched. "I'm still working on that."

As they continued, the portraits got older. The chancellors started to wear frilly shirts and grand jackets with gold braiding under their overalls. Counting the dates, Bitsy noticed a gap between one chancellor's departure in 1759 and the next chancellor's appointment in 1763. "Did something happen here? Only there are four years between the last chancellor leaving and a new chancellor being appointed."

"You have an impressive eye for detail," Chancellor Hershel remarked. "During those years, an imposter was in charge of the conservatoire – a man who called himself *Riddlejax*."

"Riddlejax?" Kosh screwed up his nose. "What kind of a name is that?"

"Riddlejax's past is a mystery. He wasn't an initiate at a conservatoire and a guild never claimed him. Historians think he was once a thief who stole a piece of farthingstone without knowing its true power. After discovering he was cosmodynamic, he taught himself to conjure by performing dangerous experiments with farthingstone. These experiments gave him the ability to shapeshift."

"You mean, Riddlejax could transform into another person?" Bitsy asked.

"That's how he became Chancellor," Chancellor Hershel answered gravely. "He murdered the then

Chancellor and masqueraded as them for four years before his true identity was discovered. Riddlejax believed that cosmodynamic people are superior to cosmotypical people. He wanted conjurors to stop helping humanity and instead use their magicores to seize power and wealth. The Alliance disagreed, so during his four years in charge, Riddlejax and his followers tried to destroy the Alliance from within. They sabotaged rescue operations, released wild magicores into cities and spread magi-woven diseases, threatening thousands of innocent lives. It was a dark time in the Alliance's history."

Bitsy swallowed. "What happened to them?"

"Nobody knows exactly what happened to Riddlejax," Chancellor Hershel replied. "Some think he was killed in a magicore battle or accidentally died when one of his experiments went wrong. But after he was gone, his message endured. His followers call themselves chaos-conjurors; their calling card is a chaosphere symbol. Hidden among us, a small number of them have been trying to disrupt our work for centuries."

Bitsy shivered, beginning to understand why the Alliance was so mistrustful.

The final portrait showed a middle-aged gentleman with rosy cheeks and a gentle smile. He wore an old-fashioned powdered grey wig and emerald conjuring overalls with gold toggles. According to the inscription, he had been Chancellor during the seventeenth century.

"And here we have the first Chancellor of the European Conservatoire of Conjuring," Chancellor Hershel said with pride, "Gilander Arkwright."

Arkwright... Bitsy stared at Kosh. "Can you tell us more about him? What was he like?"

"Gilander Arkwright was one of the most important conjurors in history. He was the founder of the Weaver Guild. An architect, engineer, writer and artist. By all accounts, a very accomplished man."

Bitsy was about to fire off another set of questions when the floor trembled, and nearly three-quarters of the doors around the atrium burst open. Initiates spilled out in all directions, laughing and chatting.

"Ah, you'll have to excuse me," the Chancellor said, glancing concernedly at her desk. "Feel free to wander around; just don't leave the atrium."

As she returned to her station, Kosh admired Gilander Arkwright's portrait. "Arkwright's Gyrowheel must be connected to this dude somehow."

Bitsy nodded, reaching for her notebook to jot everything down. But as her fingers curled around the pages, she spied a familiar figure queueing outside a door on the ground floor. *Frayed khaki T-shirt. Curly dark hair. Beaded bracelets.* The guy wasn't wearing a camera around his neck like the last time Bitsy had seen him, but it was him: the hunter who'd been searching her house. "Kosh, over there." She grabbed his shoulders and turned him in the right direction.

Kosh squinted. "Is that … the hunter from your kitchen?!"

"Yes, only he's not a hunter," Bitsy realized. "We just assumed he was because he had a hunter magicore with him. Look at his black overalls – he's an initiate. He must look older than he is."

"So … he's *not* working for Melasina Spires?"

Bitsy pictured the boy tramping uninvited through her home and clenched her fists. "The ransom note appeared right after we saw him, and he was definitely searching my house for something." She watched the boy disappear through the door with a rabble of other initiates. "It's likely he knows something about my dad. Come on, we've got to follow him."

8

Bitsy smoothed down her overalls as she and Kosh joined the gaggle of initiates funnelling through the door. Nobody seemed to be paying them any attention. "Keep your head down," she whispered in Kosh's ear. "Try to blend in."

"What if someone talks to me?"

"I don't know, improvise."

They filed into a brightly lit hall with a wooden stage erected in one corner and a bank of tiered seating opposite. Behind the chairs, the rest of the hall was divided into three sections. One part of the floor had ramps like a skatepark; there was an assault course area with ropes hanging from the ceiling, and a storage space containing shelves and cabinets filled with equipment, including multiple fire extinguishers. Banners embroidered with the coats of arms of all five allied guilds decorated the concrete walls, which were disconcertingly pockmarked with craters and scorch marks, as if they'd repeatedly taken heavy blows. The air smelled faintly of burning.

"Hurry up and take your seats, please," called a short, bald-headed man from the stage. He had dark brown skin with black freckles and wore a boldly patterned jumper under his emerald conjuring overalls. "For those of you who don't know me, my name is Master Ollennu, and this is a beginner-level conjuring module. You should not be here if you have not yet earned your *conjuring theory* badge."

A couple of initiates blushed and hastily scurried back outside. Ignoring the tutor's guidance, Bitsy pulled Kosh towards the seats, where the boy they were following had sat down. As she passed a bookshelf, she did a double take. Among the titles were a dozen copies of *Magicalia* written in different languages. They had glossy plastic covers and crisp white pages and looked much newer than the copy in her satchel. Bitsy frowned. She'd guessed her mum had woven *Magicalia* with her mudtail, but the encyclopaedia must be a commonly used reference book in the conjuring world. Perhaps her mum's copy had been altered to make it more responsive? That could be why Melasina wanted it so badly…

Trying to be discreet, she and Kosh sidled into some empty chairs two rows behind the mysterious boy.

"Today's workshop will form part of your *BONDING WITH MAGICORES* badge," Master Ollennu announced as the last few initiates took their seats. On the stage beside him was an elegant metal lectern that looked like it had been welded with glowing threads of light, reminding Bitsy of an ozoz saddle. Master Ollennu waved his hand over the lectern and a pale mist gathered above it. An image appeared in the haze, depicting a colourful heart-shaped badge.

Murmured conversation rippled through the audience. Bitsy noticed a few initiates examining the straps of their overalls. She looked down at hers. Given that the overalls' previous owner had been careless enough to lose them, she wasn't surprised to see only two badges sewn on: *CONJURING THEORY*, a circle filled with segments of all six conjuring colours, and *HUFFLUFF HANDLING*, a rectangular badge with red stripes. She saw that the previous owner of Kosh's overalls had been slightly more successful. In addition to the two badges Bitsy had, they had earned a green, star-shaped *SCRYING WITH JUBS* and a golden-yellow *RIDING LUBBERWHARLS*.

"Look there," Kosh whispered, nodding. The mysterious boy slouched in his chair with his feet resting on the base of the seat in front. His rucksack was slung on the floor, and a tatty exercise book and pencil rested in his lap. Scrawled in messy black handwriting on the front was a name: MATEO GASPAR.

Bitsy quickly copied it into her notebook.

"To earn *BONDING WITH MAGICORES,* you must demonstrate a good working partnership with one of your magicores," Master Ollennu continued. "The stronger your bond, the more easily you'll be able to communicate. Remember: our magicores learn from us, just as we learn from them. To begin with, I want us to think about the special connection between conjurors and magicores. Can anyone tell me something about it?"

An initiate in the front row raised her hand. "Our magicores have similar personalities to us. If you're a curious person, your magicores tend to be curious. If you have a short temper, your magicores will too."

Master Ollennu nodded sagely. "Our magicores are conjured from deeply personal memories, which means they often think and behave like us. They are also unique in appearance, just like we are. What else?" He gestured to Mateo with a frown. "Put your feet down, please."

Mateo snorted and answered, "Even when your magicores wear shades, you can sense their presence." He sounded bored, like he just wanted to get the workshop over and done with. "And you can feel when they've been extinguished."

"That is correct," Master Ollennu conceded. "It's even been claimed that on rare occasions you can sense their life force beating inside you." He wiggled his fingers over the lectern and the image in the mist changed to two red words written in capital letters: ALPHA-LEVEL ONLY. "I'm going to teach you all some bonding exercises you can do with your magicores. First of all, I need you to each conjure an alpha-level magicore. For many of you, this may only be your second or third time conjuring something. At this stage of your tutelage, it's important not to rush. Just conjure at your own pace. Off you go!"

The auditorium erupted into activity as the initiates pulled out various farthingstone objects. Bitsy spotted a spanner, a heart-shaped ring and a pocket watch among them. Most initiates closed their eyes and held their farthingstones tightly as if meditating. Mateo rolled up his right sleeve and clasped the beaded bracelet on his wrist. It had to be made of farthingstone.

"They're going to notice we aren't conjuring anything…" Kosh murmured through his teeth.

Bitsy tensed as Master Ollennu scanned the hall. They couldn't afford to get chucked out now. She fetched her dad's fountain pen and her mum's pendant from her satchel. "Here," she said, handing the pen to Kosh. "We'll have to try conjuring something. Giverna told us how it works."

Kosh gulped as he took Eric's fountain pen. The

barrel glowed blue, red, purple, yellow, green and white under his fingertips. "What shall I conjure?"

Checking that the coast was clear, Bitsy slid *Magicalia* out of her satchel and into her lap. Remembering a species she'd read about the first time she'd opened the encyclopaedia, she flipped to the first page. "What about a hix? It's an alpha-level clairvoyant magicore, and its source emotion is amusement. Its unique gift is that it can temporarily persuade people of something."

"Like a Jedi mind trick?" Kosh's face brightened. "That sounds awesome! A hix it is. What about you?"

"Err…" Bitsy's brows drew together as she perused *Magicalia* slowly. *Something easy…*

As she turned the pages, she spotted the listing for a springle and smiled as she remembered Crumbs. "I've got it. I'll conjure a springle. They're alpha-level, and I know exactly what they're meant to look like. Giverna said that to conjure Crumbs, she has to remember a joyous moment from her sixth birthday. You go first – do you have a memory of a time when you felt amused? Maybe when you were laughing or when you found something really hilarious?"

A grin spread across Kosh's face. "That's easy. Oddingham FC versus West Hobbledown last season. I was sitting with my mum and dad in the East Stand, watching the team mascot – a badger named Odders

– dance at the side of the pitch. Odders fell over. My dad snorted hotdog up his nose and my mum and I didn't stop laughing until twenty minutes into the first half."

Picturing the scene, Bitsy giggled. "I love it." She glanced around the room. Mateo was still focused on his farthingstone bracelet and none of the other initiates had conjured anything yet, so their cover was intact. "Now you have to hold the pen and think of the memory, I suppose."

Kosh gripped the pen. After a few moments, nothing happened. "I must be doing it wrong…"

Bitsy surveyed the room again and noticed how the initiates looked deep in concentration. "Try closing your eyes and focusing harder on the memory."

With a deep breath, Kosh shut his eyes. The muscles on his forehead tightened, and the corners of his mouth twitched. Bitsy stared at the fountain pen in Kosh's hand, willing it to work. A minute passed.

Then another.

Kosh lifted open one eyelid, checking to see if anything was happening.

"Maybe you need to immerse yourself in every detail of the memory?" Bitsy suggested. "The sights, the smells, the tastes, the colours – like you're back there at this very moment."

Closing his eyelids, Kosh tried again. After a few

seconds, Bitsy flinched as a puff of farthingdust appeared above Kosh's hand, glittering as it swirled through the air. "Kosh, it's working!" she hissed.

Kosh opened his eyes and gasped as the farthingdust formed a beachball-sized sphere that plopped into his lap. The sphere sprouted flat ears, a black nose and four stubby paws. As the farthingdust melted away, a magicore covered in flyaway reddish-gold hair emerged beneath. It looked like a cross between a giant guinea pig and a Pomeranian. It beamed up at Kosh with a milky-white gaze and then did the loudest hiccup Bitsy had ever heard.

Kosh burst out laughing. "He is the cutest thing EVER!"

"How do you know it's a *he*?" Bitsy asked as Kosh bundled the hix into his arms.

A couple of initiates turned round to look at them and Kosh hushed his voice. "I'm not sure. It just feels right." He leaned his head away as the hix rolled up his chest and started trying to lick his face with a tiny black tongue. "What shall I name him?"

"Giverna said a magicore's name must be connected to the memory you used to conjure it," Bitsy reminded him.

Kosh considered the hix carefully. "In that case, I'll name him *Odders*, after Oddingham FC's mascot." As soon as Kosh spoke Odders' name, the hix pricked up his ears and made a whooping noise like a hyena.

106

"I think he likes it," Bitsy observed.

Master Ollennu started clapping. "Excellent, up there! A beautiful hix – and one of the fastest to be conjured in the room."

As Kosh sank lower in his chair, Bitsy assessed the progress of the initiates. Several had now conjured magicores. She spotted what looked like a blue-eyed lizard on one initiate's shoulder and a hummingbird whizzing up the sleeves of another. A few more were beginning to muster clouds of farthingdust. It looked like there was a magicore moving under Mateo's chair, but Bitsy couldn't see it properly. "Do you feel OK?" she asked Kosh, thinking of the energy he must have expended.

"Yeah, fine. It's like Giverna said – you feel a bit tired and hungry afterwards. My stomach's gurgling and my muscles ache, like after a long swim." He nudged her. "Come on, it's your turn."

While Odders rolled around hiccuping in Kosh's lap, Bitsy grasped her mum's pendant. The stone teardrop was cool against Bitsy's clammy palm and Bitsy felt a rush of excitement holding it, knowing that her mum must have used it to conjure magicores, too.

"You can do this," Kosh said. "Choose a strong memory. That'll help."

Bitsy relaxed her shoulders, closed her eyes and inhaled slowly, trying to focus her brain. She scoured her memories for a time when she had felt full of joy. A few instances sprang to mind. There was Christmas morning last year when her dad had surprised her with presents in bed, or that time she and Kosh had invented the game crumble-tumble by taking turns to devour an entire chocolate cake while bouncing on his trampoline.

She considered both occasions carefully, but some of their details felt fuzzy. She needed a crystal-clear memory, something she had thought about often.

And then she realized.

She had a whole treasure trove of those memories, all connected to her mum. They were moments she had relived again and again to make sure she never forgot them.

One such moment was an evening before Halloween, when Bitsy and her mum were in the kitchen of their old house, carving a pumpkin to put on the doorstep. The scent of fresh pumpkin was so strong in the air it had made Bitsy sneeze. Her mum was wearing a sunflower-patterned blouse with her frizzy chestnut hair tied back into a ponytail. The corners of her mouth had twitched mischievously as she'd added wobbly lips and curly eyelashes to their pumpkin-ghoul. When she'd turned the pumpkin around to show Bitsy, they had laughed so loudly it had drowned out the rock music playing on the radio…

"Whoa, it's happening already!" Kosh blurted. "Well done!"

Bitsy blinked open her eyes, feeling the farthingstone go warm in her hand. A cloud of fiery-orange dust floated above her fingers, whirling like a dust devil. It fashioned itself into the shape of a squashed peach and then transformed into a fuzzy-shelled springle with heavy-lidded eyes. The creature's smooth green skin was brighter than Crumbs' – closer to the colour of freshly cut grass than seaweed – but it had the same fluffy white hair and vertical tail.

"Hi there," Bitsy said, her heart racing. She couldn't believe she'd conjured the little creature into being. Her fingers trembled as she stroked the springle's soft shell. She could sense, somehow, that it identified as a girl, and Bitsy already knew what she wanted to name her. "I'm going to call you Pumpkin."

Pumpkin wiggled her tail, beaming up at Bitsy with a grin.

"It's impossible to decide who is cuter," Kosh mused, looking back and forth between Pumpkin and Odders.

Bitsy yawned, feeling a sudden wave of tiredness. Her eyelids felt heavy like she could do with a nap. Glancing at the chairs in front, she elbowed Kosh. "Look at Mateo."

Mateo's magicore had appeared from under his chair. It was the same species they'd seen him with before – a droopy-eared puppy with leathery-grey skin and multiple tails, the shapes of which kept changing. Rather than paying attention to Mateo, the magicore was gnawing aggressively at a nearby chair leg.

"We should find out what species that is," Kosh whispered. "It might reveal something abo—"

But no sooner had he started speaking than *Magicalia* jumped open in Bitsy's lap. Hoping nobody had seen the encyclopaedia move, she leaned forward to partially conceal it. The page it had opened onto contained the entry for a species of magicore conjured from *excitement*:

excitement
FIDGLET
[*Hunter, alpha-level*]

The fidglet resembles a domestic dog with strong teeth and an acute sense of smell. It has the ability to generate "pull-throughs" – temporary gateways that pull matter from one place to another. The duration of a pull-through is linked to the distance it travels, and a distinctive rumbling noise, akin to thunder, is produced whenever one is opened or closed. The fidglet has tough grey-brown skin and communicates using its twenty-four tails, which can morph into different shapes. The species' unique talent allows it to find the fastest route to whatever its conjuror seeks. It is not, however, recommended to follow a fidglet anywhere, as their tails can be notoriously difficult to interpret, and a conjuror may find themselves being led astray.

"*Akin to thunder...*" Kosh looked up from the book. "That's what we heard the night your dad was kidnapped. Do you think Melasina used a pull-through to get into and out of your house?"

As Master Ollennu congratulated everyone on their magicores, Bitsy thought carefully. "That would certainly explain how she could disappear into thin air and take Dad with her. I heard thunder in the kitchen yesterday, too, right before we saw Mateo."

"I know he's only an initiate, but I still think he's working for Melasina," Kosh said. "The Chancellor said hunters are rebellious, arrogant and strong-willed even at a young age, and he seems to have all those qualities. Maybe Melasina's recruited him early?"

The noise in the hall dulled as the initiates settled back into their seats, and Master Ollennu started talking again. Bitsy glanced at Mateo's fidglet, still chewing wilfully on a chair leg. If magicores shared similar traits to their owners, Kosh could be right. "Whatever his agenda is, it can't be a coincidence that he broke into my house the morning after my dad was kidnapped. We need to find out what he knows."

"At the back there!" Master Ollennu waved. "I can see you discussing something. Would you like to share your thoughts with the rest of the workshop?"

Bitsy flinched as the faces of the initiates all pointed in her direction – including Mateo's. Blood rushed to her cheeks and her heart raced, although Mateo looked too disinterested to have recognized her. She tried to say something, but her throat had closed up. Sitting on *Magicalia*, Pumpkin slid her head under her shell.

"If you have nothing to share, I'd appreciate it if you remained quiet so that those around you can hear," Master Ollennu said scoldingly.

Right. Of course. Sorry.

Or at least that's what Bitsy should have said. Instead, she remembered the advice she'd given to Kosh earlier, should anyone speak to them: *improvise*. "We were just, uh, discussing … Arkwright's Gyrowheel," she hazarded, finally finding her voice.

The room went quiet. Mateo stared at her, a flash of suspicion in his dark eyes. For an excruciating moment, Bitsy thought she might have blown their cover as initiates. But then Master Ollennu arched an eyebrow. "An interesting topic. For those who don't know, Arkwright's Gyrowheel was a device engineered

112

by Gilander Arkwright about three hundred and fifty years ago. It allowed a group of conjurors to absorb energy from their environment and combine it with their own, enabling them to conjure omega-level magicores." He tapped his lectern and the images in the mist reconfigured to show a spherical contraption featuring a series of six concentric rings, each one rotating on a different axis, like in a gyroscope. In the centre was a golf-ball-sized sphere of farthingstone. The device was made of gleaming silver, stitched together by the same luminous threads as the lectern. "To activate the gyrowheel, conjurors needed to charge it with six different types of energy."

"What happened to it?" Kosh called. Odders had rolled up his arm and was now perched on top of his beanie like a pompom.

"Arkwright donated the gyrowheel to this conservatoire so that tutors might use it to conjure omega-level magicores for initiates to study," Master Ollennu recalled. "The gyrowheel used to hang over the chancellor's desk. Then in 1660 the founder of the Hunter Guild tried to steal the gyrowheel for himself. As punishment, the Hunter Guild was banished from the Alliance."

Bitsy needed to update her notes. Giverna had described that story too, but without mentioning that

Arkwright's Gyrowheel had been at the centre of it. Was that why Melasina wanted it? To finally get the gyrowheel for the Hunter Guild?

"Most historians agree that the gyrowheel was destroyed after that," Master Ollennu continued, "although a legend says Arkwright hid the gyrowheel and left behind a trail of clues so that a worthy conjuror might one day find it."

Right at that moment, *Magicalia*'s pages whirred forward, making Pumpkin jump. With a furtive glance at Mateo, Bitsy shuffled in her seat, doing her best to make it seem like she'd caused the movement.

"You can learn more about the gyrowheel and Gilander Arkwright if you attend a workshop on the history of conjuring," Master Ollennu advised. "I believe the next one is a week on Saturday, but you'll have to check the timetable." He tapped his lectern and the image of the gyrowheel dissolved in the mist. "Now, let's return to our bonding exercises…"

As Master Ollennu continued, Kosh looked into Bitsy's lap. "That's weird. I thought *Magicalia* would show us something about the gyrowheel, but the pages are all blank."

But when Bitsy peered down, that's not what *she* saw. The book lay open on a section of newer, lined sheets. In the margins of the spine, tiny green shoots were laced through the paper, as if these pages were part of another book that had been bound *inside Magicalia*. Bitsy's heart fluttered as she recognized her mother's sloping handwriting. It was interspersed with all sorts of arrows, bullet points and crossings out:

Mysterious scroll

This morning I received a call from a contact at Greenwich Observatory in London. A seventeenth-century scroll, sealed with the <u>Weaver Guild</u> coat of arms, has been discovered behind a wooden panel in the Octagon Room. The Octagon Room is an eight-sided chamber with high windows, once used by astronomers to view the night sky. It was designed by famous architect Sir Christopher Wren and completed in <u>1676</u> thanks to the work of many artisans, purportedly including <u>Gilander Arkwright</u>. Did Arkwright hide the scroll there? Why?

— 26 April 2017

Arkwright's Gyrowheel?

I have examined the scroll. It contains a ten-line riddle and a set of coordinates leading to a village called Morcote in Switzerland. The riddle talks of a further six coordinates hidden in different places:

Here are the first, where the race begins.
The second are played to the tune of the wind.
The third are on paper, written and known.
The fourth are etched into walls of stone.
The fifth look down for all to see.
The sixth are as clear as clear can be.
The seventh are hidden near a bird's-eye view,
To show where the wheel is waiting for you.
But before you can claim a tool of such wealth
You must face three tests to prove yourself.

The final lines discuss a "wheel" and a "tool of such wealth". What if this is <u>Arkwright's Gyrowheel</u>*? Legend has it Arkwright hid the wheel and wrote a set of clues to help guide a worthy conjuror towards it. This riddle could be it! I'm going to Switzerland to dig deeper and see what I can find.*

— 28 April 2017

Bitsy looked up excitedly. "I'm not sure why you can't see this," she whispered, "but there are pages from one of my mum's old notebooks inside here! She was investigating Arkwright's Gyrowheel. She'd found a riddle composed by Gilander Arkwright and thought it was a trail of clues leading to where the device was hidden."

Kosh blinked and re-examined *Magicalia*. He rubbed his eyes, even glancing at Odders for a second opinion. "I still can't see anything. What else does it say?"

Bitsy's skin tingled as she looked back at the text. Her mum's voice came across so clearly in her writing that it was as if she was sitting next to Bitsy now, speaking in her ear. Checking Mateo and Master Ollennu were distracted, she whispered the next part out loud:

Switzerland

In the seventeenth century, Morcote was home to an esteemed instrument maker and member of the Weaver Guild. Only a handful of his instruments survive today, but since the second set of coordinates are "played to the tune of the wind", I tracked down the only wind instrument I could find – a flute – and purchased it at auction. Carved on the base of the flute was another set of coordinates leading to the Bodleian Library in Oxford! *I suspect each set of coordinates was hidden by a different weaver. Back then, the guild comprised artists, stonemasons, printers and architects, so it makes sense that every clue is connected to something they were*

117

working on. This could really be a race of wonders! To Oxford I go!

— 3 July 2017

"It's like your mum was on a treasure hunt," Kosh said. "I wonder if the flute she found is the same one in that cabinet in your living room? What happened in the end? Did she find the gyrowheel?"

Bitsy skimmed ahead. "The third coordinates were hidden in the spine of a book in the library, and the fourth were carved on the walls of Fasil Ghebbi, a seventeenth-century fortress in Ethiopia. The fifth coordinates..." She turned the page and paused when she saw only one journal entry left.

"What is it?" Kosh asked.

An icicle stabbed Bitsy's heart. It was a sensation she was familiar with. "The fourth coordinates led my mum to the Theatre Royal, Drury Lane in London," she said forlornly, "but she never found the fifth coordinates. The last note is dated two days before she died."

"Oh..." Kosh gazed into his lap. "I'm sorry, Bits. The gyrowheel must still be hidden. That's why Melasina wants us to find it."

"And my mum's secret notes must be why she was searching for *this* copy of *Magicalia*," Bitsy realized, slotting the pieces together. "All the information you'd need to find the gyrowheel is here." She looked at the back of Mateo's head, wondering how much he knew about all of this. If he was working for Melasina, was he after both the gyrowheel and *Magicalia*?

Just then, an alarm blared around the hall, making them both jump. Master Ollennu raised his hands. "Everybody, stay calm. It's probably just the wild rumbleplume again. Please take your magicores and evacuate to your nearest conservatoire exit in an orderly fashion."

The scrape of chair legs reverberated around the hall as initiates gathered their belongings and abandoned their seats. Most magicores were small enough to ride on their conjuror's shoulders, but others jumped across chairs or flitted through the air.

Very gently, Bitsy scooped up Pumpkin and dropped the springle into the top pocket of her cardigan. She weighed barely more than an apple. Pumpkin wriggled until she'd found a comfortable position with her front feet hanging over the edge of the pocket so she could peek out. With Odders already settled on Kosh's head, they returned *Magicalia* to Bitsy's satchel and made for the exit.

As everyone bundled into the atrium, Bitsy rose onto her tiptoes to keep track of Mateo. "Can you see him?" she asked Kosh.

The atrium vibrated with noise as attendees from other workshops emerged from doors on every level. The air reeked of smoke, and an ominous black cloud masked the ceiling, flashing with fiery sparks. The rumbleplume, no doubt. She couldn't see Mateo anywhere…

Chancellor Hershel waved at Bitsy through the crowd. "I thought I'd lost you two! Your exit's over there." She pointed towards a door flanked by Hasim and Lars, who were ushering people through.

"I think we might have lost him," Kosh admitted, scanning the vicinity. "I can't see Giverna, either. This could be a good opportunity to sneak away."

Bitsy tried to plan their next move as they headed towards the right door. "If we're going to find the gyrowheel and save my dad, we'll have to pick up my mum's investigation where she left off, at the Theatre Royal, Drury Lane."

Odders wobbled on Kosh's head as he reached for his phone and swiped a finger across the screen. "We're in luck there. According to Google, the Theatre Royal's only a five-minute walk from Kean Street."

"Let's drop our overalls back into the lost property box on the way out," Bitsy said. "I don't want to give Lars and Hasim a reason to follow us. We're in enough trouble as it is."

9

A flock of unsuspecting pigeons took to the air with annoyed squawks as Bitsy and Kosh hurried around the corner of a building, following the directions on Kosh's phone.

As they waited to cross a busy road, Bitsy suddenly realized Odders was no longer sitting on Kosh's head. She peered into her cardigan pocket and couldn't see Pumpkin, either. Very carefully, she pushed her fingers inside…

…and felt Pumpkin's soft shell.

"Odders and Pumpkin are wearing shades," she told Kosh breathlessly.

Kosh patted the air above his beanie. "Oh yeah. I can sense Odders up there."

Bitsy remembered Mateo saying something about that in the workshop. She tried to reach out with her senses and "feel" for Pumpkin. Sure enough, she detected a buoyant presence near her chest, right where her pocket was.

"We don't have much time," Kosh panted. "Giverna will realize we're missing soon and come looking for us."

They rushed past a row of shops and cornered another road by a busy barista van. Finally, Kosh stopped opposite a grand two-storey building with a large balcony and a portico supported by square columns. A painted sign under the roof read THEATRE ROYAL DRURY LANE. On top of the portico was a plaster-moulded symbol featuring a lion and a unicorn: the royal coat of arms of the United Kingdom. Glittering, ice-blue banners flapped on either side of the main entrance, advertising *Frozen the Musical*.

Bitsy and Kosh hastened through open doors, into an elegant foyer with a shiny marble floor. Enormous vases of flowers stood in alcoves around the walls, and through an archway ahead of them was a long bar with a statue of William Shakespeare behind it. Everything gleamed like it had just been cleaned and the scent of furniture polish lingered in the air. There was a merchandise shop to the left and a box office to the right, both operated by staff in neat uniforms with red ties and gold name badges. None of them took any notice of Bitsy and Kosh.

Kosh collected a leaflet from a stand by the door and skimmed the front cover. "According to this, the Theatre Royal is the oldest theatre in London and one of the most haunted in the world. It was originally built in 1663."

"That makes sense. Gilander Arkwright and his weavers would have hidden the coordinates here in the seventeenth century." Bitsy fetched *Magicalia* from her bag and, with the book's help, returned to the section of her mum's notes that she had been reading. The last entry was titled *Theatre Royal, Drury Lane* and contained more question marks, arrows and crossings out than all the previous notes combined:

Theatre Royal, Drury Lane

According to Arkwright's Riddle, the fifth coordinates "<u>look down for all to see</u>". I suspect that I will find them <u>up high</u> – painted on the auditorium ceiling or hidden on the roof. I haven't visited the theatre due to two troubling developments: firstly, there was a break-in at Greenwich Observatory. The <u>thief</u> took nothing, but my contact believes it was a chaos-conjuror who was after the scroll. She has destroyed it to stop it from ever falling into their hands. As far as I know, the only copy of Arkwright's Riddle is now written in this notebook. Secondly, someone was following me at Fasil Ghebbi *in Ethiopia. They disappeared before I could see their face, but in their haste, they dropped a small glass bottle branded with a <u>chaosphere</u>. Further analysis has revealed that the bottle contains a magi-woven poison. I'm not sure how <u>chaos-conjurors</u> know that I am searching for the gyrowheel, but I suspect this may have been an attempt to assassinate me and steal my notebook. Using the gyrowheel, chaos-conjurors will use omega-level magicores to destroy the Alliance and threaten millions of innocent lives. I must find a way to hide my notebook so they will never find it. This is getting dangerous. I am worried about Bitsy.*

— 19 September 2017

The back of Bitsy's throat swelled as she read the last line. Not a day went by that she didn't miss her mum, but grief came in waves. She could go for ages without feeling sad, and then something small would remind her of what she'd lost and it would hit her all over again. *I am worried about Bitsy.* Her mum had been anxious about something terrible happening, which would mean she couldn't be there for Bitsy. It was eerily prophetic.

"Are you all right?" Kosh asked softly, stuffing the leaflet into his pocket.

Bitsy sniffed. "Yeah. Just thinking about my mum."

One corner of his mouth lifted. "I know I never met her, but I reckon she'd be proud of us right now."

"Yeah, me too." Bitsy examined a sketch in her mum's notes. It showed a circle filled with squiggly lines, like a ball of spaghetti. It had to be *a chaosphere*. "Chaos-conjurors were after the gyrowheel, too. One of them tried to poison my mum. She never made it to the theatre, but according to the riddle, the fifth coordinates *look down for all to see*. She thought they might be somewhere up high, like on the auditorium ceiling."

"In that case, we need to find a way into the auditorium." Kosh surveyed the foyer. A few customers were queueing at the box office, plus a couple of staff were behind the bar. "Even if we got tickets for the next show, they wouldn't let us in yet. It says over there that the matinee performance doesn't start for another two hours."

As Bitsy tried to think of a solution, Kosh scratched himself between his shoulder blades. "Odders, cut it out," he hissed.

Bitsy heard a mischievous, hyena-style whoop. The air shimmered and a ball of reddish-gold fluff materialized on Kosh's shoulder. A thin black tongue shot out of it and licked Kosh on the cheek.

"Odders!" Kosh glanced left and right. "Someone might see you."

Before Kosh could grab him, Odders rolled down Kosh's body and streaked across the floor towards the merchandise shop. "Odders!" Kosh sprang after him, with Bitsy at his heels.

Odders sped under a table and settled himself between the feet of a member of staff who was arranging merchandise. Bitsy looked around the foyer to see if anyone had noticed, but they all seemed too wrapped up in their affairs.

"What's he playing at?" Kosh asked worriedly.

Bitsy wasn't sure why Odders was trying to sabotage them until she remembered something she'd read in *Magicalia*. "Wait. I think he might be trying to help us. A hix has the gift of persuasion, remember? If Odders makes someone laugh, he can temporarily convince them of anything."

Kosh's eyebrows jumped. "The Jedi mind trick! Odders can persuade them to let us into the auditorium."

Odders bounded up and down excitedly as they approached the shop. The sales assistant was a tall man with pale skin, a neatly styled beard and piercing blue eyes. His name badge said JOHAN.

"How do you think this works?" Kosh whispered. "Obi-Wan Kenobi waved his hand and told someone what he wanted them to believe."

Bitsy shrugged. "It's worth a shot."

As they drew closer, Johan looked up from shuffling T-shirts. "Is there anything I can help you with? The T-shirts come in five different sizes…" He pointed to an information guide on the table.

Kosh grinned sheepishly. "We don't want to buy anything. We, uh, need to get into the auditorium?" He started to wave his hand in front of his face, but then chickened out and tucked a strand of hair behind his ear.

"If you have tickets for the matinee, the doors don't open for a while yet," Johan explained in a friendly tone. "If it's lost property, you need to see the box office."

"No, it's neither of those."

"Oh?" Johan gave Kosh a quizzical look. "Why do you need to go in there?"

Bitsy tensed. Whatever Odders was doing, it didn't seem to be working.

"Uh, well…" Kosh cleared his throat. "We're theatre inspectors."

"Inspectors?" Johan blinked. His lips wobbled, and he burst out laughing.

Bitsy's shoulders fell. "Why didn't you say we were doing a school project or something?" she hissed.

"I don't know. I panicked."

But Johan's laughing didn't stop. He started crying and hopping from one foot to the other. Bitsy peeked under the table. Odders was spinning around by Johan's ankles.

His feathery hair had grown an extra twenty centimetres, and he was tickling Johan's legs up to his knees.

When Bitsy looked back up, Johan's laughter had subsided to a gentle giggle and there was a glazed expression on his face. He nodded at Bitsy and Kosh. "Very well, inspectors. Follow me, please."

Bitsy raised her eyebrows at Kosh. It had worked. It had actually worked.

"Odders, you legend," Kosh muttered, scooping the fluffball off the floor and into his hoodie pocket. "Now, let's find these coordinates."

They followed Johan along a carpeted hallway, past a grand staircase, and through a set of doors marked STALLS.

Emerging at the back of the auditorium, they walked down an aisle between rows of velvet-covered seats. Bitsy had never been into an empty theatre before and, in many ways, seeing the place without hundreds of people bustling around inside was more spectacular. The walls were adorned with plaster mouldings covered in dazzling gold leaf. Balconies with sumptuous red curtains overlooked the stalls. An elaborate safety curtain protected the stage, painted to resemble a set of ornate golden gates.

She tipped her head back to study the ceiling. It was painted duck-egg blue, decorated with more gold-leaf mouldings, and three chandeliers were suspended in the centre. "I can't see any numbers from here..." she told Kosh.

"Here." He unclipped a pair of small red binoculars from behind one of the seats. "Try looking through these."

As Bitsy grabbed her own pair of binoculars, she noticed Johan giggling vacantly to himself. He appeared to be lost in a happy trance. "We should search quickly," she warned. "Odders can only temporarily persuade people. At some point, Johan's gonna snap out of it."

Moving around the floor, they examined the ceiling through their binoculars. As Bitsy scoured the plaster for any unusual markings, she couldn't help but notice how fresh everything looked. The paintwork was unchipped and the plaster looked smooth and even, unlike what you'd expect in a four-hundred-year-old theatre.

"*The fifth look down for all to see*," Kosh murmured. "Maybe the numbers aren't on the ceiling at all? Maybe they're hidden near the upper level of the seating or on a balcony, where the audience looks down from?"

Bitsy could feel a rising sense of panic. They didn't have time to search the whole theatre.

A *bang* rang out as the stalls doors swung open and a uniformed woman with poker-straight hair came marching in. "Johan! What are you doing here? You're meant to be tidying the shop." She halted as she saw Bitsy and Kosh. "Who are you?"

Bitsy lowered her binoculars slowly, uncertain how to reply. She saw Odders tumble from Kosh's hoodie and whizz along the floor towards the woman's feet. He looked like a giant dust ball.

"These are the theatre inspectors," Johan explained, a delirious smile plastered across his face. "They wanted to see the auditorium."

"Theatre inspectors?" The woman scowled and put her hands on her hips. "I don't know what you think you're—" Her face spasmed. The wrinkles at the corners of her eyes crimped, her mouth widened and her lips turned upwards.

"Ba-hahaha!" She had one of those infectious laughs like Bitsy's mum, the kind that makes others giggle when they hear it because it sounds so silly. "Theatre inspectors, of course!"

Vibrating by the woman's ankles, Odders was starting to look tired. His tongue was lolling out of his mouth and his fur had lost its sheen.

"His energy's waning," Kosh said. "Let's peek on stage and then go upstairs." As he lifted Odders back into his pocket, the information leaflet he'd collected in the foyer slipped out. He picked it up off the floor and browsed through it as they climbed the steps to the stage.

"Wait a second." Kosh lifted his hand and Bitsy

paused. "It says here that the original Theatre Royal on this site was built in 1663, but the *present* theatre was built in 1812, after a fire burned down the old one. And it's just been refurbished again."

Thinking of the fresh paintwork, Bitsy was overcome with a sinking feeling. "But then … the coordinates planted here in the seventeenth century would have been destroyed in the fire. They'd be lost. For ever." Palpitations filled her chest as she thought of the ransom note and the threat to her dad's life. She couldn't lose him. "We can't be at a dead end already! We just can't."

Footsteps sounded offstage and they both jumped as a member of the technical crew walked out, dressed in black trousers and a matching polo neck. He studied them uncertainly. "Are you two meant to be up here?"

Before they could respond, Johan called in a giggly voice, "They're theatre inspectors!"

His colleague hiccuped loudly and burst into laughter.

Bitsy could see from the look on the man's face that he knew something was afoot. He unclipped a radio from the belt of his trousers and lifted it to his lips.

"I think we've outstayed our welcome," Kosh said, edging back.

Bitsy nodded, dropping her binoculars. "Yep. Time to go."

They legged it off the stage and sprinted towards the

exit, leaving Johan and his colleague chortling happily in the aisles. Bitsy felt Pumpkin bobbing up and down in her pocket and clawed a hand across her heart, trying to stop her from falling out. Her trainers slapped loudly against the marble floor as they dashed through the foyer and tore down the steps at the front of the building.

They stopped to catch their breath behind a crowd queueing for coffee at the barista van. Looking back at the theatre, Bitsy noticed a member of staff watching them curiously – a young man with a thin face and a shock of black hair. For a moment, Bitsy wondered if he was going to chase them, but then he stepped back inside the theatre. Her gaze was drawn to the lion and unicorn crest above the entrance. *The fifth look down for all to see...* "Kosh, do you still have that leaflet? I want to check something."

Bent double, Kosh fished the pamphlet out of his pocket and handed it over. "What is it?" he wheezed.

Bitsy scanned the leaflet until she found what she was looking for: a black-and-white etching of the original seventeenth-century Theatre Royal. It depicted the exterior of the building in great detail, with horse-drawn coaches and women in long dresses passing by outside. Hanging above the entrance was the same lion and unicorn crest.

And there were numbers painted along the bottom of it.

"Kosh, the coordinates are here!" Bitsy gasped. She poked the leaflet so hard that she almost tore through the paper. "*The fifth look down for all to see* – it meant the lion and the unicorn on the outside of the building."

Smacking the leaflet against Kosh's chest, she fumbled for her notebook and pencil. Kosh flapped open the pamphlet and squinted. "Twenty-seven degrees, ten minutes, thirty seconds North. Seventy-eight degrees, two minutes and thirty-one seconds East."

Bitsy wrote the coordinates down, feeling dizzy with hope. "Only two sets of coordinates left to find. Where are we off to next?"

Kosh plugged the coordinates into his phone and shrivelled.

"What is it?" Bitsy asked. "Is it far?"

He gulped like he was swallowing sour milk. "Yeah, you could say that. Those are the coordinates of the Taj Mahal. In *India*."

10

"There's only one way we're getting to India in time to save Dad," Bitsy said, dodging out of the path of a lady with a pram. "We'll have to use the root-network."

Moving away from the theatre, they navigated across the West End and into the busy shopping district of Covent Garden. The pavements were full of people bustling in and out of stores, admiring boutique windows or gathering to watch street performers. The mouth-watering smells of freshly baked cookies and fried churros drifted over from a couple of food vendors, and a clamour of voices filled the air.

Kosh looked over his shoulder. It was the third time Bitsy had seen him do it in as many minutes. There was still an Odders-shaped bulge in his hoodie pocket, so she knew it wasn't his hix irritating him. "Everything all right?" she asked.

A line appeared on his forehead. "Someone's following us, but it's not one of the theatre staff. This person's trying to hide. They're wearing a dark green baseball cap."

The back of Bitsy's neck prickled. She waited for a beat and then looked around. She couldn't see anyone fitting that description, but it was so crowded that it wouldn't be hard to stay hidden. "I've got an idea," she said. "Follow me."

She steered them out of the busy heart of Covent Garden towards a quieter street with fewer shops. Dodging between pedestrians, she sped up and took a sharp turn along another road. "In here!" She grabbed Kosh's arm and pulled him into a recessed doorway. "If someone's following us, they'll turn this way."

They waited with their backs against the wall, taking shallow breaths. Footsteps sounded, getting closer. Bitsy's heart raced as a shadow drew around the corner…

A taller than average boy with messy dark hair and a camera swinging around his neck stepped into view. His face was covered by the peak of a dark green baseball cap, but Bitsy recognized him anyway.

Mateo Gaspar.

She clenched her fists and, before she knew it, she'd stepped out in front of him.

Mateo stopped in his tracks. "You," he said, snarling.

Bitsy immediately regretted her decision. Mateo was much bigger than her, with a fierce look in his dark eyes. Despite feeling Pumpkin trembling in her pocket, she lifted her chin. "Why are you following us? And what were you doing in my house?" she demanded.

As Kosh stepped out from behind her, Mateo flared his nostrils. "How about you answer my question first. Why were you asking about Arkwright's Gyrowheel?"

Bitsy spied a trail of paw prints around Mateo's feet and guessed he had his fidglet with him. "I'm not telling you anything unless you tell me what you know about my dad."

At this, Mateo narrowed his eyes.

Before Bitsy could probe further, the tension was broken by a comedy ringtone: the gravelly voice of Batman saying, "Your phone is ringing".

Mateo reached into his inside jacket pocket and pulled out his mobile. Glancing at the screen, his eyes softened. He answered quickly, walking behind Bitsy and Kosh towards a quieter section of the road.

Turning their backs on him, Bitsy and Kosh huddled closer. "This proves it!" Kosh exclaimed. "He has to be working for Melasina. Why else would he care so much about Arkwright's Gyrowheel?"

Bitsy was inclined to agree. "That could be Melasina

on the phone right now. Kosh, we have to make him tell us what he knows!"

Just then, thunder rumbled behind them. Bitsy spun around...

And the road was empty.

"Gone," Kosh summarized grumpily. "His fidglet must have generated one of those pull-throughs."

Bitsy ground her teeth. "We don't have time to chase Mateo *and* locate the gyrowheel." Her mind whirled as she tried to figure out their next steps. "Giverna's going to realize we're missing any moment. What shall we do?"

Kosh took a deep breath, clearly weighing up their options. "We don't know where Mateo's gone, but we do know where the next coordinates are. Let's focus on finding them. Come on, we're going to rescue your dad."

It wasn't easy to find an out-of-the-way spot in Covent Garden. Still, after investigating several promising backstreets, they stumbled upon a secluded alley behind a row of coffee shops.

Bitsy scrunched her nose as they hurried past a line of industrial-sized rubbish bins. The place reeked of mouldy banana skins and used coffee grinds, which probably explained why nobody else was there. "I can't see any CCTV cameras," she noted, scanning the rooftops and building sides. "Do you think it's safe?"

"We're about to travel halfway around the world

using a network of giant roots," Kosh said drily. "Nothing about this is safe."

He had a point. Bitsy's nerves jangled as they stopped beside a bare brick wall, hidden between two bins. They'd only ventured a short way into the root-network before and so much about it was still a mystery.

"Are you sure there'll be an exit near the Taj Mahal?" Kosh asked.

Bitsy nodded. "If the root-network connects to all the places my mum visited as a journalist, then there will definitely be one in the city of Agra. She wrote an article on untreated sewage released in the Yamuna River that runs through the city and alongside the Taj Mahal." It was one of the pieces that had inspired Bitsy to become a journalist – an article that fought injustice and gave a voice to the powerless.

Kosh glanced in either direction before fishing out the root-key from under his hoodie. He sank it into the brickwork and tendrils of damp white roots wormed through the cement with a crackle, forming an arched opening in the wall.

Switching on her phone's torch, Bitsy took the first step inside. As there were no stairs in front of her, she realized they'd entered the network in a different place. She'd forgotten how dense the darkness was and how close it felt. "Look for a glowing symbol. It doesn't matter which one. If we head towards it, we should come upon the central chamber with all the other doors."

They trawled through the gloom, up and over the sprawling tubers. Bitsy tried to keep track of their route in case they got lost, but picturing the pathways was like trying to complete a Rubik's Cube in her head. She wondered if all the pathways led to the central chamber or if some of them went elsewhere.

It wasn't long before they spotted the luminous outline of the Pyramids of Giza in the distance. They followed the symbol like it was a beacon and eventually emerged at the edge of the central root chamber. Looking up, Bitsy saw landmarks twinkling like constellations high above them.

"The Taj Mahal is a big white building with an onion-shaped dome on the top, isn't it?" Kosh said as they circled round, scanning the different symbols.

"Yeah, that's the one," Bitsy replied. She didn't know much about the Taj Mahal besides its name and iconic image. Photos of it were permanently plastered on the covers of travel magazines or books about India in the school library.

Helping with the search, Pumpkin floated out of Bitsy's pocket to survey some of the doors. In the darkness, her solid-white eyes shone like moons. Her tail swung like a metronome as she bobbed merrily through the air, keeping her perfectly balanced. Odders, who still seemed a bit drained, preferred to offer his encouragement from inside Kosh's pocket, whooping loudly and lapsing into attacks of hiccups.

Eventually, Bitsy spotted the unmistakable outline of the Taj Mahal, four levels above them. She clung tightly to the rungs of a ladder as they ascended, focussing carefully on placing her feet. When they reached the door, they paused.

Kosh checked his phone. "It's midday in London, which means it's around five in the afternoon in Agra."

Bitsy had never visited India before, although she'd always dreamed of travelling to the places her mum had. "We just need to stay together and find the Taj Mahal," she said calmly.

"If we're lucky, the door will open somewhere safe," Kosh said. "We don't want to be spotted."

As they pushed open the door, they were hit by warm air and a blast of noise – blaring car horns, shouting voices and revving engines. Sunlight streamed into Bitsy's eyes, making her blink. She stumbled out into a small, tiled courtyard with low terracotta walls. The door to the root-network dissolved behind them.

"Get down," Kosh whispered, pulling Bitsy behind a wall as a couple of men in camel-coloured uniforms and felt berets marched past.

Heart pounding, Bitsy gazed up at the nearest building. A colourful sign read:

POLICE STATION TAJGANJ, DISTT. AGRA

"I know I wanted the door to open somewhere safe, but this isn't exactly what I had in mind," Kosh grumbled.

They waited for the officers to pass and then peeked over the top of the wall. Parked outside the police station were several police-branded motorcycles and soft-top 4x4s. It was a short dash to the road, busy with electric rickshaws, cars and buses.

Kosh watched the officers carefully. As soon as they'd turned their backs, he hit Bitsy on the arm. "Now!"

They hurdled the wall and bolted to the street, quickly joining the flow of other pedestrians. Shabbily plastered hotels lined the road, alongside shops selling everything from fresh fruit and blankets to mobile phones and car tyres. Traders called to each other in what Bitsy presumed was Hindi, laughing and waving. The air was alive with so many new sounds and smells that she didn't know where to turn.

She beamed at Kosh. She'd never been so far away from Oddingham and it felt incredible.

"Come on," he said, smiling. He pointed to a nearby street sign that featured a symbol of the Taj Mahal. "It must be this way."

They followed the road around, heading north. The narrow pavements were cluttered with market stalls and they had to snake through various crates and boxes to make progress. As they brushed past the shoppers, Bitsy's eyes were drawn to the brightly coloured saris some of the women wore, adding pops of colour to the crowds.

Soon enough, a majestic red stone archway appeared in the distance. It was as tall as two double-decker buses with long queues of tourists twisting around at its base. As Bitsy and Kosh approached, they saw police officers underneath the archway, operating security scanners. Beyond the scanners was a row of ticket barriers, where tourists waved their tickets under a flashing red light and a bar lifted to let them through.

"The Taj Mahal must be through there," Kosh said. "We'll be able to pass through security easily enough, but what about the ticket barriers?"

"I suppose we could see if my dad's debit card works abroad?" Bitsy suggested. "With enough rupees, we can buy a ticket each."

Kosh glanced thoughtfully at Bitsy's top pocket. "Or … Pumpkin can levitate objects, can't she? Maybe she can raise the barriers to let us through?"

Bitsy felt Pumpkin wriggling. "What do you think?" she whispered. "Can you do that?"

Pumpkin squeezed her smooth green head out of

Bitsy's cardigan pocket. As her dandelion headdress sprang back into position, she stretched her nose towards the red stone archway like she was trying to touch it.

"I think that's a yes," Kosh said. "Let's join the queue."

The line moved quickly despite the number of tourists waiting in front of them. Bitsy cobbled together a couple of "fake" tickets using folded paper from her notebook. They only had to appear real from a distance, and she knew what the actual tickets looked like because everyone around her was clutching one.

At security, she pushed her satchel along the conveyor belt and waited nervously as it moved through the scanner. Fortunately, *Magicalia* didn't raise any alarm bells, and they were able to continue. As they approached the ticket machines, Bitsy watched the tourists ahead of her.

"We've just got to do what they do," Kosh said into her ear.

Bitsy patted her pocket. "Pumpkin, get ready. You need to time it exactly right." Jitters filled Bitsy's stomach as the woman in front of her passed under the barrier and walked off. Trying to appear relaxed, Bitsy stepped up to the ticket scanner. She moved her fake ticket towards the red light—

Too soon, the bar rose in front of her.

But none of the staff seemed to notice and Bitsy hurried through.

"Nice one, Pumpkin," Kosh said, once they were both on the other side.

Bitsy heaved a sigh of relief. All they had to do now was find the coordinates.

They'd emerged into a forecourt bordered by red sandstone porticoes and neat lawns. People were taking pictures on a paved area in the centre, gazing up at an ornate domed gateway, as tall as the archway they'd just passed under, but much broader and grander. It was inlaid with tiles decorated with Arabic writing and delicate red and green flowers. Unlike the streets outside, the forecourt had a peaceful atmosphere. People mumbled quietly to each other, moving around slowly.

"The Taj Mahal is this whole complex," a lady said softly, strolling past them. She was wearing a bib that said TREASURES OF INDIA, and a party of English-speaking tourists with rucksacks and cameras followed behind her, listening intently. "This structure is the main gate. If we walk through, we'll see the gardens and the mausoleum – the building you always see in photos."

Bitsy tugged on Kosh's sleeve, pulling him towards the back of the group. "Come on, we might learn something helpful."

"A mausoleum is a building that holds a tomb," the tour guide continued. "The Taj Mahal is often considered one of the most romantic places in the world because Mughal emperor Shah Jahan built it to house the tomb of his wife, Mumtaz Mahal. Since the seventeenth century, the building has widely been considered a symbol of love."

"That's a bittersweet story," Kosh commented, as they followed the tour guide through the gateway. "The emperor loved her this much, but she died. What does Arkwright's Riddle say about the coordinates?"

Bitsy checked her notebook. She'd jotted down the last few lines of the riddle when she'd copied out the previous coordinates. "*The sixth are as clear as clear can be*," she read. "But how can coordinates be clear?"

"I'm not sure. Maybe they're written on glass?"

Emerging on the other side of the gateway, they simultaneously drew their breaths.

A milk-white mausoleum with an onion-shaped dome rose ahead of them. It looked more beautiful in the soft, sunny light of early evening than in any of the photos Bitsy had seen. It was approached by neat formal gardens and a long channel of water, all set out in perfect symmetry. It made the mausoleum look like a mirage floating on the horizon.

"It's ... *amazing*," Kosh uttered.

Bitsy stared, instantly wishing they had time to stay longer.

The tour party shuffled forward in mute awe. Their guide directed them along one side of the pool. "Follow me, please. We kindly ask that you don't throw coins into the water."

Water...

"Kosh, that could be it," Bitsy said. "*As clear as clear can be* – the coordinates might be underwater."

They made a preliminary search of the pool end nearest to them. Although the basin was painted a pale turquoise, it was speckled with mildew, dirt and leaves, making it tricky to see any numbers. "I haven't found any coordinates yet," Kosh said. He gazed into the distance. "This pool is massive and there are another three just like it. It'll take hours to comb through them all."

"Let's split up," Bitsy suggested. She prodded her top pocket. "Pumpkin, we need the whole team searching. You're looking for eight numbers, hidden under the water."

Kosh looked like he was poking himself in the abdomen as he nudged Odders. "Yo, Odders. You're up. Stay invisible this time."

The group parted ways, arranging to meet at the far pool, closer to the mausoleum. Tackling the closest pool, Bitsy made her way slowly along one side of the water, tapping her pencil against her notebook. She imagined an invisible grid drawn on the basin's surface and carefully checked each square. She saw several brown blotches and a few squiggly lines that looked like stains from old coins or plants, but there were no numbers.

"Excuse me," someone asked in an American drawl.

A finger poked Bitsy in the shoulder and she turned around to see a middle-aged woman with a pointy chin and beady eyes. The stranger wore a green visor over her frizzy red hair and clutched a tourist map in one hand.

"Does that guidebook of yours tell you what year this place was built?" the woman asked.

Bitsy glanced at her notebook, realizing that the lady had mistaken it for a travel guide. "Oh no, this isn't a guidebook. It's just where I write notes. I believe the mausoleum was built in the seventeenth century."

The woman lifted her eyebrows. "Oh, my mistake. Thank you."

As she strolled away, Kosh waved from the other side of the pool. "Bitsy, over here!" A dozen people glared at him as he lowered his hand. "Sorry..." he whispered gingerly.

Bitsy quickly crossed to the other side. "Have you found them?"

"I'm not sure. Look there." He pointed to another wiggly brown stain near the centre of the pool. "Do you remember that science lesson where Miss Taylor drew an arrow on a piece of paper, held it behind a glass of water, and it changed direction?"

"The reversing arrow illusion," Bitsy remembered.

147

"It's because as light passes through water, it bends, distorting the images behind it."

Kosh wagged his finger. "Exactly. So, if the water is bending the numbers, they won't look like digits. They'll look like abstract marks."

Bitsy's skin tingled. She felt sure Kosh was on to something, but there was only one way to find out. She glanced in both directions. "Cover me."

Kneeling by the pool's edge, she took a deep breath and plunged her face into the cool water. As she blinked back bubbles, she glimpsed the brown squiggle that Kosh had pointed to at the bottom of the pool...

...except it wasn't a squiggle any more. It was two straight lines, forming a number 7. A metre to the left of it was written 2 and beyond that, 3.

"They're here!" Bitsy spluttered, lifting her head out of the water. She dried her face on her sleeve and motioned in a line down the centre of the pool. "Each number is written a metre apart." She fumbled for her notebook, wanting to jot the coordinates down as fast as possible.

"I've got it," Kosh said, submerging his phone in the water. He tapped at the screen, taking a few pictures. "This baby's waterproof to three metres."

They moved along the pool, snapping photos of the other numbers in the correct order. Once Kosh was finished, he lifted his phone to show Bitsy. As he zoomed in on the first number, a reflection on the water's surface caught Bitsy's attention: a dark glass bottle clenched in a hand. The front of the bottle was branded with an eerily familiar design: a tangle of swirling lines within a circle.

Bitsy's blood went cold, remembering the sketch of a chaosphere in her mum's notes. A chaos-conjuror had tried to assassinate her mum using a magi-woven poison contained in a similar bottle. She looked up, her senses alert. Standing across the water was the middle-aged woman in the green golf visor who had spoken to her earlier. She stared greedily at Bitsy's notebook, her fingers twitching around the bottle.

Bitsy's pulse spiked as she hastily tucked the notebook away. "Don't look now, but we're being watched," she told Kosh. "It's a woman holding a bottle with a chaosphere on it. I think she might be an assassin."

11

Bitsy hooked her arm under Kosh's and pulled him back towards the main gateway. "We need to get out of here. Now."

His neck tensed. "An assassin! Where?"

"Other side of the pool, the lady in the green visor."

Glancing over his shoulder, he shrank. "She's following us."

"I thought she was a tourist when she spoke to me earlier. She was interested in my notebook," Bitsy said. "My mum wrote about a chaos-conjuror who tried to assassinate her and steal her notebook because it contained information that might help them find the gyrowheel. Perhaps they're after my notebook for the same reason?"

As they snaked through the visitors, Bitsy sensed an uplifting presence near by. Her chest loosened as Pumpkin plopped back into the top pocket of her cardigan. "Pumpkin's returned," she told Kosh. "Do you have Odders?"

"I can feel him right behind us. He'll catch up."

They picked up their pace, dashing through the main gate and across the forecourt towards the exit. Bitsy checked on their pursuer. A dogged scowl lined the woman's forehead. She had disposed of her map and was walking briskly to keep up with them.

They left the site the same way they'd entered, under the red stone archway. Mercifully the exit barriers were automatic, so Pumpkin did not need to pull any levitation tricks. As they jogged into the streets of Agra, Bitsy noticed Kosh's hoodie pocket bulging. Odders had made it back safely.

"This way," she said, hopping over several empty crates as they turned down another market road. "We can try to lose her in the crowds."

The pavements were heaving. Bitsy's temperature rose as she dodged between shoppers, trying not to flinch at every clang and shout behind her. She couldn't work out how chaos-conjurors knew that she and Kosh were searching for the gyrowheel. And how had the group tracked them to Agra? It's not like she and Kosh had told anyone; Melasina had made sure of that. Something about this didn't add up.

At the end of the street, Kosh rocked onto his tiptoes. "I can't see her any more. Let's look for somewhere to open the root-network and get back to London."

After ten minutes of trawling the streets, it became apparent that finding a quiet spot in Agra would be near on impossible. Every alley they ventured down bustled with people, dogs, cars and e-rickshaws. It was even busier than Covent Garden. They cornered one building only to be confronted by a large white cow with handlebar-shaped horns and saggy skin. It mooed angrily at them and poked its tongue up its nose as if to say, *Try again, losers!*

"At this rate, we're going to have to leave the city before we can find a suitable place," Kosh said as they trudged around another corner.

He froze in his tracks.

"Hello there," said a waspish voice.

Bitsy stumbled to a halt. The woman with the golf visor was standing in front of them. Sweat shone on her pale skin and her cheeks burned the same colour as her hair. Bitsy didn't know how she'd managed to track them through Agra; they thought they'd lost her. She spotted movement near the woman's sandals. Two parallel lines twisted through the sandy pavement like an invisible snake was slithering over the ground.

Or a magicore wearing a shade…

"Stay back!" Bitsy said with as much confidence as she could muster. She gulped as she felt Pumpkin trembling in her pocket.

The woman smiled, baring her teeth. "Be a good girl and give me the notebook."

Kosh stared at Bitsy. It was a stare that said one thing: *Run.*

Kicking up dust from the road, they spun around and sprinted back the way they'd come. Bitsy's satchel thumped against her hips, her feet slamming against the hard concrete. Kosh veered left into a road of houses. Most of them had stairs outside that climbed to rooftop terraces.

"She's chasing us!" he cried, glancing over his shoulder. "And her magicore looks *massive*!"

Bitsy frowned as she pumped her arms; the magicore had seemed small and slippery to her.

A car alarm suddenly wailed behind them, followed by a loud crash. People started diving into doorways, screaming. Ahead of them, a mother grabbed her child, pulling them behind a car. In the reflection of the windscreen, Bitsy saw what they were all afraid of…

A three-metre whirlwind of dirt and litter hurtled towards them, smashing anything in its path. Between the spinning drinks cans and plastic bags, Bitsy glimpsed the shape of a giant, octopus-like creature. Its globular body was the size of a washing machine and almost invisible, with countless tentacles as thick as drainpipes. The chaos-conjuror raced beside it, her golf visor slipping up and down in her bushy red locks.

"It's horrible!" Bitsy yelled. It seemed to have tentacles everywhere. Round, sucker-shaped puncture marks materialized on the sides of buildings, and overhead telephone cables collapsed like an invisible force had ripped them down. People shrieked, slamming doors and closing windows.

Sweat trickled across Kosh's temples. "We can't outrun it. It's too fast."

Kosh was right. Bitsy's lungs already felt like boiling lava, and the magicore was gaining on them fast. "Odders and Pumpkin can't extinguish it – they'll be mincemeat in seconds!"

Pumpkin squirmed in Bitsy's pocket and suddenly appeared. She beamed up at Bitsy, her eyes bright as snowflakes. Bitsy wasn't sure exactly what she was trying to communicate. Perhaps she just wanted to bolster Bitsy's confidence.

Confidence…

Like a jolt to the brain, Bitsy had an idea. She scoured the road and pointed to the nearest exterior staircase, about two hundred metres away. "Kosh, over there! We can call an ozoz from the roof!"

"We don't even know if they operate in Agra!" Kosh replied.

"We'll have to chance it. Come on!"

They charged towards the stairs, but the magicore pursuing them was accelerating. Leaves whipped around Bitsy's ankles and rubbish clattered through the air. She ducked as an invisible tentacle crashed into the building next to her, gouging a hole in the plaster.

"It'll catch us before we get there!" Kosh warned.

Bitsy considered their options. She didn't want to endanger Pumpkin, but she had to remind herself that magicores were like candles. If they were extinguished, they could be relit. She and Kosh, on the other hand… "Pumpkin, I need you to slow that thing down. Try anything!"

All credit to the little springle, Pumpkin didn't curl up and hide. She furrowed her brow in determination, wiggled her tail and popped out of Bitsy's pocket, floating upwards.

"We can't let Pumpkin save our butts all by herself!" Kosh told Odders. "Go help!"

Odders became visible on Kosh's shoulder, his long fur billowing in all directions like grass in a storm. He launched off Kosh like he was doing a bungee jump, rolled onto the ground and sped towards the maelstrom, hiccuping frantically.

In the road ahead, a motorcycle started rattling. It creaked as it levitated into the air. Pumpkin's face strained, using all her effort to lift it higher. Bitsy and Kosh stooped as the motorcycle flew over their heads. With perfect timing, Odders rolled up the side of a wall, backflipped into the air and landed in the driving seat. Pumpkin, meanwhile, flopped against Bitsy's chest and fell back into her pocket.

To the terrified bystanders, Odders must have looked like an eccentric stunt dog with hair extensions. He twisted the handlebars, aiming the motorcycle directly at the pursuing magicore.

They collided with a riotous *thuddunk*.

The octopus magicore gave an ear-splitting screech. Dents appeared in nearby cars and circles of tarmac were ripped from the road, as if the magicore had been knocked over and was using its tentacles to right itself. The whirlwind slowed, just for a moment…

It was long enough for Bitsy and Kosh to break away. They made it to the stairs and raced to the rooftop. Bitsy could hear the chaos-conjuror yelling angrily behind her.

"ARMOURED RIDER, I'M IN NEED. PRITHY LEND A NOBLE STEED!" she and Kosh shouted in unison.

For a heart-stopping moment, Bitsy feared the hail would not work unless they spoke it in the local language…

But then a whoosh sounded above. A gust of wind blustered around them, making the awning on a neighbouring building flap violently. Bitsy's legs shook as the rooftop quaked. Cracks appeared in the middle of the concrete and, out of nowhere, a magnificent blue ozoz materialized in front of them. The magicore was wearing a saddle identical to those Bitsy had seen before, although its rider had on a looser red uniform of a more lightweight material. She was tall and broad-shouldered with a long dark plait that ran down her back. She waved cheerfully and said something in Hindi.

Kosh replied by pointing into the street.

Down below, the whirlwind had gathered speed. It crashed into the side of the building, making the ozoz rider wobble in her saddle. With menacing strength, the octopus magicore started climbing the walls, ripping plaster off with its tentacles.

The ozoz rider pulled a lever on her saddle, releasing two chairs. "Get on!" she screamed.

As Bitsy and Kosh scrambled on board, Bitsy saw the chaos-conjuror charging up the stairs towards them, and a shiver traced her spine. She had a horrible feeling it wasn't the last they'd seen of her.

The ozoz bent its knees and jumped.

Never before had rocketing into the sky in a flimsy metal chair felt so wonderfully safe. Bitsy inhaled deeply as they whizzed into the air, climbing into the evening sky over Agra. Far below, people were starting to emerge into the chaos of the rubble-strewn streets.

"Where do you want to go?" the rider called back.

Bitsy cupped her hands around her mouth and shouted, "Somewhere quiet with no one else around!"

"You got it!" The rider pulled on the ozoz's reins and the magicore adjusted, angling its head and feet so their course bent to the right.

Kosh's face tightened as he touched his heart.

"You OK?" Bitsy asked.

"It's Odders," he replied, miserably. "He's been extinguished. I can feel it."

Bitsy immediately looked down at Pumpkin. Her eyelids were heavy and her downy fluff had wilted like she'd been drenched in water. She must have been holding on to say goodbye because she managed one last sunny smile ... before she burst into farthingdust.

A cold feeling spread through Bitsy's chest, followed by a sense of emptiness. *Until next time,* she thought sadly.

They landed minutes later in an empty car park between buildings on the city's outskirts. After bidding farewell to their ozoz rider, Kosh opened a door to the root-network and they were swallowed back into darkness.

"That was seriously close," he muttered, turning on

his phone's torch as they shuffled along a pathway. "How did she manage to follow us?"

Bitsy coughed. "I don't know." Her throat was thick with dust and the muscles in her legs were throbbing, but they'd made it. She patted her jeans pocket, checking that her notebook was safe.

"Where to now?" Kosh asked.

"To the next coordinates, I suppose. The sooner we find the gyro—"

A light switched on, making them both jump. A stocky figure with pale hair stood silhouetted in front of them.

"Giverna!" Bitsy spluttered, recognizing the chopstick sticking out of her hairdo.

Giverna had her hands on her hips and another root-key – identical to theirs, but with a G woven into it – hanging around her neck. Her cheeks were pink and her eyes were bloodshot. "Oh, I don't think so," she snapped irritably. "You two are coming with me."

12

Water bubbled through the copper pipes in Giverna's kitchen as the soothing smell of chamomile tea drifted over from a pot on the stove. In the middle of the ceiling, the stained-glass candelabra swayed from its chain. Its jewelled light swept back and forth across the kitchen table, illuminating Giverna, Kosh and Bitsy, a half-empty platter of sandwiches and three glass mugs of steaming tea resting between them.

"Let's see if I have this right," Giverna said, drumming her nails against the side of her mug. "After the conservatoire was evacuated, you ran off to *find ice cream*."

"I … had a craving," Kosh offered sheepishly. "Double chocolate with salted caramel sprinkles. It's the best."

Bitsy let her hair fall in front of her face so Giverna couldn't see her cringing. Giverna had practically marched them back through the root-network in silence, making it impossible for them to invent a good cover story without her overhearing.

"And what about this?" Giverna held up the root-key she'd seized from Kosh – the one shaped like an E. "How long have you been root-walking?"

"That's what you call it?" Bitsy asked, lifting her head. *Root-walking?*

Giverna grumbled. "That's what your mother called it. When she and her mudtail created that place, they made an additional key for me and also one for your father. I don't know how you got hold of Eric's key; he certainly wouldn't have given it to you himself. Root-walking is incredibly dangerous. You could have been hurt inside and I wouldn't have known where you were to help you. I only ventured in there on a hunch."

Bitsy peered guiltily into her glass mug, running her fingers up and down the strange markings on the outside. Perhaps she had been reckless, but it was only because she was desperate to save her dad. Thinking of him, she felt a pang of sadness. She wondered where he was right now and hoped he wasn't scared.

"I'll return this to your father when we find him," Giverna decided, tucking Eric's root-key away in her apron pocket. "Where did you root-walk to? Did anyone see you?"

Kosh side-eyed Bitsy and started slurping tea.

We got chased by an octopus magicore who destroyed half a street in Agra, Bitsy thought. Obviously, she couldn't say that. "We opened a door to New York, but we never went through it," she admitted. It wasn't a lie; it just wasn't the whole truth.

"Hmmm." Giverna narrowed her gaze on the notebook poking out of Bitsy's pocket and Bitsy curled her fingers around it, determined not to let Giverna confiscate it, too. "I heard you talking about *coordinates*," Giverna said. "Think very carefully: is there anything else you want to tell me?"

Bitsy squirmed in her seat. Adults only ever asked that question when they knew exactly what you were hiding and were offering you the chance to fess up. She glanced at Kosh, who had frozen with his lips on his mug. Maybe it would be better to tell Giverna the truth – about the ransom note, *Magicalia*, and their hunt for the gyrowheel – but they couldn't risk it while her dad's life hung in the balance.

More softly this time, Giverna said, "I can't help you unless I know what's going on."

"I've got an idea," Kosh announced, putting down his mug. "Can we borrow your thinkerchief?"

Giverna looked puzzled, but she fetched the square of white fabric from her pocket and spread it on the table between them. Bitsy wasn't sure what Kosh was planning until he leaned into her ear, saying, "The ransom note said *speak of this to no one*. But perhaps there's a way to communicate without speaking?"

Of course. Bitsy's hopes crept up. Using the thinkerchief, they could show Giverna everything without the need to say it out loud. "Good thinking," she whispered. And, turning to Giverna, she continued, "Can you help us take some precautions first? We need to close all the windows and draw the blinds. You'll understand why when we start to explain."

The kitchen darkened as they got to work. Giverna even shut off all the pipes and stuffed the taps with rags. Afterwards, they drew back around the table and turned their attention to the thinkerchief.

"Ready?" Kosh asked Bitsy.

She took a deep breath. "Ready."

They both placed a hand on one corner of the thinkerchief.

The polka dots bounced around frenetically before resolving into an image of the ransom note attached to Bitsy's front door. In quick succession, they reconfigured to show Bitsy studying her mum's notes in *Magicalia*, jotting facts in her own notebook, and then her and

Kosh searching for coordinates at the Theatre Royal, Drury Lane.

Giverna lifted a hand to her mouth as she watched. "When did you find the ransom note?"

"Yesterday morning," Bitsy said, feeling the burden ease a little now that someone else knew. "We're sorry we didn't tell you sooner, but we were scared about what might happen."

"It's all right. You haven't done anything wrong." Giverna's eyes crinkled with sympathy. "I might have done the same in your situation. But you cannot continue hunting for the gyrowheel. It's too dangerous." Something in her tone made it sound like she was talking from experience.

"Did you know that my mum was looking for it?" Bitsy ventured.

With a heavy sigh, Giverna moved her mug aside. "Your mother came to me at the beginning of her investigation. I told her to be careful. Powerful tools attract dangerous people, and I didn't want to see her get hurt. Your mother assured me that only two other people knew what she was doing – your father and..." From the ghostly wash on Giverna's face, Bitsy could tell that whatever she was about to say was very painful. "...and Melasina Spires."

"*What?*" Kosh jerked his head back. "But that makes no sense."

Bitsy frowned. "Why would my mum trust Melasina Spires?"

"Because," Giverna said, bitterly, "they're sisters."

A sledgehammer walloped Bitsy in the stomach. If she hadn't been sitting down, she might have fallen over. "W–what?" she stammered.

"Your mother's maiden name is Spires. Melasina is two years older than her. I taught them both at the conservatoire." Giverna touched the thinkerchief and the polka dots rearranged into the image of two teenage girls, standing with their arms around one another's shoulders. The shorter of the two Bitsy recognized as her mum. Her frizzy hair hung loose around her shoulders and her scrawny arms were nearly lost in the folds of the T-shirt she wore under her black conjuring overalls. The taller girl had a bolder haircut and dark eyes outlined with kohl.

Bitsy blinked, unable to believe it. The two girls had the same-shape nose and a similar curve to their jaws. She could see they were related.

"As initiates, the two of them were inseparable," Giverna continued. "When Melasina joined the Hunter Guild, and it was forbidden for the sisters to see each other, they did so secretly. I warned Matilda against trusting her sister, but your mother always saw the best in people. In the end, that's what Melasina took advantage of."

Bitsy's throat contracted. "What do you mean, '*in the end*'?"

Giverna's face wobbled. She reached a hand across the table and squeezed Bitsy's arm. "I'm so sorry, Bitsy. There was nothing I could do. At first, Melasina helped your mother with her investigation. But one day, while Matilda was driving, Melasina demanded to see her notebook. When your mother said that she'd destroyed it, Melasina attacked her. The car swerved and…"

Giverna's voice faded as Bitsy was transported back to the last time she and her dad had discussed her mum's accident. With misty eyes, he'd told her there had been ice on the road that morning, and the tyres had lost grip. "No," Bitsy said, shaking her head. "No, that's not what happened. My dad wouldn't lie about that."

Giverna parted her hair to reveal a gnarled red scar on her scalp. "I was sitting in the backseat. After the car skidded, I blacked out. When I came to, Matilda was injured and Melasina was nowhere to be seen. Matilda used the last of her energy to tell me a secret: that morning, she had used her mudtail to conceal the pages of her notebook inside an old copy of *Magicalia*. Her mudtail had woven them so Matilda's handwriting could only be read by someone she loved."

Tears stung in the corners of Bitsy's eyes as she realized that Giverna was telling the truth. It would explain why

Bitsy could see her mum's writing and Kosh couldn't; and why Melasina needed Bitsy to read *Magicalia* and find the gyrowheel for her. It had always seemed unfair that her mum had been taken from them in a car accident, but that she had been betrayed by her sister – Bitsy's aunt – was even more painful.

"This is why you must stop looking for the gyrowheel," Giverna added. "A tool that powerful cannot be delivered into the hands of someone like Melasina Spires."

Bitsy wiped her face on the back of her sleeve. Although she agreed with Giverna, she couldn't just give up on her dad. And the ransom note had been very clear: if she wanted to see him alive again, she had to find the gyrowheel. "What happened at the meeting with the Alliance? Have they located any of the Hunter Guild's barracks?"

"They have found one," Giverna said with a sigh. "The rescue team went in, but the site was abandoned. They're still looking for others. It's going to take time."

Bitsy chewed on her lip. If she stopped looking for the gyrowheel, the hunters might find out. Her dad would only be safe if the Alliance rescued him before that. It was a massive risk. "Is there anything we can do to speed up the Alliance?" she asked eagerly.

"They're working as fast as they can," Giverna said. "I recommend you drink some more tea and try to get some sleep. I'll tell you as soon as I hear anything."

Waiting was unbearable. Bitsy spent most of the evening combing through her notes, trying to identify something to help the Alliance rescue team. Kosh paced up and down the kitchen, nervously eating his way through the contents of Giverna's cupboards. After conjuring Crumbs, Giverna sat silently with the springle curled in her lap, waiting for a telepathic call.

By the time they all went to bed, it was late and there had been no news.

"This sucks," Kosh said, crashing back into his pillow. He and Bitsy were lying on makeshift beds on the two sofas in the front room. "At least when we were out hunting for the gyrowheel, it felt like we were actually doing something to help your dad."

"Yeah, but we were also playing right into the hands of my evil aunt," Bitsy said with a shudder.

Kosh rolled onto his side so he was facing Bitsy. "Do you want to talk about it?"

She stared up at the ceiling, feeling shivery even with a duvet wrapped around her. "I just want my dad back. Everything Giverna told us about my mum and Melasina – I can't process it without him." Wriggling to get comfy, she accidentally kicked her satchel off the end of the sofa and *Magicalia* slid out onto the floor.

"Do you think we should have told Giverna about

that chaos-conjuror in Agra?" Kosh asked. "We still don't know how they managed to find us."

Bitsy swallowed, thinking of their near escape. Given that anyone could be a chaos-conjuror, it was difficult to know whom to trust. "The chaos-conjurors must need the information in my notebook to find the gyrowheel, otherwise they'd already have it by now. I reckon Melasina knows that chaos-conjurors are hunting for it too. She's probably been spying on us this whole time. One of her hunters will be watching us, ready to swoop in and snatch the device if we ever find it. I suppose it could even be Mateo Gaspar."

"Wait a second..." Kosh sprang upright. "If that's true, then why don't we use it to our advantage? We could set a trap for whoever's spying on us. Lure them somewhere, give them the slip, and then follow them back to wherever your dad is being held!"

Bitsy turned to Kosh. "You mean, spy on a spy? That's impossible! For starters, how are we going to lure them anywhere?"

"By going after the next set of coordinates!" Kosh said, excitedly.

As he grabbed his phone and began tapping wildly at the screen, Bitsy hesitated. Giverna had expressly told them to stop looking for the gyrowheel. If they were going to try this, they'd have to keep it a secret from her. Again.

"But we don't have the root-key any more," Bitsy reminded him, pushing herself up on her elbows. "How are we going to travel anywhere?"

The light from Kosh's phone illuminated his widening grin. "Not a problem. The next coordinates point to the Palace of Versailles in France. That's only twenty-five kilometres from Paris and—"

"—and we've already got a trip booked there tomorrow morning!" Bitsy sat bolt upright, her skin prickling. She didn't believe in destiny, but this felt like that. She'd helped her dad plan the holiday, so she knew the arrangements. She grabbed her phone and opened a browser. "I should be able to access our tickets. I've still got my passport in my bag. Do you still have yours?"

Kosh nodded. "I never unpacked it. We can do this: get to Versailles, find the coordinates, spy on the spy, rescue your dad."

"One small snag," Bitsy said, biting her lip. "Children under thirteen years old aren't allowed to travel on the Eurostar alone. We need to bring an adult with us."

Just then, *Magicalia*'s cover burst open and its pages flipped forward as if a breeze were moving them. Kosh drew back his duvet and collected the book off the floor. He brought it over to Bitsy's sofa and they sat together to examine it. It had opened in the middle of the *A* section, where the first entry at the top of the page read:

arrogance
COPYCAT
[*Metamorph, beta-level*]

The copycat is a medium-sized, scaly magicore with a long tail. Its name derives from its physical similarities to the common feline, and it has the power to shapeshift into any human, once it has eaten one of their belongings. It is best known for its gold, almond-shaped eyes and the distinctive purring noise it makes when tired.

Cold fingers traced Bitsy's spine at the word *shapeshift* – it reminded her of the murderous conjuror Riddlejax, whose twisted beliefs had inspired the chaos-conjurors.

"Umm … is the book suggesting what I think it is?" Kosh asked. "That we conjure a copycat to shapeshift into your dad and have it escort us to Paris?"

Bitsy shifted in her seat. All she'd dreamed about these past two days was seeing her dad again. The thought of being around a weird doppelganger of him was unsettling to say the least. "I think you're right. I don't like it, but what other choice do we have? Time's running out and this is our only plan."

Kosh ran his finger across the page. "A copycat is a beta-level species, so it'll take more energy to conjure one

171

than Odders or Pumpkin. Let's conjure it now. We can recover while we sleep."

"Good plan." Bitsy reached under her pyjama top for her mother's teardrop pendant, which she'd started wearing around her neck. "Arrogance is a copycat's source emotion. That's like when you feel smug. Or superior."

Grinning, Kosh withdrew Eric's fountain pen from his rucksack. The barrel glowed different colours under his touch. "I can think of plenty of times when I've felt that way. Mostly while beating you at *Mario Kart*."

He tightened his grip on the pen and closed his eyes.

Bitsy waited patiently as Kosh took deep breaths, his brow furrowed in concentration. A few minutes passed in silence, and then Bitsy shuffled back as a swirling cloud of farthingdust appeared over the sofa between them. It resolved into a pointy-eared cat with glowing yellow eyes and an oversized head. The creature's scaly skin reminded Bitsy of the flaky chamois cloth her dad used to clean their car. Folds of skin were draped around the copycat's neck and the base of its ears, and giant flaps hung under its belly, as if its skin had continued growing long after its skeleton had stopped. Its shiny scales were round as coins and coral pink.

The copycat trotted forward, its chin held high.

"Whoa..." Kosh muttered, beaming. As he stroked the magicore's back, its scales made a *shhhht* noise like a maraca. "You're a girl, aren't you? I think I'll name you…"

Bitsy had a feeling she knew what Kosh was going to say. There was one character he always chose to play as whenever they raced in *Mario Kart*.

"…Princess Peach," Kosh decided happily. "Peach for short."

Peach arched her spine, rubbing against Kosh's hand. Despite her baggy skin, she had long, elegant limbs and graceful movements.

After consulting *Magicalia*, Bitsy fetched her dad's battered leather wallet, removing his passport, all his cards, coins and any scraps of paper inside it. "She can eat this. It's the only thing I have of Dad's that we don't need."

Peach sniffed the wallet curiously.

"I need you to shapeshift into Eric Wilder," Kosh said. "Can you do that?"

The copycat tossed her head, as if to say, *Me? Of course! I'm incredible!* She picked up the wallet in her teeth and flung it into her mouth. Her eyes shone as she chewed.

And then her scales started to shift position. It was like watching Tetris blocks move. Some scales rotated. Others shifted left or right, up or down. Peach's saggy skin stretched in all directions, making a *wibble-wobble* sound like jelly. Her legs extended and her chest widened, pushing her head upwards.

173

"This is beyond weird," Bitsy said, looking away. "Tell me when it's over."

After thirty seconds, the transformation was complete. Bitsy turned back and jumped, seeing her dad in front of her. He was dressed in cotton chinos, a striped shirt and a pair of leather brogues the same tawny-brown colour as the wallet Peach had eaten. The shape of his face and all its features were exactly as Bitsy knew them; his hair was combed in the usual way, and he had the correct pattern of freckles across his nose. There were only two odd things about him. Firstly, he was sitting in the same pose as Peach had been before she'd shapeshifted, meaning his legs were tucked under his bottom and his hands hanging in front of his chest. Secondly, amber flecks were glittering in the whites of his eyes.

"That is amazing!" Kosh said, staring. Peach-Dad gave a haughty smile.

Bitsy quickly turned her attention to her phone, desperate for a distraction. "I'll set the alarm for tomorrow morning." She stuffed *Magicalia* back into her satchel and tucked her notebook under her pillow. "We'll need to sneak out of here before Giverna wakes if we're going to catch our spy and find my dad!"

COPYCAT

13

The lights on the Eurostar were far too bright. Bitsy yawned and rubbed her eyes as Kosh arrived back from the onboard buffet.

"This was all they had for breakfast," he said tiredly, tossing a bag of croissants and two bottles of orange juice onto the table. He handed Bitsy her dad's debit card and slumped into the seat opposite. "At least the contactless payment was working."

Bitsy pushed the card back inside her satchel. The pressure changed as the train entered a tunnel, making her ears pop. "See that man over there?" She signalled covertly to an elderly gentleman across the aisle. "While you were gone, he caught sight of Peach and spat out his coffee. We've got to do something about her face. It's getting worse."

Glancing at the seat next to Bitsy, Kosh recoiled. Peach-Dad was sitting with her hands in her lap, smiling proudly. This wouldn't have drawn attention if the entire left side of her face didn't look like it had *melted*. One of her gold-flecked eyes had slipped down beside her nose and her cheeks sagged so much that they were now draped over her shoulders. Bitsy shuddered. Beholding Peach-Dad still gave her chills. She had to keep reminding herself that the person who appeared to be her dad was actually a golden-eyed magicore with pink scales.

"She must be running out of energy," Kosh said. He grabbed a newspaper off an empty seat. "Here, Peach. Cover your face with this and pretend to be asleep."

On command, Peach-Dad took the newspaper and relaxed back in her seat with her head against the headrest, placing the newspaper across her face. Bitsy looked around the carriage, checking for other curious passengers. The newspaper seemed to be working for now, but Bitsy couldn't help but worry what would happen if Peach turned into farthingdust before they reached Paris...

Bitsy's seat vibrated as the train sped on. She rolled her neck from side to side, trying to dispel some of the tension in her shoulders. Supervising Peach-Dad had made for a stressful journey so far. Although the three of them had managed to navigate through security and passport control in London without arousing suspicion, when they'd passed a traveller carrying an *actual* cat in a basket, Peach-Dad had started meowing at them, much to the consternation of the confused owner. Only in the last twenty minutes had the copycat's appearance deteriorated.

A buzzing sounded from Kosh's pocket. Frowning, he pulled out his mobile phone and blinked at the screen. "Oh no, it's my parents. I forgot – they promised to ring me this morning to wish us well in Paris."

"You'd better answer it," Bitsy said, feeling a flash of guilt that Kosh was putting himself in danger to help her.

Holding his phone between them, Kosh answered the call and the beaming faces of his mum and dad appeared. They were sitting at their kitchen table, framed by two coffee mugs, a milk carton and several potted plants.

"Morning!" Kosh's mum called cheerily. She had a narrow face with delicate features and wore her centre-parted black hair in a wavy ponytail down one shoulder. "Did you three make the Eurostar all right?"

Kosh signalled to their surroundings. "Yeah, we're on our way. Eric's gone to the toilet, so it's just Bitsy and me here."

"Hi," Bitsy added, waving. Her heart warmed, seeing their familiar faces. "I hope you had a great weekend away. We might enter a tunnel soon and get cut off."

Kosh's dad – a broad-chested man with dark hair as messy as Kosh's – nodded. "Thanks Bitsy, it was lovely. We'll make it quick, then. We hope you both have lots of fun in Paris. Take some photos to show us when you get back."

"We will," Kosh assured them, his forehead tightening. He thought for a moment and then asked, "Have either of you ever been to Kean Street?"

His dad scratched his chin. "*Kean Street?* Is that somewhere in Paris?"

"No, in London," Kosh replied. "You've never been there?"

When his parents both shook their heads, the muscles in Kosh's face relaxed. "In that case, never mind. It's not important."

"Well, have a great time both of you," Kosh's mum said. "Tell Eric we said hi."

"Will do," Bitsy promised.

Kosh waved. "Bye then!"

"Bye!" his parents replied.

After Kosh had ended the call, Bitsy sat back in her seat. "Why did you ask them about Kean Street?"

"I wanted to see their reactions to find out whether they're conjurors or not," Kosh explained with a shrug. "I've still got no clue why I'm cosmodynamic or who might be a conjuror in my family. They didn't recognize Kean Street, though, so I guess it isn't them."

Thinking of everything they'd discovered in the last three days, Bitsy realized that while Kosh had been helping her to find the answers to her conjuring heritage, he'd also collected some questions about his own. "Perhaps one of your grandparents is a conjuror, like you said before. We can investigate together. I'll help you."

"I know you will," Kosh said with a small smile. "Just think, we might need to visit Sri Lanka. You'd finally get to meet my Great-Aunt Ravi and Elvis!"

Bitsy beamed. She'd been watching videos of Elvis, Kosh's great-aunt's German Shepherd, since he was a puppy. "That would be awesome!"

A line appeared on Kosh's brow. "But that's a project for another time. Right now, we've got to save your dad."

Returning to the mammoth task ahead, Bitsy felt a wave of nausea. Doubts and fears churned through her mind like the litter tornado they'd escaped in Agra. She had no idea how they would identify the hunter that was spying on them, or what would happen when Giverna realized they were missing. She gazed past Peach-Dad's chest to her reflection in the dark glass. There were shadows under her blue eyes and pencil smudges on the cuffs of her cardigan. With her curls hanging loose, she looked similar to her mum in Giverna's thinkerchief. She wondered what a young Matilda Spires would have done in this situation and whether she was anything like her.

Inspired, she fetched her notebook from the pocket of her raincoat. "I made some notes on the Palace of Versailles this morning before our alarm went off." She flicked back a couple of pages, scanning through her bullet points. "It's a ridiculously extravagant palace built during the seventeenth century by King Louis the fourteenth of France. It's filled with expensive artwork and furniture and has over *two thousand three hundred* rooms, including ballrooms, private apartments and even an opera house!"

"That's wild," Kosh said, unscrewing the lid on his orange juice. "What's the clue from Arkwright's Riddle?"

"*The seventh are hidden near a bird's-eye view, to show where the wheel is waiting for you,*" Bitsy read from her notes. "A bird's-eye view – what do you think that might mean?"

"A bird's-eye view is when you're looking down on something from above," Kosh said. "Maps are nearly always drawn using a bird's-eye view. Blueprints, too. Maybe there are some on display in the palace?"

Bitsy logged in to the Eurostar Wi-Fi on her phone and navigated to the Palace of Versailles website. "There's an online database of all the items in the palace collection – art, furniture and historical documents. We could scroll through and— Oh, you've got to be joking. There are over twenty-two thousand items listed!"

Kosh stuffed a chunk of croissant into his mouth and turned his attention to his phone. "In that case, we'd better get started. To save time, you should begin searching on page one, while I'll search backwards from the final page. We can meet in the middle."

They trawled through the database while tearing off croissant pieces and sipping juice. Peach-Dad started snoring, which sounded worryingly like a cat's purr. Swiping past photos of candelabras, porcelain soup terrines and mantel clocks, Bitsy paused only to examine documents or paintings. Cross-referencing her notes, she ignored anything made before 1656, when the farthingstone meteorite was first discovered; or after 1689, when Gilander Arkwright died. There were lots of portraits of men and women in extravagant clothes, with fine jewellery and huge wigs. Bitsy paused on one portrait of Louis XIV himself because she couldn't get over how self-important he looked – even more so than Peach, who was literally born from arrogance.

Her attention wavered as the air crackled and a voice came over the loudspeaker: "*Ladies and gentlemen, it is approximately nine-twenty a.m. local time and we will shortly be arriving at Paris Gare du Nord…*"

As the announcer switched to French, Bitsy tensed. "We can't be there already! I've still got hundreds of items to check through."

"Me too," Kosh admitted, rubbing his eyes, "*and* my phone's almost out of battery."

As passengers started pulling on their coats and reaching for bags from the overhead shelves, Bitsy peeked under Peach's newspaper. She expected to see some horrifying plasticine version of her dad's head, but what she found was worse. "Yikes. We've got another problem. Peach's face is gone."

"What do you mean, *gone*?"

Checking none of the other passengers were looking, Bitsy lifted away the newspaper, revealing … nothing. Peach-Dad's head was completely missing. All that remained was the collar of her shirt and a neck-shaped lump covered in pink scales.

"Right," Kosh said, his voice wobbling. Casting around, he picked up the paper bag that had once held their croissants and blew air into it. He twisted the end tightly and passed it over. "See if you can create a head out of that. We've just got to make it off the platform and into the train station without anyone noticing."

They waited until everyone had left their carriage before affixing Peach-Dad's new paper bag skull. Kosh gently pulled his Oddingham FC beanie over the top and instructed Peach to keep her head lowered and cover her face with the newspaper should anyone look at her. Then, with a deep breath, they got off the train.

Blood thudded in Bitsy's ears as they shuffled along the concourse with the last of the remaining passengers. There was a woman in a dark coat, wheeling a large suitcase, and a family with three young children, all too interested in their affairs to notice. Ahead, people had bunched together as everyone funnelled through a gate into the main station.

Bitsy could hear Peach-Dad's purring getting louder. Not only would the sound draw more attention, but she remembered reading in *Magicalia* that this meant the copycat was tired. They didn't have much time.

"We've just got to make it to the crowd," Kosh said, picking up his pace. He grabbed Peach-Dad's arm and jumped as he saw he was only holding a floppy shirt sleeve. "Bitsy, go!"

As the newspaper fell from Peach-Dad's other hand, Bitsy caught it and stuffed it under her arm. Jogging now, she hooked a finger through Peach-Dad's belt, trying to keep up her trousers.

Peach-Dad swayed from side to side as they approached the crowd's edge.

"Is everything OK?" a concerned voice asked over Bitsy's shoulder.

Bitsy tensed and rushed forward without looking back, pulling Kosh and Peach-Dad into the crowd. As they passed through the gate into the main station, she

183

felt a release of pressure against her finger and she turned to see Peach-Dad finally disintegrate into farthingdust, the paper bag with Kosh's beanie on it falling to the concourse floor.

Kosh clutched his chest and groaned with relief, bending down to pick up his beanie and place it back on his head. "We did it! Next stop: Versailles."

They took the train from Gare Du Nord, changing at Saint-Michel-Notre-Dame for the line to Versailles-Château-Rive-Gauche, which the Versailles website informed them was only a ten-minute walk from the palace. On the way, they resumed searching the palace database until Kosh's phone died and Bitsy's was down to just two per cent battery.

The streets of Versailles were packed with sightseers. Bitsy and Kosh scanned the crowds warily, trying to identify Melasina's spy, but everyone looked like a genuine tourist. They followed a German-speaking tour group along a wide tree-lined avenue, past a statue of Louis XIV on horseback, towards a row of ornate gold railings. Beyond the bars stood a resplendent palace of jaw-dropping proportions. It was laid out in a U-shape, with brick and stone walls and a slate roof decorated with gleaming gold leaf. With thousands of windows and hundreds of chimneys, it made Buckingham Palace look positively feeble.

In front of the palace, long queues of visitors snaked across a stone courtyard. Unlike at the Taj Mahal, there were no automatic ticket barriers. Instead, palace staff wearing lanyards checked tickets using hand-held scanners.

"There's no point me conjuring Pumpkin, as I don't think she can help us here," Bitsy said, trying not to feel daunted by the scale of the place. It was easy to understand why Gilander Arkwright had chosen to hide a set of coordinates there. "We'll have to buy tickets the old-fashioned way."

Kosh spotted a sign for the ticket office and they joined the queue. While they waited, Bitsy got out her phone. If they could narrow the search even slightly, it would save them time. She might as well use the last of her battery trawling through the database.

She scrolled to the bottom of the page, browsing ornamental vases, upholstered chairs and fine porcelain. As the queue shuffled forward, she tapped to move to the next page…

…and her eyes sharpened.

The first item was an oil painting titled *View of the Château de Versailles and the gardens from the Avenue de Paris in 1668*. It depicted a detailed aerial view of the palace and gardens as they had looked long ago. There were figures on horseback parading into the palace and people in seventeenth-century costume walking around the grounds. The caption beneath the painting described it as *"The only known painting of Versailles from a bird's-eye view"*.

Bitsy gasped. "Kosh, look—!"

He huddled closer to see her phone screen. "No way. That's got to be it. Can you see any coordinates in the painting?"

Bitsy zoomed in, but the image quality wasn't good enough for her to view the smaller details. "No, but Arkwright's Riddle said the coordinates are *hidden near* a bird's-eye view, so we probably need to search around where the painting is hanging." She skimmed the information listed on the webpage. "It says the painting is displayed in the Gallery of the History of the Palace, on the ground floor of the North Wing."

"This is perfect," Kosh said as the queue moved forward. "It'll be easier to identify Melasina's spy if we're confined to one room in a gallery. We just need to be on the alert for someone carrying farthingstone who looks like they might be a hunter in disguise."

After purchasing two tickets using Eric's debit card, they entered the South Wing of the palace through the main entrance. An information desk operated by smartly dressed staff ran along one side of a modern hall. With Bitsy's phone finally out of juice, she grabbed a couple of maps from the desk and handed one to Kosh. "Here, let's plan our route."

But Kosh had frozen, staring into the mass of people ahead of them. "I knew it," he muttered. Grabbing the map, he opened it and lifted it to hide their faces. "Look over there, by the cloakroom."

Bitsy peeked out from behind the map. She started as she recognized a scrawny figure in dark clothing. "Mateo Gaspar!"

"This settles it," Kosh said. "He *is* Melasina's spy! He was at your house right before the ransom note appeared. The next morning, he was at the conservatoire with us and tailed us after we left the theatre. He's been close by the whole time."

Mateo grunted as he barged past a group of tourists, his face scrunched in anger. Watching him, Bitsy noticed something odd. "But he's not trying to hide. If he was following us, you'd expect him to keep his head down and not draw attention to himself. Instead, he's acting like he doesn't know we're here."

Kosh frowned at Mateo from around the corner of the map. "He's moving off. Why don't we split up? I'll follow Mateo while you head to the North Wing to find the coordinates. If Mateo is the spy, I'll end up there, anyway. If not, I'll come to you."

Bitsy shifted her feet. She didn't like the thought of

them parting ways. "What if something bad happens? How will I contact you now that our phones are out of battery?"

"Umm..." Kosh cast around for a solution. "What about Pumpkin? She could help us communicate telepathically, like Giverna did with Crumbs. That way, we can talk to each other no matter where we are."

Bitsy considered the people milling around them. Conjuring in a public place would be impossible with a large magicore, but with a teacup-sized springle, it might just be doable. She transferred *Magicalia* into Kosh's rucksack, clearing a space in her satchel for the farthingdust to swirl around.

With her mum's pendant pressing against her heart, she closed her eyes and recalled her joyous memory: her mum's laughter echoing around their old kitchen, the smell of freshly carved pumpkin in the air, the seed-splattered apron her mum was wearing...

It was the second time she'd recalled the memory in as many days and it felt much easier to draw upon the details than before. After a few minutes' concentration, she peered into her satchel to find Pumpkin shaking off a few sprinkles of farthingdust. "Nice to see you again," Bitsy mumbled. "We need your help."

Pumpkin gurgled as Bitsy and Kosh teased away a piece of white fluff from her coat. "How do you think this works?" Bitsy asked, stuffing the fuzz into her ear.

"I'm not sure." Kosh tapped the side of his head like a security guard wearing an earpiece. "Can you hear me?"

"Yes, because you're still speaking aloud," Bitsy replied drily. "Try talking in your head."

WHAT ABOUT NOW?

She jolted as Kosh's voice resonated somewhere behind her eyes. It sounded tinny like the train guard speaking over the Eurostar loudspeaker. *I can hear you,* she tried responding. *Can you hear me?*

His eyebrows jumped. *THIS IS SOOO WEIRD!*

It works! Bitsy intoned. She briefly wondered why Kosh didn't have a glazed expression on his face, like Giverna did when she was communicating telepathically, but figured that must only happen on long-distance calls. *Come on,* she told him. *Mateo's getting away. There's no time to lose.*

14

As Kosh raced after Mateo, Bitsy consulted her map. She needed to cross the Royal Courtyard before entering the North Wing and proceeding to the Gallery of the History of the Palace. Holding her satchel close to her hip, she squeezed between groups of visitors in the courtyard, striding as fast as possible. The area rang with shouts and chatter as teachers wrangled students and tour guides rallied holidaymakers. Overlooked by hundreds of palace windows, Bitsy imagined all the places a spy could be hiding and shivered at the thought of someone watching her. As she pushed through another group of camera-clad tourists, she locked eyes with a bald man in a black puffer jacket. For a moment, she froze, but the man's gaze swept past her and he walked over to join a group on the other side of the courtyard. Bitsy took a deep breath – she was being paranoid. She had to focus if she was going to find the coordinates.

Entering the palace's North Wing, she jostled past a queue of visitors waiting to get into the Royal Chapel, and came into a magnificent study. It was decorated with flocked ruby wallpaper, sumptuous velvet and gold.

So much gold.

WHAT WAS THAT? Kosh yelled. *HAVE YOU FOUND THE COORDINATES?*

Bitsy flinched, briefly having forgotten that Kosh could hear her thoughts. *No, not yet. What's Mateo doing?*

HE'S FOLLOWING HIS FIDGLET. IT KEEPS POPPING IN AND OUT OF VISIBILITY TO COMMUNICATE WITH HIM. IT'S MOVING IN YOUR GENERAL DIRECTION, TOWARDS THE NORTH WING.

Maybe you're right about him being Melasina's spy, Bitsy admitted. *Keep following him.*

She drew her breath as she crossed into the next room, where a towering four-poster bed filled the floor. More gold had been used to decorate an elegant fireplace, and a dazzling crystal chandelier hung from the ceiling. Every centimetre of the room was so opulent and over the top, it was strange to think that a real person had lived there. It felt more like a room in a fairy-tale palace or a doll's house.

Exploring further, Bitsy reached the Gallery of the History of the Palace, a series of small rooms with grey wallpaper and polished parquet floors. The walls were hung with oil paintings and information boards; glass cabinets lit by spotlights dotted the floors. Tourists meandered around, talking quietly and studying the exhibits. Bitsy noticed palace staff stationed at every doorway, wearing radios clipped to their belts.

She scanned the walls carefully, looking for Pierre Patel's painting. Several portraits of finely dressed men and women with rosy cheeks were displayed in the first room. The next room was dominated by a huge scale model of the palace and gardens, protected under a glass case. As Bitsy approached it, a little boy with spiky hair rushed up beside her and pressed his nose against the glass.

A woman, presumably his mother, pulled him away. "Recule, tu vas salir le verre!"

The boy pulled a face, trying to shrug her off. As he moved aside, Bitsy spotted a familiar reflection in the glass. With a burst of excitement, she turned around to find Pierre Patel's painting on the wall. It was set within a wooden frame carved with leaves and flowers.

I've found the painting! she told Kosh triumphantly. She shuffled closer, studying the trees, roads, rooftops and fountains, but there were no numbers painted anywhere. She considered the clue from Arkwright's Riddle. The nearest place the coordinates could be hidden was ... well, the frame. Examining the detailed wooden carvings, her heart jumped as she spotted a string of numbers concealed in the tumbling leaves and flowers. *The coordinates are hidden in the frame!* she projected. *Fifty-six degrees, twenty-four minutes, thirteen seconds North. Five degrees, one minute and forty-four seconds West.*

She fetched her notebook and pencil, but when she tried to write she realized the lead was blunt. She tucked the palace map under the page to stop it from tearing and, pressing hard, just about managed to scratch the numbers into the paper.

Kosh? Kosh, are you getting any of this? she intoned. *I've found the coordinates. Where are you and Mateo?*

HE'S DEFINITELY MELASINA'S SPY! came Kosh's flustered reply. *I OVERHEARD HIM TALKING TO HIS FIDGLET ABOUT THE GYROWHEEL. HE MUST HAVE THE COORDINATES ALREADY BECAUSE HE TOLD HIS FIDGLET TO LOOK FOR A QUIET PLACE TO OPEN A PULL-THROUGH.*

Bitsy shoved her notebook into the pocket of her raincoat. *If he's leaving, then we have to follow him! Where are you now?*

APPROACHING THE HALL OF MIRRORS.

She checked the map. The Hall of Mirrors was in a long gallery connecting the palace's two wings. If Bitsy followed the route the map recommended, she'd have to pass through over thirty rooms to get there. There was, however, a shortcut through a section marked PRIVATE TOURS ONLY.

I'm on my way, she told Kosh. *Don't let him out of your sight!*

Exiting the gallery, she steered around a couple of corners to where an arched opening was cordoned off with a rope barrier and a sign that read NEW EXHIBITION COMING SOON in English and French. Waiting until no one was looking, she hopped over the rope and slipped under the arch.

The hall beyond was dark and eerily quiet. Empty podiums crowded the floor, creating a forest of shadows. Bitsy's nose tingled with the smell of fresh paint, like the place had been newly decorated. A single door was lit on the far wall by a fire-exit sign that cast a green glow.

There was nobody else there. Bitsy zigzagged through the display plinths to the far wall and pressed her ear against the fire-exit door. She couldn't hear movement on the other side, so she tried the handle.

It was unlocked.

Very slowly, she nudged the door open and peeked around the corner.

She found herself gazing halfway up an impressive marble staircase. To the right, it climbed towards a ceiling painted with clouds and cherubs. To the left, it sank into a dingy corridor. The area was silent. Pushing the door open further, Bitsy lifted her foot over the threshold. An alarm pierced the air.

The noise was so unexpected that Bitsy almost lost her footing on the stairs. She steadied herself against the doorframe as the sound reverberated up the walls. Footsteps thundered above her. *Kosh, I'm in trouble!*

Her pulse raced as she retreated back inside the exhibition room and shut the fire-exit door behind her. She leaned her shoulders against it, breathing heavily.

WHAT'S HAPPENED?

She frantically explained her situation. *I need you to buy me some more time. Can you slow Mateo down?*

I CAN TRY.

Suddenly, she felt the door judder. *Kosh, someone's coming!*

She dived behind the nearest podium, tucking her satchel between her knees to ensure she was completely hidden.

The door creaked. Footsteps plodded across the carpet. Bitsy risked a peek around the corner of the plinth and spied a brawny, bald man with a square jaw. He was dressed in a black bomber jacket, under which he wore rugged utility trousers, combat boots, and a camo-print T-shirt that pulled across his bulging muscles. Bitsy's chest tightened as she recognized the man she'd seen earlier staring at her in the courtyard.

WHAT'S HAPPENING? Kosh communicated. *ARE YOU OK?*

The security alarm was still wailing, making it difficult for Bitsy to think. Trying hard not to panic, she did her best to describe the scene. The man scanned the room with a cold gaze, walking steadily forward. Slowly, he lifted open his bomber jacket to reveal a farthingstone dagger tucked into his waistband, alongside …

She stifled a gasp.

… a small leather pouch branded with a chaosphere.

He's a chaos-conjuror! she projected at Kosh.

WHAT? he replied worriedly. *HOW HAVE THEY FOLLOWED US AGAIN? BITSY, YOU HAVE TO GET OUT OF THERE!*

Heart thumping, Bitsy watched as the chaos-conjuror closed his left hand around his farthingstone dagger, which briefly glowed red, and a swarm of farthingdust materialized beside him. The particles resolved into a black insectile magicore, the size of a large dog. Its sleek, segmented body was supported by at least twenty pairs of thin, spidery legs that sprouted from a ridge along its back. It had a curled tail like a scorpion and an arrow-shaped head with a small mouth and two mandibles. On the crest of its head was what looked like a dollop of wobbly red frogspawn. It wasn't until the black dots inside each frogspawn moved that Bitsy realized what they really were: eyes.

Covered in a layer of greasy black fur, the magicore looked like it had just emerged from a tar pit. Its legs rippled as it slunk forward, lifting its feet off the carpet with a distinctive *schhht* noise like ripping Velcro. Bitsy had no idea what emotion the creature was conjured from, but the very sight of it made her skin crawl.

The conjuror pulled a piece of springle fluff out of the chaosphere pouch. "Stay alert," he growled at his magicore. "She's around here somewhere."

Obeying its master, the magicore's legs vibrated and, in a streak of shadow, it rocketed up the wall and onto the ceiling. Suspended overhead, its frogspawn eyes began scanning the room unnervingly.

Blood rushed to Bitsy's face. She could feel Pumpkin shaking in her satchel. Guards were probably still rushing towards the hall, but she'd rather be accosted by them than the chaos-conjuror. They had to get out of there. Now.

As the conjuror stuffed the springle fluff into his ear, Bitsy crawled around the edge of the podium towards the door. Her fingers trembled as she placed one hand in front of the other, trying not to make a sound. She flinched as she caught the conjuror's reflection in a glass display case. For a heart-stopping moment, she thought he'd spotted her, but he was staring into the middle distance, just like Giverna had when she'd been communicating telepathically. Bitsy wondered if the man was speaking to another chaos-conjuror; it was becoming clear that the group was a lot bigger than Chancellor Hershel thought.

Steeling her nerves, she rose to her feet and dashed to the door. Her blood pounded as she turned the handle and slipped outside, hoping the chaos-conjuror and his magicore hadn't seen her.

There were several guards talking urgently at the top of the stairs, so she sped off towards the corridor at the bottom.

BITSY, ARE YOU ALL RIGHT? Kosh's voice sounded loud and urgent in her head.

No! she replied, projecting her panic. Her thighs pumped as she sprinted down the stairs. *The chaos-conjuror has a weird spiderpede magicore that's really fast and can crawl up walls. Pumpkin and I don't stand a chance!*

THAT'S ... BAD, Kosh acknowledged. *I'LL CHECK MAGICALIA FOR HELP. IN THE MEANTIME, I'VE STALLED MATEO. I TOLD PALACE STAFF THAT I SAW HIM TRYING TO GRAFFITI ON A WALL, AND THEY STOPPED TO QUESTION HIM.*

Grateful for Kosh's quick thinking, Bitsy reached the bottom of the stairs and tore along the corridor towards a door at the far end. She was only a few metres away when a spine-tingling *schhht* noise sounded directly above her. Her arm hairs stiffened as she looked up. The spiderpede was hanging upside down on the ceiling, ogling her with its mound of jelly eyes. A blob of radioactive-green mucus sat on the tip of its curled tail. With incredible speed, it drew its tail back like it was setting a catapult, then launched the projectile straight at Bitsy's head.

She ducked just in time to see the substance splatter onto the marble floor. It looked like a mix of dental floss, chewing gum and melted cheese – stringy, sticky and altogether disgusting. A plume of foul-smelling smoke rose from the area where it had landed.

Update! Bitsy told Kosh as she skidded to a halt by the door. *The spiderpede also fires acidic snot bombs.*

She yanked on the handle and pulled the door open with an unfortunate bang. A darkened hall of pink marble stretched ahead of her. Velvet chairs stood at intervals along the walls, which were decorated with glinting crystal sconces and Greek style statues.

Bitsy didn't have time to admire the décor. She bolted through the door, snatched one of the chairs and jammed it under the door handle behind her. It might not prevent the spiderpede from escaping the corridor, but it would hopefully slow it down.

I'VE GOT GOOD NEWS AND BAD NEWS, Kosh

announced in Bitsy's head. *GOOD NEWS: I FOUND A SPECIES OF MAGICORE YOU CAN CONJURE TO HELP YOU.*

Bitsy dived behind one of the statues as voices sounded at the far end of the hall. In the reflection of a marble panel, she saw a group of security guards carrying torches and radios, no doubt looking for her.

She squeezed her clammy palms, feeling trapped. With the chaos-conjuror and spiderpede behind her, and the guards ahead of her, she had no escape. *But if I conjure a different magicore, Pumpkin will be extinguished and we won't be able to communicate any more,* she warned Kosh.

GONNA HAVE TO RISK IT, he projected. *YOU HAVEN'T HEARD THE BAD NEWS YET.*

The shuffle of bodies filled the hall. Bitsy pressed her back flat against the wall as the security guards waved their torches, altering the shape of every shadow. Her heart stopped as a beam hovered over the statue she was hiding behind.

She clutched her satchel, hoping against hope that nobody spotted her.

After a few beats, the light glided away and the guards turned back the way they'd come. Bitsy let out a breath as the sounds of their footsteps faded. *What's the bad news?* she asked Kosh reluctantly.

THE BAD NEWS IS THAT I KNOW THE MAGICORE THAT'S CHASING YOU. IT'S A DELTA-LEVEL ARMOURER SPECIES CALLED A SCUTTERFLIX AND IT'S CONJURED FROM PANIC.

Over Bitsy's shoulder, the door to the stairwell suddenly rattled. She tensed as the chair she'd jammed under the door handle fell away...

Heart racing, she sprinted down the corridor, her trainers slapping loudly against the marble floor. She pushed through the door at the end into a jarringly modern stairwell with a stainless steel lift in the centre. The area was mercifully empty, although the call buttons by the lift doors were glowing as if they were in use. Remembering the route to the Hall of Mirrors, she dashed towards the steps and began to ascend.

Delta-level! Bitsy glanced worriedly over her shoulder as she ran up the stairs. *There's no way I can conjure a magicore strong enough to beat that.*

JUST DO WHAT I TELL YOU, Kosh intoned. *TRUST ME.*

Bitsy reached under the neck of her T-shirt for her mum's pendant. As her fingers curled around it, she tried to have faith. Maybe this magicore could turn her invisible or defend her in some way. *All right,* she told Kosh. *Tell me what to conjure.*

QUIGGLE

15

Kosh's voice buzzed loudly in Bitsy's head. *IT'S A BETA-LEVEL WEAVER-TYPE MAGICORE CALLED A QUIGGLE. ITS SOURCE EMOTION IS DISAPPOINTMENT.*

Disappointment? Bitsy scowled as she raced up the steps. Why couldn't it be confidence or excitement? She was trying to escape an acid-shooting scutterflix. A disappointing memory was not what she wanted to think about right now.

Approaching the top of the stairwell, she heard voices. With her back flattened against the wall, she peeked around the corner and saw the same security guards she'd just escaped gathered outside the lift. One had a radio clipped to their belt; the others wore earpieces.

She retreated a few steps to consider her options. There was no way she could sneak past without them noticing. She'd have to wait there until they disappeared into a lift … and hope the chaos-conjuror and his scutterflix didn't find her first.

"Patrouille à la sécurité," one of the staff said curtly into his radio, "des mises à jour?"

The radio crackled, echoing down the stairwell. A broken voice replied in French. "…*problème d'alarme… fille aux cheveux blonds et à la veste rouge.*"

Bitsy tensed. She couldn't be sure, but she suspected "*cheveux blonds*" might mean "blonde hair" and "*veste rouge*", "red jacket". They had her description.

Suddenly, a door scraped open a few flights below. The distinctive crunch of scutterflix steps made the hairs on the back of Bitsy's neck go rigid. She pictured the creature's snapping mandibles and swallowed. *It's now or never,* she told Kosh. *If I don't conjure the quiggle or make it to the Hall of Mirrors in time…*

YOU WILL, he projected. *YOU'VE GOT THIS.*

Bitsy said a silent farewell to Pumpkin and tightened her grip on her mum's pendant. She concentrated on the first disappointed memory she could think of: reading the news headlines for the last episode of Poddingham, three days ago.

She summoned all the details of the memory to mind:

the scribbled words in her notebook; the wheeze of Kosh's laughter; and the sagging feeling inside her own stomach as she said the word *potholes*.

Seconds passed and nothing happened.

Schhht.

Bitsy's heart rate spiked as the scutterflix grew louder. She wasn't sure why she couldn't conjure the quiggle. It could be that the memory she'd chosen wasn't strong enough, or maybe she was too panicked to concentrate. Taking a deep breath, she gave it another go.

Her hand trembled on her mum's pendant, but she tried to relax and immerse herself in the same memory. She remembered sitting at her desk, her headphones pressing into her hair, the low crackle of the microphone buzzing in her ears. As she'd opened her notebook, she'd felt a heavy weight of disappointment, knowing she had to tell her listeners the same old boring stories...

Suddenly, the farthingstone turned warm in her hand and a puff of farthingdust appeared before her. It swirled through the air and settled into the shape of a tiny mouse with a pointed face and long tail. The creature dropped to the floor and, as its coat of twinkling dust evaporated, a layer of short olive-green fur emerged beneath. The quiggle had a grumpy face with beady green eyes and droopy whiskers. It gave Bitsy a dissatisfied look and huffed.

Bitsy's first thought was that she was going to kill Kosh. The quiggle was the size of a vol-au-vent that the scutterflix might devour at a party … but there wasn't time to do anything about it now.

"Your name is … Headline," she decided hastily. She sensed that Headline didn't identify strongly as male or female. They weren't either. "I need your help getting out of here. There's a scutterflix and a conjuror chasing me."

As if on cue, the security alarm fell silent and Bitsy heard the stomp of heavy footsteps approaching. She scanned the walls, but couldn't see the scutterflix.

Headline rolled their eyes, like it was just their luck to have been conjured by such a loser, and scurried around the corner of the stairs. Realizing she couldn't hear the palace security staff any more, Bitsy followed.

The coast was clear by the lifts, but Bitsy could see shadows moving behind a set of glass doors leading to another corridor. Headline darted to an area beside the doors, turned their back to the wall and lifted their tail.

For a worrying second, Bitsy thought that Headline might be about to poop, but then they touched the tip of their tail against the plaster...

...and with a soft crumbling noise, a series of Swiss cheese style holes expanded in the wall, like ink spreading through wet paper. On the other side of the holes, Bitsy could see cobwebs and the dusty brickwork that lined the cavities between the walls of the building. The space looked big enough for her to fit. *Kosh, you genius,* she thought as she hurried forward. Headline might not be able to turn Bitsy invisible, but they had provided a way for her to move around unseen.

Headline aimed their tail at the largest hole in the wall, roughly the size of a dustbin lid. Bitsy got to her knees in front of it. "Thank you," she whispered.

Headline gave a tired squeak as if to say, *Whatever.*

Bitsy was about to crawl through when she sensed movement behind her. She flinched as a ball of stringy green goop hit her right trainer and began sizzling through it. Sour-tasting gas filled her mouth, making her cough. Over her shoulder, she saw the scutterflix streaking towards her across the ceiling. The chaos-conjuror was tearing down the stairs after it.

"Go!" Bitsy told Headline.

With a flick of their tail, Headline vanished into one of the smaller holes. Several acid bombs splattered on either side of Bitsy's legs as she scrabbled forward, her raincoat scraping against the plaster. One of her pockets snagged on an exposed brick and, as she yanked it free, she heard a loud rip. A fresh blob of scutterflix goop hit her right heel as she clambered to her feet, squeezing up into the narrow gap between walls. She felt a stinging pain as the heat of the acid corroded her skin.

Lumps of green sludge continued to sail through the Swiss cheese holes, but no sooner had they landed, than the holes started closing. There was a faint snap as they finally sealed shut and everything went black.

Panting heavily, Bitsy was about to shuffle forward into the darkness when she noticed a green light by her ankle. Headline was glowing like a radioactive gooseberry. Bitsy felt a pang of guilt for ever underestimating them.

Fearing the scutterflix might burn through the wall at any moment, Bitsy reached down and pulled off her damaged trainer. The melted rubber sole snagged on her sock, pulling that off, too. She winced as she saw the wound: three swollen red blisters the size of fifty-pence pieces. It was painful, but she'd live.

Headline nudged Bitsy's ankle with their nose, eager to get going.

"I need to get to the Hall of Mirrors," Bitsy said, awkwardly pulling the clean sock off her other foot and putting it on the blistered one. She showed Headline the map. "It's here."

Headline looked left and right along the passageway, their whiskers twitching. They shrugged their mousy shoulders and scurried ahead, lighting the way like a beacon.

Dust crumbled down the walls as Bitsy hobbled after them, the shoulders of her raincoat grating against the bricks. Headline turned two corners – particularly difficult to navigate with a satchel – and arrived at a long expanse of stonework.

After sniffing the air, Headline tapped their tail against the concrete and another set of Swiss cheese holes developed. Bitsy peered through the largest one and felt a surge of hope. Huge mirrored panels, gilded stone columns, baroque furniture – it had to be the Hall of Mirrors.

She waited a minute or so, listening out for tourists or security guards, but the place was quiet. After counting to three to steady her nerves, she crawled out of the wall and limped to her feet.

The Hall of Mirrors was a spectacular gallery of shining marble and gleaming gold. Sunlight flooded the large windows along one side, reflecting in a row of dazzling mirrored panels opposite. Gold sculptures holding crystal candelabras flanked the parquet floor and at least a dozen chandeliers hung from the painted ceiling. A bustling tour group had stopped at the far end of the hall to listen to their guide, but Bitsy couldn't see Kosh or Mateo anywhere. A chill swept over her skin, fearing she was too late. Perhaps Mateo had already gone?

Pausing to admire the hall must have lowered Bitsy's adrenaline because it was right then that conjuring Headline caught up with her. The blood rushed to her head, making her vision go blurry. Swaying with dizziness, she steadied herself against a wall. "Headline?" she whispered, hoping the quiggle was paying attention. "I've got to find my friend. He's—"

"—right behind you," a voice whispered, making Bitsy jump.

As her sight cleared, Kosh appeared at her shoulder, grinning. Sweat beaded his brow and his breathing was ragged. "Good to see you." He glanced at her missing shoe. "You'll have to tell me what happened later. There's no time."

Grabbing her arm, he pulled her into an adjoining room, empty of tourists, with more sunlit windows and opulently decorated walls. A shimmering, metre-wide square of light was hovering close to the ceiling, making an ominous rumbling noise. As Bitsy drew closer, she realized it was an opening through which she could see a sunset horizon. "A pull-through?" she guessed.

"Mateo eventually gave the palace staff the slip. He disappeared through this a minute ago, but I don't know how long it'll stay open. *Magicalia* said the duration of a pull-through is directly linked to the distance it travels." Kosh crouched in front of the portal and locked his fingers together, forming a step with his hands. "Come on, I'll give you a boost."

Despite still feeling giddy, Bitsy's senses sharpened.

If there was even a slight chance that her dad was on the other side, it was a chance worth taking. She placed her surviving trainer in Kosh's hands and pushed up, clambering through the opening.

16

Bitsy felt like she'd been thrown into a giant tumble dryer. Wind blasted her from all directions. Thunder rumbled in her ears. Her chin dug into her chest and her ankles pitched over her head as she did a backwards roly-poly.

All at once, she was surrounded by warm air and dropped to the ground in a crouch. As Kosh landed beside her, she saw the pull-through dissolve into farthingdust behind them.

"That was even worse than ozoz travel," Kosh moaned, readjusting his beanie. "Can you see Mateo?"

Shaking off her dizziness, Bitsy assessed their surroundings. They were perched on a rocky outcrop overlooking an expanse of sandy desert. Close by, a complex of ugly concrete buildings was half-buried in the sand, enclosed by a tall barbed-wire fence. Judging by the setting sun, they had to be in another time zone to Paris. "Those structures look a bit like the Hunter Guild's barracks Giverna showed us on her thinkerchief!" She pointed to a scruffy-haired boy, trudging towards the main gate. Two guards wearing long leather jackets emblazoned with the Hunter Guild's coat of arms were standing with their arms folded outside. "That's Mateo!"

"I told you he's Melasina's spy," Kosh said, squeezing his fists.

Anger boiled in Bitsy's stomach, thinking of how deceitful Mateo had been. But the feeling quickly dissolved into hope. "My dad could be inside!" she realized. Her heart lifted as she imagined seeing him again. "We've got to find a way in."

Kosh surveyed the complex. "I can't see any magicores, but that doesn't mean they're not there, wearing shades. We have to be careful."

As Mateo approached the guards, Bitsy squinted. The two men looked ... off. One had lumps in his jacket like he had stuffed a load of tennis balls underneath; the other had a sickly-green hue to his skin. Mateo said something to both men, and the one with the bulges spoke into a radio. A moment later, the gates opened.

"Headline, I need your help," Bitsy murmured. A ticklish feeling spread down Bitsy's arm as Headline tunnelled along her coat sleeve and popped into her hand. The quiggle sniffed the air toward the barracks and then scrunched their nose.

Kosh jerked his head. "*That's* your quiggle? They're so much … smaller than I was expecting."

Squeak! Headline exclaimed indignantly.

Bitsy almost laughed. "Trust me, the size of their attitude makes up for it. Headline can get us through the fence and the walls of the building, but we need to stop the guards from seeing us."

"We could try to distract them," Kosh said. "Although, there might be other conjurors inside, watching on CCTV. We've got to think stealthy." He reached round to his rucksack, pulled out *Magicalia* and began flicking through. "Do you remember that balloon-shaped magicore Lars was holding outside the European conservatoire? Giverna said the species can turn the conservatoire entrance invisible in an emergency."

It took him a few seconds to find the correct entry in *Magicalia,* and he turned the book around so Bitsy could see:

boredom
BUNDLER
[*Metamorph, alpha-level*]

Bundlers are slow-moving beasts, often pink or orange in colour. When first conjured, they appear flat and shrivelled, but their bodies can stretch to up to ten times their original size. Their gift allows them to expand the perimeter of their personal shades, rendering nearby objects, people or entire buildings invisible. As their energy depletes, they shrink in size. They communicate by pushing air through the holes in their bodies, resulting in an array of musical sounds.

"This could work," Bitsy realized excitedly. "A bundler should be able to keep us hidden while we sneak inside."

Kosh stashed *Magicalia* back in his bag. "I've already got a boring memory – last Tuesday's German class with Frau Huber."

Remembering the lesson, Bitsy groaned. Frau Huber was their new German teacher – a sweet-natured lady with an unbelievably dull voice. For twenty minutes on Tuesday, she'd read aloud a long list of German words and made the class repeat them over and over. It had been a total snorefest.

Retrieving Eric's fountain pen from his pocket, Kosh took a deep breath. A line of concentration formed on his brow and, after a few seconds, fireflies of copper dust swirled around his fingers. They resolved into a shrivelled tangerine-orange magicore covered in silky blond fur. The magicore's pancake-like body was about the size of a shopping bag and, between the crumples of its skin, Bitsy discerned slitted nostrils, a pair of sleepy yellow eyes and a thin, toothless mouth.

"He's so wrinkly," Kosh observed, gently stroking the bundler's body. "I'm going to call you Frau Huber."

The bundler contracted, making a long, whistling note. Bitsy couldn't tell by the tone whether he liked the name Frau Huber or not.

"I need you to cast your shade over my friend and me to keep us hidden," Kosh instructed. "Can you do that?"

Frau Huber flapped like a fish out of water and, with a long *pfft* noise, started to inflate. His mouth and nostrils elongated. His skin smoothed as his body stretched until he had almost quadrupled in size. As he floated off the ground, a thin tail unravelled beneath him.

Bitsy sensed a shift in the air and noticed a hazy curtain of light drawing around them that had to be Frau Huber's shade. She reached out, her fingers creating twinkling channels in the rays. "Do you think we're invisible now?"

"Only one way to find out." Kosh gazed hopefully up at Frau Huber, now hovering over them like a sunset cloud. "Let's go."

Headline scurried along by Bitsy's ankles as the group snuck across the sandy ground towards the barbed-wire fence. Sharp gravel pierced the sock on Bitsy's shoeless foot, making her hop and wince. She kept a watchful eye on the two hunter-conjurors at the gate, but they didn't seem to notice her presence. Frau Huber's party trick had worked. They were invisible … for now.

"What happened to your shoe?" Kosh whispered, as they stopped beside the fence, a reasonable distance from the guards.

"The scutterflix fired acid at me," Bitsy hissed. "Headline, can you get us through this?"

Headline snorted as if to say, *If I must*. The quiggle tapped their tail against the metal wire and a cluster of holes materialized in the centre. Kosh's eyebrows jumped. He gave Headline an appreciative nod before crawling through the largest opening. Once Bitsy had wriggled after him, Frau Huber floated through.

When they reached the building, Headline repeated their trick in the concrete, allowing the group to pass right through the wall. They all emerged into a long, dimly lit corridor with a lino floor. Although nobody was around, Bitsy could hear faint activity elsewhere in the building: doors opening, mumbled conversations and clanging equipment.

Headline slumped against Bitsy's foot. There were dark circles under their beady green eyes and their whiskers were droopy. As Bitsy reached down to scoop the quiggle up, Headline gave a spluttering wheeze ... and burst into farthingdust.

Bitsy's lungs went cold like she'd just inhaled winter air. She blinked, realizing Headline must have exhausted the last of their energy breaking them all in there.

OK? Kosh gestured with his thumb and forefinger.

She nodded, knowing she could always reconjure Headline if they needed. Although ... she was feeling weaker. Without food or rest to replenish the energy she'd spent conjuring Pumpkin and Headline, there was only so much remaining in her body.

Kosh pointed at Frau Huber. Crinkles had started to appear in his stretched hide. He was consuming energy, too, and as soon as he extinguished, they would all become visible. They had to act fast.

Listening for signs of danger, they crept along the corridor and turned a corner. There were glass doors dotted along the walls of the corridor. Peering through, they saw what appeared to be disused sleeping quarters, where rows of metal-frame bunk beds were arranged with neatly folded woollen blankets. There were photos of smiling faces pinned to the walls beside each bunk. Bitsy wondered grimly if they might be estranged family members.

Another room looked like it was used for recreation, with a cosy space furnished with beat-up sofas, a coffee table and a shabby patchwork rug. A kitchen area with a large fridge sat off to one side, along with a flashing Star Wars-themed pinball machine and a snooker table. A noticeboard on one wall was pinned with posters advertising a karaoke night and a chess club. A sign read: THE STRENGTH OF A TRUE FAMILY LIES IN THE LOYALTY OF ITS MEMBERS.

Bitsy hadn't expected the Hunter Guild's barracks to feel so … friendly. But that wasn't what surprised her most. "Where is everyone?" she whispered to Kosh. The complex had obviously been designed as a place for hundreds of hunters to live, yet it was eerily empty.

"I don't know," he replied ominously. "Giverna said that the Alliance rescue party had found another barracks abandoned... We should follow the noise. If your dad's being held here, he'll be under guard."

Heading towards the murmured voices, they hurried down another passage and across a shadowy hall with damaged walls. From the pits and scorch marks in the concrete, Bitsy guessed it might have been used for magicore combat training. Slinking through another door, they entered a corridor with stark fluorescent lighting. The air smelled like disinfectant and gravy.

The stomp of boots sounded at the far end. Kosh grabbed Bitsy's arm and pulled her behind a wall as several hunter-conjurors appeared around the corner, wheeling a metal trolley with a pot of steaming liquid wobbling on top. Bitsy covered her mouth as the conjurors walked past. One had a giant crab's claw *growing* out of their neck; another had oily blue scales covering half their face. She gave Kosh a horrified look. What had happened to them?

Once the coast was clear, they continued along the corridor and heard voices at the first door they came to. Behind the glass, they saw what appeared to be a hospital ward with six beds surrounded by hi-tech medical equipment. Six male patients, whom Bitsy assumed were other hunters, lay resting under blankets. A few looked around sixteen and must have only recently graduated from a conservatoire. They all seemed to be suffering from bizarre afflictions. One man had scarlet feathers sprouting through his hospital gown; another was floating a metre above his bed, tethered by soft straps around his waist and shoulders. Bitsy spotted a boy in one corner with downy fluff growing off his face, exactly like the fuzz on Pumpkin's shell.

A couple of conjurors wearing white coats and

stethoscopes were gathered in the middle of the room. The taller of the two had a worrying purple tinge to her lips, while her colleague had bulges under her white coat, similar to the guard outside the building.

"They're all sick," Kosh realized, keeping his voice low. "It's like they've been infected with something."

Given the nature of the hunters' symptoms, whatever they'd contracted had to be magicore-related. The patients' faces looked washed out, their mouths were twisted in pain and their eyes had glazed over. Despite knowing that they were all spies and thieves – and that their leader had kidnapped her dad – Bitsy couldn't help but feel sympathy for them. She scanned the room, wondering how their illness was being treated. There didn't seem to be any medicine vials, brown bottles or bandages, like those she'd seen in Giverna's medical bag.

Kosh elbowed Bitsy in the ribs and her attention was drawn to a scrawny figure in frayed black jeans, further along the corridor. *Mateo Gaspar.*

Mateo paused outside the door to a different room and took a deep breath before entering. Tiptoeing after him, Bitsy and Kosh found themselves in another ward with six female patients. Mateo waved at a bed in the far corner. The older girl sitting there had the same golden-brown skin and tousled dark hair as him. She looked perfectly healthy, except for one thing…

She was turning invisible.

From the chest down, her body had completely vanished. All you could see was the squashed pillow at her back and the indentations of her legs on top of her bedsheets.

"Hey, Esme," Mateo said, pulling a chair up at the side of her bed. "I came as soon as I could. How are you doing?"

Bitsy and Kosh moved closer as Esme gave Mateo a shaky nod. "Still alive," she croaked. "You were careful travelling here, weren't you? If a conjuror from the Alliance sees you…"

"I don't care about any of that." Mateo flared his nostrils. "You're my sister. No stupid Alliance rule is going to stop me visiting you."

Esme smiled weakly. "Where were you just now? There were voices in the background when I called."

"I was in France, at the Palace of Versailles," Mateo said, lowering his voice. "I asked my fidglet to find the fastest route to the gyrowheel and she led me there."

"The gyro—?!" Esme glanced warily around the room. "You shouldn't be looking for that. You shouldn't even know it still exists."

"I'm just trying to help," Mateo argued. "When I was visiting last Friday, I overheard Melasina saying that she needed the gyrowheel to heal you all."

Esme shook her head, her curls swinging above her shoulders. "Hunting for the gyrowheel is too dangerous. You don't know who else is looking for it." She looked at Mateo imploringly. "Promise me you'll stop searching for it. *Promise me*."

Mateo's eyebrows jumped. "OK, OK. I promise. My fidglet has been leading me to different places, anyway. It's like the gyrowheel has been moving."

Bitsy frowned, confused. Mateo couldn't be Melasina's spy if he'd been looking for the gyrowheel of his own volition. She had a sinking feeling that she and Kosh had made a terrible mistake, like they'd forced the wrong puzzle piece into place. Before she could communicate this to Kosh, a whistle sounded overhead and Bitsy gasped. Frau Huber was the size of a prune and shrinking fast. There were probably only seconds before he extinguished.

Springing into action, she grabbed Kosh's arm and pulled him towards the exit. They'd just emerged into the corridor when there was a squeaky *pop* and a twinkling shower of farthingdust rained over them. As Frau Huber's shade dissolved, two figures in white coats came out of another door, further along.

This time it was Kosh that acted quickly. He ducked behind a metal trolley parked at the side of the hallway. "Bitsy, down here! They're going to see you!"

But Bitsy's body had turned to lead. She stared at the two people in white coats. One was a solemn-faced woman with beaded dreadlocks and a furry antler protruding out of one side of her head. The other was a slim man dressed in corduroy chinos and a striped shirt. Bitsy's heart fluttered as she studied his sandy-blond hair and steel-framed spectacles.

The resemblance was unmistakable.

It was her dad.

17

Bitsy reeled. Ever since the kidnapping, her head had been swirling with fears about her dad. She'd worried about him being alone or scared or badly hurt. She'd spent so long terrified that she might never see him again that she could barely believe he was real.

Come to think of it…

Suppressing the temptation to run straight to him, Bitsy crouched beside Kosh and peeked out from behind the trolley. Princess Peach had taught her that appearances could be deceiving and this man didn't look like someone who had been held hostage for the last three days. His face was clean-shaven; there were no marks on his wrists or ankles to suggest he'd been tied up, and his shirt was freshly pressed. Suspicious, she watched carefully as the conjuror with the antler asked her so-called dad a question. As he offered a reply, Bitsy noticed him rubbing circles between the thumb and index finger on his left hand.

Her pulse skipped. She'd recognize that gesture anywhere. Her dad did it whenever he was deliberating a problem. It *was* him.

"Dad!" She sprang out from behind the trolley and sprinted forward, her single trainer slapping an irregular beat against the lino.

Her dad lurched. "Bitsy! What in the name of—?"

She crashed into his chest and threw her arms around him, burying her face in his shirt. "I'm so happy you're safe," she sobbed, taking great gulps of his pencil-shavings-and-aftershave scent. Tears stung at the corners of her eyes as the emotion of the last three days rushed out of her all at once. "I was worried I might lose you."

Her dad squeezed her tightly before pushing her shoulders back. There was a fraught look in his eyes as he wiped her cheeks dry. "How did you get here? Are you hurt?"

"I'm fine." Bitsy sniffed. "Kosh and I came here to rescue you."

Right on cue, Kosh stepped out from behind the trolley and raised his hand. "Good to see you, Eric!" He skirted nervously past the lady with the antler, who was observing everything with muted interest.

A line appeared on Eric's brow as he pulled Kosh in for a hug. "*Rescue* me? Didn't you get Melasina's note?"

"The ransom note," Kosh replied. "Yeah, we got it. That's what we've been doing this whole time – trying to find Arkwright's Gyrowheel to keep you safe."

"You've been doing *what*?" Eric staggered back, gazing at them like they'd just confessed to a crime. "Melasina's note said that I had been forced away on emergency business and that you weren't to leave the house until I returned. She sent it on Friday while I was unconscious. There were instructions to eat the food in the freezer and use my Amazon password if you wanted to rent a movie."

Bitsy and Kosh shared a nervous glance. "That's not … the note we read," Bitsy said, momentarily imagining how different their weekend might have been if they'd followed that advice.

"As soon as I recovered consciousness this morning, I borrowed a phone and tried calling you both, but your phones were switched off," Eric explained, pushing a hand through his hair. "I rushed home, but you weren't there. I was about to call Kosh's parents to check if they'd heard from you, when I received an email on my laptop thanking me for travelling on Eurostar! Have you been to Paris? What happened?"

Bitsy reached into her satchel and pulled out the now tatty ransom note scrawled with Melasina's handwriting.

She swallowed, remembering the panic she'd felt when she'd first read it. "I found this attached to our front door on Saturday morning, right after we saw a boy ransacking our kitchen. We followed him here – that's how we found you. His sister is a hunter."

As Eric took the ransom note, he shook his head. "How do you know what a hunter is?"

"That's a long story," Kosh admitted. "It all started when that grobble appeared on the landing and started eating your dirty laundry..."

Eric's face paled as Kosh and Bitsy recounted everything that had happened to them in the last three days, including meeting Giverna, learning how to conjure magicores, and their adventures through the root-network.

When they were finished, Eric studied the ransom note. Behind his spectacles, his eyes shone. "You could have been hurt or..." He closed his fingers around the paper, colour rising to the surface of his freckled cheeks. "Melasina didn't write this. Whoever did put you both in grave danger. I'd wager they're also responsible for intercepting Melasina's real note." He scowled at the lady with the antler. "Find the boy they talked about and bring him to the command room. Bitsy and Kosh, follow me. We need to get to the bottom of this."

Bitsy's brain felt like porridge. If Melasina hadn't

written the ransom note, then who had? And why was her dad here if he hadn't been kidnapped? As he directed her and Kosh around a corner, her shoulder blades stiffened. There was something she needed to tell him; something she'd left out before. "Giverna told me what really caused Mum's accident," she said in a small voice. "And ... I know Melasina is my aunt."

Her dad's forehead tightened. He reached for Bitsy's hand and gave it a squeeze. "I'm sorry I never told you about Melasina. I wish being an adult meant you always knew the right thing to do, but it doesn't. Your mum wanted you to meet Melasina, but I argued against it. I thought I was protecting you." His tone soured. "As for your mum's accident, the truth is more complicated than even Giverna knows. I've only just learned it all myself."

They entered another ward, similar in size to the last two. The walls were pinned with a chaotic jumble of scribbled notes, pictures and maps, all connected with red string. There were various sketches of chaospheres and grainy photos of shady-looking people taken from afar. A single patient sat in bed by a window in the corner. The setting sun painted shadows across her strong jaw and her raven-black hair was arranged in a plait on top of her head. Despite her sunken cheeks and sickly complexion, Bitsy recognized her instantly.

Melasina Spires.

Fire burst in Bitsy's veins. She ripped her hand out of her dad's grasp and charged forward. "YOU! It's your fault my mum's dead!"

"Bitsy, no!" Eric lunged forward and pulled her back. "Melasina didn't have anything to do with that."

"But Giverna said…"

"Giverna believes I caused Matilda's accident because the culprit looked exactly like me," Melasina said. Her voice was wheezier than Bitsy remembered, although her dark eyes glittered fiercely. "The truth is, I wasn't there. It was Riddlejax."

"Riddlejax?" Bitsy staggered as she recalled Chancellor Hershel's story about the murderous conjuror with the ability to shapeshift. "But he's dead. He died hundreds of years ago."

Melasina snorted. "If only that were true. In reality, he has been living in disguise for centuries, using stolen energy to keep himself alive, and manipulating people's weaknesses to persuade more and more to join his cause. He wants to destroy the Alliance so that conjurors can rule over cosmotypicals. All chaos-conjurors take their orders directly from him, and their numbers are growing. The Alliance believes there are only a dozen or so, but we know there to be closer to two hundred."

"The Hunter Guild has been gathering intelligence on Riddlejax and his followers for the last few years," Bitsy's dad explained, motioning to the maps and photos on the wall. "They discovered that, through his experiments, Riddlejax learned how to extinguish another conjuror's magicore by 'dragging' its energy back through a piece of farthingstone and into his own body. This 'stolen' energy repairs Riddlejax's cells, making him heal faster and age more slowly. It has also given him special abilities, like the power to shapeshift."

Bitsy steadied herself against the foot of Melasina's bed. It was terrifying to think that someone like Riddlejax was that powerful. The idea that he had been there when her mum had died made her feel sick. "But why was Riddlejax even posing as Melasina?"

"I suspect he impersonated me from time to time when he needed to gather information about the Hunter Guild for another of his schemes." Melasina grimaced as she tried to sit up straighter. "While disguised as me, he must have spoken to Matilda, learned that she was searching for Arkwright's Gyrowheel, and decided to steal her notebook so he could find the device himself. With the help of his chaos-conjurors, he can use the gyrowheel to conjure omega-level magicores – weapons in his fight against the Alliance."

"But Riddlejax can't read Matilda's notes, right?" Kosh said anxiously. "Giverna told us that only people Matilda loved could see her handwriting."

"That's true," Eric confirmed. "Bitsy, Melasina and I are the only people that can read those notes."

Bitsy felt embarrassed she'd got it so wrong. Melasina had always been able to read Matilda's notes. She frowned at her aunt. "Why didn't you tell everyone you were innocent?"

"I did, but the Alliance didn't believe me. It was the same when I tried to warn them about Riddlejax." Gazing out of the window, Melasina gave a crooked smile. "Matilda would have known it wasn't me in that car. She never stopped trusting me. It's a shame you did, Eric. Then we might have avoided that argument on Friday."

Eric's cheeks burned.

"That was really you at our house?" Bitsy pulled over a couple of chairs for her and Kosh. The more she learned, the more her knees felt like jelly and she needed to sit down.

When Melasina nodded, Kosh spluttered, "But your grobble tried to impale us against a wall!"

"My grobble can be a little … unfriendly," Melasina said. "It's not his fault. He gets it from me."

Unfriendly was putting it lightly. Still, there was something about Melasina's response that made the corners of Bitsy's mouth twitch. It was so unapologetic.

"I turned up on Friday to ask your father if I could borrow *Magicalia*," Melasina explained. "I had anticipated it would be tricky, seeing as he still believed I was responsible for Matilda's death. In the end, I had no choice but to bring him here. The only way to prove to him that Riddlejax is still alive was by showing him what Riddlejax has done to us."

With a chill, it slowly dawned on Bitsy what her aunt might be saying. "Did Riddlejax make you all sick?"

Melasina's jaw stiffened. "As soon as I read the reports of Matilda's death, I knew that someone or something had been impersonating me. So, I did what Matilda would have done – I set out to uncover the truth. It took a long time to piece the clues together, but I eventually learned that Riddlejax was still alive and had been behind everything. From then on, I made it the Hunter Guild's mission to find Riddlejax and stop him. Then about a month ago, in retaliation, Riddlejax infiltrated one of our barracks, posing as a hunter. He concocted a vile magi-woven poison and released it into the water supply. One by one, the hunters there fell ill. Their bodies started transforming in the most painful ways, assuming the physical characteristics of various magicores."

That's why they have different symptoms, Bitsy thought. *Their bodies are morphing into different species of magicores.* A shiver traced her spine as she imagined how scary it must be to wake up one morning and find you have tentacles growing out of your stomach or scales instead of skin.

"By the time we realized what Riddlejax had done, it was too late," Melasina continued. "He had infected every hunter in every barracks. We are a family. The strong among us have continued working, but some are too weak."

"Can't you treat it?" Kosh asked, perched on the edge of his seat. "There must be a way. Maybe there's a magicore that can help you?"

Melasina smiled thinly. "One species could help – an *everwing*, an elemental-type, conjured from hope. It first materializes in a cocoon which, when eaten, will cure any magicore-related ailment. The problem is, it is an omega-level species. It can only be conjured using Arkwright's Gyrowheel. That's why I asked your father for *Magicalia* – so I could use Matilda's notes to find the gyrowheel and, with the help of your father and another hunter, conjure an everwing to heal everyone."

"Which is another reason why Riddlejax poisoned the Hunter Guild in the first place," Bitsy's dad said through gritted teeth. "Riddlejax has always believed that Matilda destroyed her notebook; that's why he didn't come looking for it after she died. The only people who knew the truth about it – myself, Giverna and Melasina – kept it secret. Now that's changed. Somehow, Riddlejax knows that the pages were hidden inside *Magicalia*, and that Melasina, Bitsy and I can read them. By infecting everyone in the Hunter Guild, he aimed to make Melasina desperate enough to locate the gyrowheel for him."

Heat surged through Bitsy's veins. She didn't understand how anyone could be so cruel and manipulative.

"After Melasina explained the truth, I agreed to let her have *Magicalia*," Eric continued. "Only when I returned home, you were both missing and the encyclopaedia was gone. I returned to the barracks so Melasina could help me locate you." He showed Melasina the ransom note, briefly adding, "Your message never reached them. They received this instead."

Melasina read the note and scowled. Before Bitsy could explain that she had *Magicalia* in her satchel, there was a commotion by the door as the antler-lady arrived with Mateo. He glared at Bitsy and Kosh. "What are *they* doing here?"

"Never you mind," Melasina snapped. She signalled to the ransom note in Eric's hand. "Do you know anything about that?"

Mateo trudged closer to read it. "No. I've never seen it before."

"Then what were you doing at my house?" Bitsy questioned. "Kosh and I saw you there."

"I didn't know it was *your* house until you told me so the next day," Mateo said, shirtily. "I was there because…" He paused, glancing at Melasina.

"Yes?" she prompted.

He swallowed. "Because I was searching for Arkwright's Gyrowheel. I overheard that you were looking for it and thought I could use it to save my sister, so I told my fidglet to find the fastest path to it. Initially she took me to their house, then she brought me to Covent Garden – where I saw them again – and then to the Palace of Versailles. I'm still trying to understand why."

Despite her ill health, Melasina's face flushed. "*Overheard* me? First these two sneak into the barracks, and now I find an initiate has been listening in on top-secret discussions. I know there are fewer of us patrolling the building, but I didn't realize security had become so lax. Are you sure you understood your fidglet correctly? Their tails can be difficult to interpret."

"Actually, I think his fidglet might have been following *us*," Bitsy interrupted, feeling her suspicions about Mateo dissolve. "Kosh and I have been carrying Mum's copy of *Magicalia* this whole time and the notes inside are essential if you want to find the gyrowheel." She added softly, "I'm sorry about your sister, Mateo."

Eric pushed his spectacles further up his nose. "Well, if the ransom note has nothing to do with Mateo, then it must be Riddlejax who left it. Perhaps he wanted to double his chances of obtaining the gyrowheel by forcing Bitsy to look for it, too. I suppose he might have had another plan concocted to manipulate me, but I've mostly been unconscious."

"I didn't *see* you two at Versailles," Mateo noted suspiciously.

"That's because we tried to stay hidden," Kosh explained. "I followed you in the hope you might lead us to Eric while Bitsy got chased by a chaos-conjuror."

Eric grabbed Kosh's shoulder. "A chaos-conjuror? Are you sure?"

"He was carrying a pouch of springle fluff with a chaosphere on it," Bitsy described. "Another chaos-conjuror came after us in Agra. We don't know how they've been tracking us."

Melasina reached for an iPad on her bedside table. "Did you get a good look at their faces? I have photos of several conjurors we suspect Riddlejax may have tried to recruit. Perhaps you could take a look?"

Bitsy and Kosh shuffled closer as Melasina flipped her iPad around. The screen was divided into a dozen headshots of people in different coloured overalls. Bitsy pictured the face of the chaos-conjuror who'd chased them in Agra. They'd almost run into her, so they'd got a good look. She had a long nose, frizzy red hair and a pointy chin.

"No, sorry," Kosh said. "I don't recognize any of them."

Bitsy was about to agree when her gaze fell on the last photo on the screen. "Him!" she blurted. "He was the one who chased me in Versailles with a scutterflix."

Her dad squinted at the brawny, bald man in red overalls. "Is that *Clyde Hess*? I studied with him at the conservatoire."

Melasina reversed her iPad. "According to our intelligence, he now works closely with Chancellor Hershel."

"I have to warn her," Eric said stiffly. He wiggled a hand towards Melasina. "Lend me your key. I can go to the conservatoire right now and expose him. He must be feeding Riddlejax all kinds of information about the Alliance. I'll try to fill them in on everything else that's been happening. Hopefully they'll believe me."

"OK. Bitsy and Kosh will be safe here with me." Melasina reached under the neck of her robe and pulled out a thumb-sized wooden key woven into a letter M.

"Mum made you a key to the root-network," Bitsy realized.

Melasina smiled mischievously. "How else do you think we met up in secret?"

There was a crackle as Bitsy's dad used the key to open a door to the root-network in the wall next to Melasina's bed. Thin, milk-white roots snaked up and across the plaster, forming an arch. A shadowy opening materialized in the centre.

Mateo jerked his head. "What is that?"

"The only way to enter a conservatoire by magicore-means," Melasina said with a wink. She collected her key from Bitsy's dad. "Good luck, Eric."

He wrapped an arm around Kosh before pulling Bitsy into a hug. "Everything's going to be OK. Just stay here and wait for me. Look after your aunt."

Bitsy nodded, although she couldn't stop her bottom lip from wobbling. She'd only just been reunited with her dad and it felt unnerving for him to leave her again so soon. "Promise me you'll be careful."

He scuffed a hand through her curls. "I promise."

"Here," Kosh said, fetching Eric's fountain pen from his pocket. "This belongs to you. You might need it."

"Thanks." With the pen clutched in his hand, Eric took a deep breath before vanishing into the gloom.

As the archway of roots melted back into the plaster, something worrying tugged at the back of Bitsy's memory. She reached into the pocket of her raincoat…

…and froze.

Her fingers went straight through a gaping hole in the bottom. Threads hung loose where the material had torn. Bitsy panicked, suddenly remembering it ripping while she'd been escaping Clyde Hess in Versailles…

"What is it?" Kosh asked.

Heat rushed to her face as she patted her other

pockets, searching for her notebook. She frantically threw open her satchel and rummaged through. A heavy feeling slipped down her throat as she realized the notebook was gone. "My notebook – I think it fell out of my pocket when Clyde Hess was chasing me. The last thing I wrote in it were the coordinates I found around Pierre Patel's painting."

"But that means…" Kosh's eyes widened. "If Clyde Hess found the notebook, then Riddlejax now knows the final resting place of the gyrowheel! He could be en route to collect it right now!"

Mateo thumped his fists against the wall where Eric had just disappeared. "Open the door! We need to tell your dad so he can warn the Alliance."

"Root-walking doesn't work like that," Melasina grumbled, shuffling to the edge of her bed. "Every door to the root-network opens in a random place. Eric could be anywhere inside and you'll only get lost trying to find him. Besides, there's no time. Do either of you remember the coordinates?"

"Uh, forty-something degrees North?" Kosh mumbled hopelessly.

Bitsy tried to remember writing down the coordinates, and was struck with an idea. She reached into her intact pocket and pulled out the palace map. Fetching a spare pencil from her satchel, she gently rubbed the nib over the surface of the paper. She'd seen the trick used by detectives in TV shows, but she wasn't sure if it would really work.

Her skin prickled as numbers started to appear. It was as she'd hoped: when she'd leaned against the map, she'd written with enough pressure to leave an imprint. She shaded the paper until the rest of the coordinates were visible.

Mateo hurriedly typed them into his phone. "It's Kilchurn Castle in Scotland. That's where the gyrowheel is hidden!"

"Then that's where I'm going." Melasina threw back her bedsheets and swung her legs over the side of her bed, making them all recoil. Piercing through her cotton pyjamas were a dozen jagged red spikes, the size of icicles.

"You can't go anywhere like that!" Bitsy protested, rushing to support her. "You can barely walk."

Melasina smirked through her pain. "Someone has to stop Riddlejax from getting his hands on the gyrowheel. With an omega-level magicore, there's no telling the suffering and destruction he'll cause." She studied the map on Mateo's phone. "Matilda and I often met in Scotland. If memory serves, there's a root-network exit near the monument to Duncan Ban MacIntyre, five kilometres from Kilchurn Castle. All I have to do is beat Riddlejax to it."

"No." Bitsy felt a sudden surge of determination. "I'm faster than you. I'll go."

Kosh snorted. "Fast? I've beaten you at the hundred metres every sports day for four years. I'll go."

"The three of us can go together," Mateo said. "The sooner we find the gyrowheel, the sooner we can heal the hunters."

The trio gazed at Melasina for approval. Bitsy half expected her aunt to forbid it – that's what her dad or Giverna would have done – but instead, Melasina's eyes narrowed. "Fine, but you're taking Yamaha with you. He can help you go five kilometres in five minutes."

"Who's Yamaha?" Bitsy asked.

She immediately wished she hadn't.

Melasina batted a hand towards the bed next to her. The air shimmered, and a familiar purple-furred magicore with preposterously large cheeks materialized, lounging back against the pillows. Yamaha's rhino horn sliced through the air as he rolled forward onto his belly. He grunted at Bitsy, Kosh and Mateo, sounding decidedly grumpy about Melasina's proposal.

"You're going to need supplies, too," Melasina said, hobbling forward. "Follow me."

18

The Hunter Guild's supply room smelled of sweat and muddy football boots, reminding Bitsy of the changing rooms at school. It was large and dimly lit, with long benches in the centre and various cupboards, shelves and racks fitted to the walls.

"You should be able to find a pair of replacement trainers in here," Melasina told Bitsy, pulling open a drawer. Inside was a jumble of second-hand shoes with coloured laces. Bitsy selected a few pairs in her size and carried them to a bench to try them on.

"You've got an unusual selection of stuff in here," Kosh observed, removing three battery-powered torches from a cabinet containing a net launcher and several American football helmets.

242

As Bitsy flexed her toes inside some plimsolls, she noticed a rack of strangely shaped leather saddles. She guessed they'd been crafted for magicores, although they weren't stitched together with threads of light like an ozoz saddle. "Why don't you have any magi-woven items?"

"The Alliance refuses to trade with the Hunter Guild," Melasina explained, sniffily. "If they did, we might have used some of the Clairvoyant Guild's medicines to delay the symptoms of Riddlejax's poison." She turned abruptly towards the door, where Yamaha was about to toss an entire silo of tennis balls into his mouth. "Don't even think about it, Yamaha."

Yamaha's furry ears flattened as he gingerly put the silo down, making Bitsy smile. "Why did you call him Yamaha?"

"It's my favourite brand of motorbike," Melasina answered, taking a seat beside Bitsy. "I've always been a bit of a petrolhead. When I was younger, I loved engines, mechanics and motocross racing. The first time I walked into a Yamaha shop, I felt overwhelming greed. I didn't need any of those motorbikes, but I wanted them *all*."

Bitsy nodded. She felt the same way whenever she walked into a bookshop. There was something else she wanted to ask Melasina; only she was worried it might make her angry. "Giverna told us hunters have attacked, robbed and spied on the Alliance for hundreds of years.

She said the Hunter Guild refused to help the Alliance against Riddlejax centuries ago. Is that true?"

"Hunters have always hated the Alliance for shunning them," Melasina replied plainly. "For a long time, while Alliance conjurors used magicores to help cosmotypical people, hunters used magicores to help themselves. We learned how to become soldiers, spies and thieves, stealing what we wanted and clashing with any conjurors who stood in our way. Our actions were driven by anger and a need to survive." She winced, rubbing a spot on her leg between two crimson spikes. "But people change. Times change. Needs change. I became guild leader on a promise to repair our relationship with the Alliance so we can work together to stop Riddlejax. The problem is, whenever I extend my hand, the Alliance pushes it away."

Bitsy understood why the Alliance had misgivings about the Hunter Guild, but it would be impossible for Melasina to repair trust between the two organizations if the Alliance wouldn't even communicate with her. "Mum didn't let the Hunter Guild's reputation cloud her judgement about you. She continued seeing you even when she wasn't allowed to – just like Mateo and his sister have."

"That's because love is stronger than hate," Melasina said, her eyes sparkling with rebellion. "Love breaks all the rules."

Bitsy smiled at her aunt and a tingly feeling of hope

spread through her chest. Not only was Melasina a new family member Bitsy could grow to love, but she was another connection to Bitsy's mum. When this was all over, Melasina would be able to share stories about Matilda and teach Bitsy things she'd never known before.

After trying on several pairs of trainers, Bitsy sank her heels into some battered leather combat boots, which felt comfier than anything else. As she fastened the laces, Mateo tossed a length of rope and a metal crowbar into a small rucksack, along with the torches Kosh had collected. With great difficulty, Yamaha swallowed a wheelbarrow. Bitsy had no idea why, but as Melasina didn't scold him, she presumed it was part of some plan.

Melasina prepared three bowls of soup which Bitsy, Kosh and Mateo slurped down hurriedly alongside some crusty bread and a couple of apples. Soon enough, the five of them gathered around a wall in the corridor outside. Melasina handed Kosh her root-key and he used it to open another entrance to the root-network.

"You keep it," she told him when he offered it back. "You'll need it to return here. You should also conjure your own magicores to take with you. You never know when you might need their help."

Bitsy considered which of her two magicores to choose: Pumpkin or Headline. They both had valuable gifts and were small enough to carry in her pocket. After careful thought, she decided on Pumpkin. She was fond of Headline but suspected that Pumpkin's positivity might boost everyone on a risk-all mission such as this.

It took a few minutes to conjure the little springle, who materialized out of a cloud of farthingdust and dropped into Bitsy's top pocket. A grin spread around Pumpkin's jaw as she wriggled to get comfy. Borrowing Bitsy's farthingstone, Kosh conjured Odders, while Mateo summoned his fidglet, Swift.

"The symbol you're looking for is a circular temple on top of a square mound," Melasina croaked, leaning against the wall. "Stay together."

The barracks disappeared behind them as they set off into the darkness. Within moments, their torch beams were swallowed by the murk.

"What's wrong with this place?" Mateo asked, trying to waft away the gloom as if it were smoke.

"You get used to it after a while," Kosh said. "Just don't slide down any ramps without checking what's at the bottom. I learned that the hard way."

Bitsy checked on Yamaha, plodding behind them. With the wheelbarrow wedged sideways in his cheeks, he looked like he might overbalance at any second and fall into the chasm below. "Tread carefully," she warned everyone. "And keep a lookout for any glowing symbols. We'll need to follow one to get to the centre."

"Not necessarily," Mateo said. He crouched down and patted Swift on the head. "Hey girl, can you show us the fastest route to Kilchurn Castle?"

Swift's ears pricked. She sniffed the air in all directions, her wet nose shining in the dim light. It wasn't easy to discern the shapes of her tails, but Bitsy could hear all twenty-four of them wagging. They sounded like propeller blades. "*Magicalia* said that fidglet tails are notoriously difficult to interpret. How do you understand Swift?"

Mateo aimed his torch at Swift's rear end. Her tails were shaped into hearts, stars or arrows. "There isn't a one-size-fits-all method. It takes time and practice to understand your fidglet. Most hunters are too impatient to learn, which is why fidglets have gained such a bad reputation. But it isn't their fault."

Swift's leathery tails rippled. The hearts transformed into plus signs and all the stars became capital letter As.

"That means she knows where to go," Mateo said. "I think I learned a lot about reading fidglet tails from watching my sister with her fidglet. Esme *is* patient. A few years ago, she took me to my first stadium concert. I remember being so excited right before the lights went up that I could barely stand still. It's that moment I think of when I conjure Swift. She's named after the artist we saw."

Connecting the dots, Kosh blinked. "You're a Taylor Swift fan?"

Mateo shrugged. "Who isn't?"

A lump formed in Bitsy's throat as she pictured Esme on the ward in the Hunter Guild's barracks. She couldn't imagine how frightening it must have been for Mateo to watch his sister slowly turning invisible. "How long has Esme been infected?" she asked gently.

"A couple of weeks." Mateo scowled as he trudged on. "She lost visibility of her toes first, then her feet and legs. It's been creeping up her body."

Swift bounded forward, taking a left-hand turn along a rougher branch. "Do your parents know what's happening to her? Have they been to visit?"

He grunted. "I can't tell my parents. They hate the Hunter Guild. They'd kick me out if they knew I'd been seeing Esme. They acted like she was no longer their daughter when she was banished. I worried I might never see her again, but we found a way to keep track of each other using a pair of proxicups."

"Proxicups?" Bitsy asked.

"Goblets made by proxiwigs, weaver-type magicores conjured from impatience. The cups are difficult to weave, making them exceptionally hard to get hold of." Mateo blushed. "I had to steal mine and Esme's from a supply vault at the conservatoire. People that drink from the same set of proxicups can locate each other on special maps. Esme and I would drink from our proxicups, find

248

out where we were and then get one of our fidglets to generate a pull-through so we could meet up."

"That makes Bitsy and me sneaking out of our bedroom windows seem really basic," Kosh commented. "The Alliance rules are so unfair. You shouldn't have to do all that to see someone you love."

With Swift as their guide, they continued at speed through the darkness. As they clambered under and over roots, Bitsy and Kosh told Mateo everything they'd learned about Arkwright's Gyrowheel in case it proved helpful when they reached the castle. Watching Mateo, Bitsy reflected on how her opinion of him had changed. Two days ago, he'd been a suspected enemy. Now he was a reassuring presence. He knew far more about magicores than she and Kosh and he wanted to keep the gyrowheel away from Riddlejax just as badly as they did. She was glad to have him on their side.

Soon enough, Swift found the central chamber of the root-network and, from there, the exit to the Duncan Ban MacIntyre monument that Melasina had told them about. The symbol on the door looked like a giant snowglobe with a flat top. When Mateo pulled on the handle, an icy gust blew in from outside, along with a splatter of raindrops.

"Scotland," was all Kosh said, drying his face.

Dragging up their hoods, they tramped out into a dark and stormy evening. Wind howled through the black sky and rain lashed the land in thick diagonal lines. Bitsy aimed her torch into the distance, assessing their surroundings. They were in a muddy field next to a remote country road. No streetlamps or buildings were in sight, except for the Duncan Ban MacIntyre monument – a moss-covered, grey stone temple – that rose on a hill behind them. Mountains loomed in the distance.

Mateo wiped his phone screen on his jacket sleeve. "According to Google, this road leads all the way to the castle. We need to head in the direction of the mountains."

A sopping-wet Yamaha plodded grumpily to the roadside. His fluffy purple coat had been flattened by the rain, making the shape of the wheelbarrow even more evident in his cheeks. Aiming his horn at the ground, he gargled and vomited up the wheelbarrow with a shrill bang. He then screeched at them all, pointing into the wheelbarrow with one of his claws.

"I think he wants us to get inside it," Kosh called, lifting his voice above the wind. Water dripped off a few strands of Odders' fur hanging out of Kosh's hoodie pocket.

"Melasina *did* say Yamaha could help us travel the five kilometres to the castle in five minutes," Bitsy reminded them. "This must be how."

Mateo scooped Swift into his arms. Water was running in rivulets down her leathery hide. "I don't know much about grobbles, but I trust Melasina. Let's go."

It took a fair amount of rearranging for the three of them, plus their magicores, to fit inside the wheelbarrow. In the end, Mateo and Swift sat at the front with Mateo's legs hanging over the rim, while Bitsy and Kosh crouched by each of his shoulders.

Bitsy ensured her raincoat was carefully zipped up, covering Pumpkin's dandelion shell. Water sloshed around in the wheelbarrow basin as the rain continued to pour, sounding like a snare drum against the metal.

"All right, we're in!" Kosh told Yamaha. He gripped the sides of the barrow. "Whatever you're going to do, do it now."

There was an awkward moment where Yamaha turned his back on them, and Bitsy suspected he might be about to stomp off in protest. But then he wriggled backwards under the rear of the wheelbarrow, so that the barrow handles were resting on his shoulders and only the wheel was touching the tarmac.

Bitsy wasn't sure what Yamaha was going to do. If grobbles had the gift of super-strength, maybe he intended to throw them to the castle? She steadied herself inside the barrow, preparing to be launched into the sky.

The wheelbarrow started to vibrate as Yamaha's chest rumbled. His claws tightened around the handles. His incisors flashed as he opened his jaws…

And so began the longest and loudest burp Bitsy had ever heard.

It was like something out of a nightmare. The sound filled her ears – a wet, warbling belch that made the very mizzle in the air tremble. Her hood blew back as they were propelled forward, zooming over the road at speed.

"Wahoo!" Kosh cheered, grasping his beanie.

Rain pummelled the wheelbarrow, soaking Bitsy's face and shoulders. Her body juddered as they whooshed past fields and trees, tearing over the road like a Formula One racing car. Mateo crossed his arms around Swift's chest, acting like a magicore seatbelt. "There's a left-hand bend ahead," he cried. "Get ready to lean in one, two…"

On *three*, they all did as Mateo had instructed, and the wheelbarrow's path shifted left around a corner.

As the mountains drew closer, Bitsy's thoughts turned to the task ahead. *"Before you can claim a tool of such wealth,"* she shouted above the continuous thunder of Yamaha's burp, *"you must face three tests to prove yourself* – that's the final part of Arkwright's Riddle!"

"What sort of tests?" Mateo yelled, his dark curls flapping in the wind.

Bitsy thought carefully. The challenges would have been devised by Gilander Arkwright three hundred and fifty years ago. "I'm not sure. More puzzles, maybe?"

Kosh's rucksack suddenly started jumping up and

down on his back. "I think *Magicalia* wants to tell us something…"

He removed the encyclopaedia from his rucksack and passed it to Bitsy. She gripped the cover tightly as the pages flapped against the wind. Eventually, they stopped on a sheet of her mum's notes. Squinting through the rain, she read them aloud:

Arkwright's Legacy

By all accounts, Gilander Arkwright believed that the gyrowheel was a thing of wonder that should be used to help others. I think he wanted the device to be claimed by someone who felt the same, which is why the final line of his riddle talks about facing "three tests to prove yourself". By this, Arkwright means to prove yourself <u>*worthy*</u>*. Arkwright was the proud founder of the Weaver Guild. My hunch is the three tests will require creativity, courage and conviction – qualities written in the guild motto. The gyrowheel's resting place may also be marked by the Weaver Guild coat of arms.*

— 6 June 2017

"Creativity, courage and conviction," Kosh repeated as Bitsy slid *Magicalia* back into his bag. "We've got that, right?"

"Uh huh," Mateo replied, although he sounded unconvinced.

Bitsy was still pondering her mum's words when Kilchurn Castle came into view. The ruins were located on a craggy outcrop in the middle of a loch, surrounded by steep mountains. Only a fraction of the original fortification stood – a mossy section of the outer wall, part of the gatehouse, and the lower half of one tower. Everything was blanketed in low-lying mist, so it looked like the dry-ice-swamped set of a horror movie. As Bitsy heard water lapping and gurgling against the rocks, she realized that Yamaha's burp was getting quieter.

The wheelbarrow began to lose speed as the belch lost power. Eventually, they came to a stop near the castle walls and, after a few elbow-shoves, managed to all scramble out in one piece.

Yamaha crawled out from under the wheelbarrow, panting. He looked like he'd just completed an assault course. His fur was splattered with mud and gravel and his whiskers were kinked and torn.

"Thanks for all your help," Bitsy said, offering him an appreciative smile.

Yamaha huffed and tossed his horn. Then he burst into farthingdust. Bitsy staggered back as his twinkling embers dissolved into the wind.

"And then there were six," Kosh muttered, adjusting

the straps of his rucksack. "Come on; time is of the essence."

With the burp-barrow section of their journey firmly behind them, the trio retrieved their torches and ventured into the castle. Despite being partially sheltered from the wind, it felt colder inside the ruins than it had outside. Some of the site was still open to the elements, so Bitsy kept her hood up as they looked around.

"There are no signs that anyone else has been here," Mateo observed, creeping forward.

Bitsy studied the ground. There were no footprints anywhere – not on the dry stone or in the wet mud. "That's good. We must have made it here before Riddlejax."

Odders wriggled out of Kosh's hoodie and rolled onto the dusty floor of the gatehouse, hiccuping. He jumped when the sound echoed back to him, reverberating off the walls of the ruins.

Then he hiccuped again. And again. Each time whooping like a hyena.

Kosh grinned sheepishly, quickly bundling Odders back into his pocket. "Sorry about him."

Mateo smirked. "Swift, show us the way to the gyrowheel."

Swift's tails morphed from diamonds to zigzags as she sniffed the air. She bounded towards the far corner of the ruins, where an arched opening led to a spiral stone staircase. A chain hanging across the steps rattled as Swift ducked under it. Attached to the chain was a sign that read: DANGER – NO PUBLIC ACCESS.

"Of course it's that way," Kosh muttered resignedly. "Come on."

As they followed Swift inside the tower, Mateo switched on his torch. "Smells like a toilet," he said, coughing.

A foul stench hung in the cold air. Bitsy covered her nose with her cardigan as Mateo aimed his torch up the mossy walls and across the cobwebbed ceiling. Pumpkin poked her head out of Bitsy's top pocket, gazing around curiously.

"We should keep our eyes peeled for the Weaver Guild coat of arms," Bitsy suggested. She remembered Giverna pointing it out on her thinkerchief. "It looks like a shield with a harp in the centre."

Swift scampered ahead as they ascended slowly, scouring the stonework for markings. Bitsy listened out for voices or footsteps, just in case, but the place was eerily quiet. All too soon, moonlight filled the stairwell and they found themselves on a windy landing at the top of the tower.

"Plenty of bird poo but no coat of arms," Kosh summarized, kicking the floor in protest.

But as his trainer scuffed the stone's surface, Bitsy spied a curved channel, partially concealed by moss. "Look! There's something underneath us. Here, help me remove this stuff."

Together, they scraped off the green sponge, exposing the lines of a design covering the entire floor. Bitsy's pulse quickened as she traced it with her eyes – the strings and frame of an old-fashioned harp.

"This is it," Mateo hissed, his eyes lit with wonder. "It's got to be."

As he circled the design, Bitsy noticed a raised stone platform had appeared in the centre of the harp. "Mateo, be careful. Don't step—"

But her warning came too late.

Mateo's boot touched the platform and it retracted with a loud *click*. Something groaned in the tower's base, and Bitsy screamed as the floor disappeared from under her.

Her stomach pitched into her mouth as she tumbled into darkness. Limbs flailing, she clawed uselessly at the air, trying to slow her fall.

"Bit-seeeeeeeeee!" Kosh yelled somewhere above her.

Wind whooshed in Bitsy's ears as she plummeted down a dark stone shaft into a torchlit chamber. She landed abruptly in a bouncy pile of straw.

Panting heavily, she took stock of her surroundings. She was in a small, brick-lined room with a vaulted ceiling. Ahead of her stood a heavy metal door etched with the Weaver Guild coat of arms.

"Look out beloooooow!" Kosh hollered.

Bitsy rolled aside as he came hurtling out of the shadows and plopped bottom first into the straw, sending a cloud of dust into the air. "Bleurgh!" He wiped pieces of straw off his tongue as Odders wriggled out of the pile, laughing deliriously. "Are you OK?"

Pain throbbed in Bitsy's side as she pulled her satchel out from under her. She checked on Pumpkin, who was still beaming. "Just bruised, I think. Thanks for jumping down after me."

"Of course." Kosh pushed himself to his feet. As he gave Bitsy a hand up, a rustle sounded above them.

"INCOMING!"

They jumped out of the way as Mateo and Swift bellyflopped into the straw. Swift sprang up immediately, her tails sounding like windscreen wipers as they wagged back and forth. Mateo groaned and raised his head. "Sorry. I saw a pressure plate up there. It must have triggered a trapdoor."

Bitsy tipped her head back and peered into the gloom. Given how far they'd fallen, they had to be underground. She considered the red brick walls and vaulted ceiling. "It looks like we're in an undercroft – a castle basement."

Swift nudged her nose against the door, panting

excitedly. Her tails had all changed shape. They now looked like upside-down exclamation marks.

"It's that way," Mateo said, brushing himself clean as he stood up. "But there's something dangerous ahead. She can sense it."

Bitsy took a deep breath to steady her nerves. "Remember what Melasina told us: stay together." She lifted a heavy metal latch and the door swung inward. Stale air drifted out from a shadowy room beyond.

Swift charged forward and everyone jumped as torches crackled to life along one wall. They illuminated a vast, sprawling series of chambers separated by round stone columns and brick archways. All sorts of dusty old objects, ranging from tottering stacks of books to wooden crates filled with bottles, were piled high against the walls.

Kosh's jaw dropped. "This place is enormous!"

"How did all this stuff get down here?" Mateo asked as they shuffled over the threshold. He reached for a dusty violin resting on top of a piano.

"Careful," Bitsy warned, nudging his arm. "If this is where the gyrowheel is hidden, these items were placed here over three hundred years ago. There might be centuries-old booby traps among them. We probably shouldn't touch anything."

Retracting his fingers, Mateo blushed. "You're right.

In movies, bad things always happen whenever anyone touches the treasure."

Bitsy wasn't sure she'd call any of this stuff treasure. Mismatched furniture, mothballed clothing, cracked wooden picture frames, Venetian masks and paper lanterns – it was a load of random junk.

"Maybe this stuff has to do with the three tests we have to face?" Mateo said.

Bitsy was about to respond when Kosh yelped and pointed back the way they'd come. "Uh, team?" His voice was a half-octave higher than usual. "There's a magicore in the doorway."

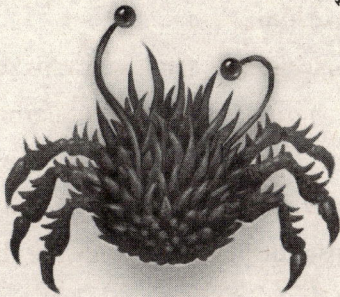

19

The giant magicore watching them was like nothing Bitsy had ever seen. As big as a car, its body was a ball of jagged crimson spikes, jutting out at different angles like an exploding firework. Six massive crab's legs protruded under its belly, protected by thorny greaves. The magicore had no discernible head or face, but had what looked like two flies buzzing around it. Bitsy realized with a jolt that they were beady black eyes attached to long, thin antennae.

"Everyone, stay calm!" she spluttered, edging back.

With a terrified squeak, Pumpkin retracted into her shell. Swift ran behind Mateo, her twenty-four tails trembling between her legs. Despite Bitsy's warning not to touch anything, Kosh snatched a tarnished flute from a table of musical instruments and brandished it like a sword in front of him. "What is it?"

"A thornsprout," Mateo said, swallowing. "It's an armourer-type species conjured from annoyance. Delta-level."

The thornsprout plodded forward, its claws *click-clacking* against the flagstones. A round dark mouth opened at the front of its body and two razor-sharp pincers unfolded from inside.

Kosh's flute started to wobble. "Its eyes are solid black. That means it's a *wild* magicore. Whoever conjured it is dead."

"It must be the first test," Bitsy hazarded, her mind whirring. "I bet it was conjured during the seventeenth century and has been waiting here all this time." Inching further away, she turned to Mateo. "Do you know anything else about thornsprouts?"

His brow furrowed. "I know their armour is completely impenetrable unless exposed to sunlight. The species has a unique gift, but I can't remember what it is."

"Exposed to *sunlight*?" Kosh flapped his arms. "But we're underground!"

Bitsy remembered her mum's notes. *Creativity. Courage. Conviction.* "If this is the first test then we need to figure out a way to extinguish the thornsprout without using sunlight. And we'll need to be creative."

The thornsprout stopped a few metres away and squatted like it was about to lay an egg. As its antennae twitched, its spikes started to vibrate.

"Uh oh," Mateo said. "I've just remembered what—"

But his voice was drowned out by the sound of a hundred popping champagne corks as the thornsprout's spikes exploded out of its body.

Bang! Bang! Bang!

An onslaught of scarlet javelins streaked through the air, demolishing anything in their path. A wooden rowing boat blasted into splinters; a chandelier crashed to the ground, shattering into a thousand crystals. Bitsy ducked as a spike sailed past her ear and speared the wall behind, leaving a crumbling chasm in the brickwork.

Kosh chucked his flute at the thornsprout. "RUN!"

Launching into a sprint, Bitsy lifted her knees and pumped her arms, hoping they weren't all about to be turned into human kebabs. A racket sounded behind them as the thornsprout gave chase.

"We need to find a place to hide!" Mateo shouted as they raced deeper into the undercroft. Swift kept pace by his heels, charging so fast her ears had folded back.

A bright red spike suddenly shot over Kosh's shoulder and clattered into a pile of birdcages. "Quickly!" he yelled.

Bitsy glanced in both directions at the endless labyrinth of chambers and took a sharp left into an area full of Egyptian sculptures. Among them was a sand-coloured tablet carved with hieroglyphics, a colossal granite bust and several stone sarcophagi. "Over here!" She squeezed behind a mammoth statue of a pharaoh's head. "Hurry, before the thornsprout turns the corner!"

Just in time, the others wriggled in beside Bitsy as a volley of red spikes whizzed into the room and collided with the Egyptian stonework, which cracked and crumbled. A spike struck the pharaoh's head, sending a cloud of dust raining over them.

Click-clack, click-clack. The thornsprout thundered in, snapping its pincers angrily. Bitsy's throat burned as she tried hard not to cough. She risked a peek from behind the pharaoh's cheek. The thornsprout looked like it had undergone a patchy haircut. Many of its spikes were missing, although Bitsy could see tiny red thorns regrowing all over its body.

The thornsprout's eyes swayed on their stalks, scanning the area. It gave a frustrated hiss and then tramped off into the next room.

As the clicking of its claws faded, Bitsy's lungs deflated. "I don't suppose either of you have a bright idea for how we can extinguish that killing machine, do you?"

"If this is a test of creativity, then we probably need to think outside the box," Mateo said, cleaning dust off his face. "Perhaps there's something in the undercroft that can help us?"

As quietly as they could, they shimmied out from their hiding place and hurried in the opposite direction to the thornsprout. They passed a room full of old pottery and dodged through a maze of broken grandfather clocks. Their footsteps crackled as they stepped over the shattered glass and splintered wood. Scarlet spikes of various sizes lay scattered across the floor and poked out from piles of rubble.

"I don't think any of this junk is going to help us," Kosh commented as they turned in to an area full of cooking equipment. A rack of old-fashioned pots, ladles and skillets hung from the ceiling, and several wooden barrels and cauldrons sat off to one side. "What if we try to extinguish the thornsprout by making it fire its spikes so much that it uses up all its energy?"

Bitsy shook her head. "There's no telling how long we'd have to survive for that to work. Especially as it's already been here for hundreds of years! It's too risky."

Odders poked his nose out of Kosh's pocket, sniffed the air and then zoomed up Kosh's arm to sit on his shoulder. After getting soaked in the rain, his reddish-gold fur had dried in matted clumps, giving him a punk rock hairstyle. "In that case," Kosh said, scratching Odders under the chin, "maybe we can trick the thornsprout into jumping through one of Swift's pull-throughs?"

"Not an option." Mateo huffed, kicking a red spike across the flagstones. "Swift can't generate pull-throughs that big."

Watching the spike roll over the floor, an idea sparked in Bitsy's brain. "I've just realized: there *is* something that might pierce a thornsprout's armour – one of its spikes."

Mateo stopped and stared at her. "You could be right." He lifted the spike and weighed it in his hands. "These are too heavy to be thrown accurately. If we want to use them to extinguish the thornsprout, we'll have to set a trap." He scanned the room until his gaze fell on the rack of pans hanging from the ceiling. "I think I have an idea."

Under Mateo's instruction, they worked fast, scavenging wire and rope from the rubble to affix six thornsprout spikes, pointy end down, to the rack on the ceiling. The rack was suspended by a chain fixed to the wall with an iron latch. The latch could be lifted with a gentle shove to release the spikes and impale the victim below. Kosh found a jar of marbles and spread them over the surrounding floor, hoping to slow the thornsprout down when it got close.

As soon as they were finished, they got into position. Kosh, Mateo and Swift hid behind a couple of barrels while Bitsy kneeled beside the latch, ready to activate the trap. After losing a round of rock, paper, scissors, the responsibility fell to her.

"Now we've just got to lure the thornsprout into the right spot." Mateo turned to Odders, perched on Kosh's shoulder. "That means we need bait."

Odders gave a nervous hiccup.

"I know you're scared, but I need you to be brave," Kosh encouraged. "You're the fastest of all of us. If anyone can outrun the thornsprout, it's you. Just find it and lead it back here."

Strengthened by Kosh's words, Odders seemed to find some confidence. With a battle-cry squeak, he rolled down Kosh's body and spun off into the undercroft.

Once he was out of sight, everyone waited in silence. Bitsy's heart thudded as she ran over their plan in her head. If she released the trap too soon or too late, it would fail. She had to hold steady until the thornsprout was in the right place.

Minutes passed.

Wondering why Odders was taking so long, Bitsy glanced at Kosh to see if he'd felt Odders extinguish—

A furious *click-clack, click-clack* resonated in the distance. The thornsprout was coming.

"Get ready," Mateo warned. "We'll only have one shot at this."

Bitsy stiffened as the beat of the thornsprout's claws grew louder. She heard pottery smashing and shelves collapsing. Chimes rang as grandfather clocks went tumbling.

In a sudden dramatic burst of red, the thornsprout came tearing out of the maze of grandfather clocks with its eyestalks pointed at Odders, who was speeding over the floor ahead of it. Odders' tiny black tongue flapped out of his mouth as he dodged left and right, desperately trying to avoid the thornsprout's claws.

Hands trembling, Bitsy reached for the latch on the wall. *Not yet,* she thought as the thornsprout drew closer. *Wait, wait…*

The thornsprout skidded on the marbles, its claws flailing. Just before it slid under the trap, her fingers flexed. *Now!*

She pushed the latch up. The chain rattled as it unwound, sending the deadly rack crashing down onto the thornsprout's back.

The thornsprout screeched and tried to shake the rack off, sending an assortment of kitchen utensils shooting out of its quills. Saucepans clattered into walls; cauldrons rolled over the floor and cutlery went flying. Bitsy had to dive behind a barrel to avoid being smacked in the face with a frying pan. As the thornsprout dropped into its egg-laying position, she feared they'd made a terrible mistake. Perhaps the thornsprout spikes hadn't been able to penetrate its armour after all…?

But then the monster's tiny eyes bulged and, with an annoyed hiss, it erupted into farthingdust. Bitsy collapsed onto her bottom as a haze of twinkling copper particles rained around her. "It worked!" she cried, gasping for breath. "We did it!"

Odders blew a raspberry with his long black tongue, bouncing up and down triumphantly.

"Thank goodness," Mateo panted, getting to his feet. "Everyone OK?"

Kosh crawled out from behind a barrel, scooping Odders into his arms. "Better than OK. Look!" He nodded into the next room, where a section of brick wall had retracted into the floor, leaving behind an arched opening.

"We must have passed the first test," Bitsy exclaimed, pushing herself up.

"There are still two more to go," Mateo reminded them, gloomily. "And if this was a test of creativity, then the next one is probably designed to challenge our *courage*."

20

As they ventured into the next section of the undercroft, Bitsy wiggled a finger into her top pocket, giving Pumpkin a reassuring tickle. Even though the thornsprout had gone, Pumpkin still felt tense.

Through the archway, flickering torchlight reflected off the surfaces of myriad strange objects, including bottles filled with different-coloured fluids, empty animal cages, brass weighing scales and alchemy books. The air smelled faintly of smoke.

"This looks like the kind of stuff an old magician might have used," Mateo said, examining a dusty crystal ball.

Bitsy glanced warily at some faded tarot cards, trying to suppress an ominous feeling about their next challenge.

"Bitsy, look out!" Kosh jabbed her in the ribs and she

jumped when she saw a small, foxy creature curled up on the floor. It had pointed ears, a bushy tail and what appeared to be a third eyelid on the back of its head. Its iridescent, peacock-blue fur was patterned with swirly black markings and two curved white fangs protruded over its bottom lip, like a sabre-toothed tiger's.

"What is it?" Kosh asked, backing away. "Is it going to kill us?"

Mateo considered the magicore warily. "Whatever species it is, I've never seen one before."

Unlike the thornsprout, this magicore seemed calm. At the sound of their voices, it arched its back into a yoga-like stretch and opened its three sets of eyelids one by one. Its eyes were completely black and there was something … *off* about them. It looked like they were juddering at high speed in their sockets, like the magicore was part of a video game and its eyes were glitching.

"Another wild magicore," Kosh said, rolling his neck like he had an itch between his shoulder blades. "It's making me feel really twitchy."

Bitsy understood what he meant. Although this magicore didn't seem to be hostile, there was something deeply unsettling about it. Its fangs and dark, quivering eyes – all three of them – made her skin bristle.

Taking a deep breath, Mateo kneeled down and stretched his hand towards the creature.

271

"Careful!" Bitsy warned.

"I know, I know." His fingers trembled as he reached closer. "I'm trying to be courageous. That's what we have to do to pass this test."

The magicore sniffed Mateo's fingers and opened its jaw. For a split second, Bitsy thought it might be about to chomp down on Mateo's wrist, but it only yawned and gently licked his hand with its shiny tongue. Mateo sighed with relief. "Hello, Blue," he said, scratching the magicore between their three eyes.

"How do you know their name is Blue?" Kosh asked.

"I don't," Mateo replied. "That's just what I'm calling them. If we make friends, they'll be less likely to want to kill us."

Blue made a low chattering noise and trotted to an imposing black cabinet pushed against one wall. As large as a wardrobe, it was painted with bold red flames and the words:

HESTIA THE MAGNIFICENT'S
DISAPPEARING CHAMBER
DARE YOU BRAVE THE PIT OF DEATH?

Nudging the cabinet door open, Blue looked back at them over their shoulder.

"They want us to follow them inside," Bitsy deduced. She shuddered as she inspected the cabinet's design. "But what's *the pit of death*?"

"The next test, probably," Kosh said grimly. "Come on, let's get this over with."

They filed through the door one after another. Given that the cabinet had been advertised as a disappearing chamber, Bitsy wasn't entirely surprised to find a dark hole at the back, leading to a long, torchlit tunnel. With a flick of their tail, Blue bounded inside and beckoned for them to follow.

"I'll go first," Mateo offered, ducking under a cobweb.

Their footsteps echoed as they tramped along the tunnel. Light flourished at the end, along with a worrying roaring noise. It didn't sound like an animal; more like something … mechanical.

"Well, this is nice," Kosh said sarcastically. "Welcome to the pit of death."

They emerged into a vast brick-lined chamber with a high ceiling. A pit filled with jagged iron spikes sat in the middle, with a narrow strip of floor on either side. The only way to cross was via a ramshackle wooden bridge suspended from the ceiling by tatty ropes. The structure looked so old and rickety that Bitsy thought she could probably sneeze and the entire thing would disintegrate.

That didn't stop Blue, however. Swaying their bushy tail, they skipped gracefully across the bridge to safety on the opposite side. Bitsy spotted an arch-shaped outline on the far wall. "That's got to be the exit over there. We must have to cross the bridge to pass the test."

She was about to say that the challenge seemed too simple, when the air thrummed. There was a loud roar, and multiple jets of flame exploded from the pit, billowing up towards the ceiling.

Everyone staggered back. Swift's tails transformed into throbbing exclamation marks as Mateo grabbed her and pulled her to safety.

Once the flames had subsided, Bitsy peered over the edge. Between the iron spikes, the floor was fitted with large metal crossbows with vats of petrol attached to the back – seventeenth-century flamethrowers.

Kosh tugged one of the rope handles on the bridge and it gave a worrying creak. "Can Swift create a pull-through to take us across?"

"Pull-throughs move matter over *long* distances," Mateo explained. "If Swift generated one, the exit would need to be miles away, which won't help us. Unless anyone has any better ideas, I think we might have to cross the bridge without magicore-means."

"I agree," Bitsy said reluctantly. "Pumpkin once levitated a motorbike for a few seconds, so she can probably lift Odders, Swift and maybe even our bags to the other side. That might help a bit."

They dumped their bags in a pile with Odders and Swift sitting on top. Under Bitsy's orders, Pumpkin floated out of her top pocket. She scrunched her tiny nose and the bags hovered into the air and sailed to safety on the opposite side of the pit.

As the flamethrowers launched another burst of fire, Bitsy, Kosh and Mateo lined up at the start of the bridge. It was too narrow for them to fit three abreast, so they would have to cross one behind the other. "As soon as the flamethrowers pause, we start moving," Bitsy said, her palms sweating. "Tread where I tread. Be careful."

At the back of the line, Kosh pulled down his beanie. "We're right behind you."

Bitsy's insides did somersaults as they waited, trying not to think about what would happen if any of them took a misstep. Finally, the flamethrowers sputtered out and the plumes fell back into the pit. *Here goes nothing.*

She stepped forward. Although the bridge groaned under her weight, the ropes held firm. With a steadying breath, she took another step and then another, advancing slowly.

Some of the wooden slats were broken or missing, so Bitsy was forced to hop from one foot to another to traverse the gaps. This made the bridge sway, and they all had to grip the rope handrails to stay balanced.

When the next round of fireballs blasted into the air, Bitsy jumped.

"It's OK!" Kosh called. "None of the flames are close enough to burn the bridge. Come on; we're over halfway!"

Bitsy's heart was going like a train, but Kosh was right. There were no signs of singed ropes and Bitsy couldn't even feel the heat from the flames, despite them being near by. She placed a foot onto the next slat…

…and it crumbled beneath her.

"Wah!" She windmilled her arms, trying to stop herself from falling.

Lunging forward, Mateo snatched her hood and pulled her back from the edge. "I've got you."

"Thanks," she mumbled, breathless.

The gap ahead of them was at least three metres long.

"That's too far to jump," Mateo observed. He took hold of the rope handrail with both hands, sliding his feet onto the parallel rope below. "We'll have to shimmy across like this."

Bitsy wiped her palms on her jeans before gripping the handrail. One slip of her boots and she'd be barbecued. Leading the way, she started sidestepping across. On the other side of the pit, Odders, Swift and Pumpkin bounced up and down like a trio of cheerleaders, spurring them on. Blue watched everything unfold with an eerie gaze. Bitsy wondered what their third eye might reveal about their source emotion. It had to be a feeling that made you want to see in all directions around you. Nervousness, maybe? Or paranoia?

The bridge rocked as the three of them shuffled across. After the first few steps, Bitsy noticed that the lower rope felt springier under her feet. She flinched when she saw the problem: a metre from the very end of the bridge, there was a rip in the rope.

And it was getting bigger.

"Faster!" she yelled. "It's going to snap!"

She scrambled to the end of the bridge and leaped onto the cold stone. Mateo was right behind her, but before Kosh had reached safety, there was a loud crunch … and the rope tore in two.

"Yahhhh!" he screamed as the lower rope fell away, leaving him dangling from the upper handrail. "Help!"

Bitsy's gut twisted. "Hold on!"

She ripped open Kosh's rucksack and reached for *Magicalia*. There had to be something she could conjure that could save him. Too desperate to wait for *Magicalia*'s help, she flipped frantically through its pages. Her eyes landed on the word *nervousness* and she thought of Blue.

nervousness
FRETFAWN
[*Metamorph, beta-level*]

Fretfawns are nimble, four-legged magicores weighing between nine to twelve stone. Due to their timid disposition, they usually hide their faces behind their disproportionately large ears. They have a chestnut coat with white mottles and small, black antlers. Their ability to alter the size of objects has often been exploited by conjurors to enlarge jewels and precious metals.

Blue didn't sound anything like a fretfawn. Bitsy skipped forward a few pages to *paranoia*:

paranoia
VISTIS
[*Clairvoyant, delta-level*]

A beautiful magicore with unique black markings and cobalt-blue fur. Its distinctive features include oversized canines, a long tail and a third eye in the back of its skull. It has the ability to create illusions, making people see and hear things that aren't there.

278

That's Blue, Bitsy thought. Her mind churned as she slammed *Magicalia* closed. If a vistis could create illusions, then perhaps that explained why Bitsy couldn't feel the heat from the flames.

Because they weren't really there.

Testing a theory, she fetched a pencil from her satchel and tossed it into the pit. It vanished into thin air after a few metres.

"Bitseeeee!" Kosh warbled. "Do something!"

Bitsy gestured for him to release the rope. "You have to let go!"

"What?" The muscles in his neck strained as he struggled to hold on. "What are you on about?"

Even Mateo, who was crouched at the edge of the pit, reaching for Kosh, looked doubtful. "Bitsy, are you sure?"

"None of this is real," she told them both. "It's an illusion. Kosh, you have to trust me!"

Tears watered in Kosh's eyes as he stared at Bitsy. She could tell by the lines on his face that he was fighting every survival instinct he had. He clenched his jaw ... and his fingers slipped from the rope.

Mateo gasped as Kosh fell into the pit of death...

...except it was no longer there.

There were no spitting flames or deadly spikes; just an expanse of dusty grey stone, only a couple of metres lower than the bottom of the bridge.

It had all been an illusion of Blue's creation.

Kosh bent his knees as he landed and threw his arms into the air. "Still alive!" he cheered.

While Odders, Swift and Pumpkin offered a chorus of congratulatory howls and hiccups, Bitsy and Mateo helped Kosh clamber out of the pit. As soon as he touched the surface, the ground shuddered, and with a long groan, the wall behind Blue descended into the floor, revealing a darkened room beyond.

Bitsy gave Kosh a celebratory hug. "Second test passed. We're almost there."

Everyone collected their bags and fetched their torches. As Bitsy plopped Pumpkin back inside her top pocket, she realized that Blue had vanished. She scanned the pit, but there was no trace of the tricksy vistis anywhere.

Judging by the echo of their footsteps, the next room seemed bigger than all the others, although it was difficult to tell because it was so crammed with stuff that the walls were no longer visible. Bitsy aimed her torch left to right, illuminating paintings on easels, artists' palettes, jars of paintbrushes and flasks of oil. There was a stack of battered leather trunks splattered with paint dollops, some empty bookshelves and a chest of drawers filled with old rags. A strong smell of white spirit lingered in the air.

With *Magicalia* still tucked under her arm, Bitsy ventured towards the only light source in the room: a flickering candelabra suspended from the ceiling. As she drew closer, a small hole opened in the floor and a stone podium spiralled out. Mounted on top of it was a spherical contraption made of bright silver. It featured a series of six concentric rings rotating on different axes and Bitsy recognized it immediately.

"Arkwright's Gyrowheel! It's right here!"

The others raced over. Kosh reached for the device, but as his fingers drew close, a sphere of light shimmered around the podium and he hissed in pain. "Argh, that burns!" He sucked his fingers as he stepped back. "There's some sort of force field around it."

"Then we need to find a way to deactivate it," Mateo said.

Bitsy was about to consult *Magicalia* when she caught a waft of something rank. It smelled like the inside of the food waste bin her dad filled with vegetable peels and used teabags – damp, fusty and rotten. A crackle sounded somewhere in the distance. Slowly, she pointed her torch beam ahead of her…

Fifty metres away, the ground was *moving*. A carpet of the most disgusting-looking fungus she'd ever seen was creeping towards her, crunching and sputtering as it spread across the dusty concrete floor. It looked like a horrific patchwork of every shape, texture and colour of mushroom you could imagine. There were bulbous grey toadstools, furry green mildew, dark brown mushrooms shaped like brains and spindly yellow fingers of fungus covered in slime. There were even fine grey strands of mould that looked like animal fur. Each organism was multiplying so fast that Bitsy felt like she was watching time-lapse footage from a nature documentary.

Behind the rug of fungi came a fog of festering spores that made every nearby canvas shrivel and turn black. A chill spread through Bitsy's veins as a magicore with cold blue eyes appeared out of the murk.

Magicalia vibrated so violently under Bitsy's arm that she dropped the encyclopaedia onto the floor. The cover burst open and the pages whirred forward, stopping somewhere in the middle. Looking down, Bitsy skimmed the text:

despair
DOOMICORN
[Elemental, delta-level]

A foul magicore of terrible power. The doomicorn is a heavy, four-legged beast with a festering coat and rotten odour. It has the ability to spawn a unique and deadly fungus from its hooves. The fungus spreads quickly through living matter, decomposing it in seconds. Human contact with the fungus is known to result in

death within thirty minutes. The doomicorn can control the movement of its fungus like a blanket across the land, laying waste to vast areas of life. It is considered extremely dangerous.

21

Bitsy's torch beam wobbled as her hand shook. The doomicorn was as large as an elephant, with broad shoulders and a muscular back. A scabby, oozing crust of green and white fungus covered its entire body. Rotting mushrooms sprouted along its spine, and patches of black mould grew out of its nostrils and around its muzzle. Its straggly mane and tail looked like the slimy hair you pull out of a plughole. As it clomped forward, it spewed puffs of deadly spores from its hooves. Its icy gaze seemed to bore into Bitsy like two frozen daggers.

"What in the—?" Mateo blurted, stumbling back.

Kosh retched and covered his mouth with his sleeve. "That's got to be what nightmares smell like."

The stench of decay filled Bitsy's nose, making her eyes

water. Edging away, she snatched *Magicalia* off the floor and shoved it back into her satchel. "It's a doomicorn," she told the others, quickly relaying everything she'd read. "So, if that fungus touches us, we'll turn into—" Her throat closed. She couldn't say it.

"Fertilizer," Mateo managed, staring at the doomicorn in horror. "Run!"

In a fit of panic, they all turned in different directions. The doomicorn stomped its hooves and the fungus sped up, racing across the floor with increased vigour. Easels clattered to the ground and frames rusted in seconds as noxious fumes filled the air.

"Climb onto something!" shouted a familiar voice suddenly. "Get to higher ground!"

Bitsy turned in the direction of the voice and staggered when she saw her dad hurrying towards them. He was wearing a long, navy raincoat over his corduroy chinos and shirt.

He pointed at a bookcase. "Up there, Bitsy! Now!"

Shaking off her shock, she stuffed her torch into her coat pocket and launched herself at the shelves. In the dim light, it was difficult to see where she was treading. She planted the ball of her foot on the first shelf and pushed upwards, throwing her arms above her head to catch the top of the bookcase.

"Boys, get on those suitcases!" Eric directed, indicating to two stacks of leather trunks.

Mateo lifted Swift onto his shoulders and started clambering up one pile. Kosh scaled the other. "What are you doing here?" Kosh cried happily.

As Bitsy reached the top of her bookcase, she saw her dad clamber onto the chest of drawers filled with rags.

"No time to explain," he replied. "Let's focus on getting the gyrowheel."

Bitsy guessed Melasina had somehow told her dad where they were. She wasn't sure whether to feel relieved that her dad was helping them, or terrified that they were now *all* in danger from the doomicorn. "The gyrowheel is protected behind a force field," she told him, reaching for her torch. She directed the beam at the podium and the gyrowheel glinted in the light. "To claim it, we have to pass three tests and we've only faced two so far."

As the doomicorn's blanket of death crackled nearer, Eric pointed left of the podium. "There's something over there, on the wall."

Bitsy aimed her torch. A space had been cleared among the paintings and art equipment. Above an empty metal easel, words were painted in white on the bricks:

> To *claim the wheel and leave this place,*
> *one final challenge you must face.*
> *Answer this, precise and true:*
> *what does the wheel mean to you?*

Make your choice and then stand fast.
Your first guess shall be your last.

"That's the final test!" Mateo said. "But what's the answer?"

An easel clattered against Bitsy's bookcase, making it sway. Holding tightly to the sides, she saw that the doomicorn's fungus had encircled her. It appeared to advance much more slowly in a vertical direction, as if it had to fight against gravity. Her dad's tip to get to higher ground might just have bought them some time.

"*What does the wheel mean to you*?" Kosh rubbed his temples like he was trying to massage an idea out of his brain. "What's the answer to that? It's so cryptic!"

Bitsy considered the puzzle carefully. "It says *your first guess shall be your last*. That means whatever answer we give, it has to be correct. We won't get any do-overs."

"Look." Eric signalled to the top of the podium. "There are nozzles buried in the surface of the stone. I'll bet if we get the answer wrong, flames will shoot out and the wheel will be destroyed."

As her dad spoke, Bitsy noticed something peculiar about him: he was completely dry. There were no raindrops on his coat or damp patches on the bottom of his trousers. His shoes hadn't even left wet footprints on the floor. She and the others were still soaked from the storm outside, so why wasn't he?

"Dad, how did you get here?" Bitsy asked.

"Ozoz," he answered hurriedly. "What do you think the answer to this puzzle is?"

Bitsy frowned. If her dad had travelled by ozoz, he'd still be drenched from the rain. Either he was lying, or he'd arrived there before them and had time to dry off.

With a growing sense of unease, she studied her dad more closely. She spied the black spiral rings of a dog-eared notebook in his coat pocket and gasped. That was *her* notebook. The one she'd lost in Versailles.

And then it struck her: just as Blue had created the firepit illusion, so too her dad's appearance was a mask, a façade. Fear gripped her chest, making her whole body shake. "You're lying," she said, glaring at her dad.

Kosh looked puzzled. "Bitsy, what are you—?"

"That's not my dad," she said hollowly. "That's … Riddlejax."

Eric went very still. A deep scowl formed on his brow. He groaned and stood up, balancing on top of the chest of drawers. With a smirk, he swung one arm behind his back and took a bow. As he straightened up, his face, hair and clothes transformed into flakes of ash, which fluttered away to reveal a slim man in a dark red tuxedo.

Riddlejax was surprisingly slight, with a bony face and sloping shoulders. His skin had the sickly yellow hue of soured milk and his flame-red hair was slicked back against his scalp. He carried a farthingstone cane in his left hand, the top of which was carved into a chaosphere.

Bitsy's jaw stiffened. This man was the reason her mum's car had swerved off the road. It was his fault that her aunt was now suffering, along with so many other hunters, including Mateo's sister. He was a murderer, a poisoner, a cruel and devious manipulator.

"I commend you," Riddlejax remarked, rocking his cane towards Bitsy. "I thought my disguise would fool you long enough for us to break the gyrowheel free, but alas. Endymion, you can stop for now."

The doomicorn froze and so did the fungus carpet.

With a sinking feeling, Bitsy realized two things. One, the doomicorn's name must be Endymion, which didn't sound remotely scary enough; and two, Endymion belonged to Riddlejax, which meant the doomicorn had nothing to do with Arkwright's final test. She kicked herself for not figuring it out sooner; Endymion didn't have the black eyes of a wild magicore.

Riddlejax hopped gracefully off the chest of drawers and walked towards the podium. Wherever he stepped, Endymion's deadly fungus retreated. Bitsy gulped, realizing that by telling them to climb up high, he'd surrounded them with fungus so they couldn't move. They were trapped.

Mateo's face reddened as he glowered at Riddlejax. Swift flattened her ears and growled.

"Have you been Eric this whole time?" Kosh spluttered, brokenly.

Bitsy shook her head. *He can't have been...*

"No, this is the first instance I've used *his* face, although you may recognize some of my others." Riddlejax twitched his neck and his features again transformed into ash. The flakes blew away to reveal a young man with a shock of black hair, whom Bitsy recognized as one of the staff at the Theatre Royal, Drury Lane. This façade then dissolved into the woman with the golf visor who had pursued them through Agra. When the ash disappeared again, Riddlejax's true form returned. The whole process had taken seconds.

The blood chilled in Bitsy's veins. It wasn't just chaos-conjurors who had been following her and Kosh, it was Riddlejax himself. Although ... she still didn't understand how Riddlejax had been tracking them.

"I always thought that your mother had destroyed her notebook and, with it, the only copy of Arkwright's Riddle," Riddlejax told Bitsy very matter-of-factly. "But I recently discovered that your mother had hidden her notes inside a copy of *Magicalia*. I poisoned the Hunter Guild so that your aunt would retrieve *Magicalia* and find the gyrowheel for me. Annoyingly, Melasina decided to appeal to your father for help, so I was forced to switch tack. I wrote the ransom note, propelling you and your friend on the hunt instead. My chaos-conjurors and I have been monitoring your progress ever since."

Hearing Riddlejax talk, Bitsy shuddered. He sounded cold and methodical, like a robot. Melasina and her dad were right – Riddlejax had been behind everything. He didn't seem to care what damage or pain he caused as long as he got what he wanted. But Bitsy couldn't work out how he'd discovered the truth about her mum's notebook…

Beside the podium, Riddlejax studied the gyrowheel closely. "It wasn't until I saw you writing in your notebook in Agra that I realized I might not need you any more; I might only need your notebook. I told my chaos-conjurors to get hold of it via any means necessary." He reached into the pocket of his tuxedo, pulled out Bitsy's ring-bound notepad and slammed it on the floor. "Yes, it contained the coordinates to lead me here, but the rest of it is full of childish junk. Your mother's notes included all sorts of clues and information she'd pieced together during her investigation. I need them to help me crack this last puzzle. I was able to put the thornsprout to sleep and cross the pit of death with ease, but this is more difficult. I've been trying to work it out, but I cannot risk a wrong answer." He gestured lazily to Kosh and Mateo with his cane. "Endymion, if you please?"

A mass of festering mould rippled across the flagstones towards Kosh and Mateo. It crackled louder as it sped up, easily climbing both stacks of trunks and turning the leather to dust.

Panic flashed in Mateo's eyes. Hugging Swift against his chest, he jumped towards an empty patch of ground. But his leap fell short and the fungus caught his right foot.

"Garr!" he howled, hopping. Toadstools exploded out of the right leg of his jeans as he fell against a wall. Swift instantly burst into farthingdust.

Kosh tried kicking away the mould, but it only latched onto him sooner. A puff of farthingdust left his hoodie pocket as he slumped to the floor, groaning – Odders must have been extinguished. Kosh's trainers looked like they'd been used as garden planters. Fetid brown mushrooms sprouted through the toes and hairy green mildew covered the soles and sides. His shoelaces had already decomposed, leaving behind thin black stains.

Bitsy's heart wrenched seeing how much pain they were in. "Stop it!" she yelled, her belly hot with anger. "You're killing them!"

"In thirty minutes, they will both be dead," Riddlejax

agreed. "Unless you give me the answer to this final puzzle, so I can claim the gyrowheel. You've read your mother's notes; use them to figure it out."

Bitsy's pulse raced. "You can still save them?"

"Endymion is an elemental-type magicore," Riddlejax said, sniffing. "He doesn't just generate the fungus, he controls it. If he removes it from your friends, they will survive."

The possibility of saving Kosh's and Mateo's lives focussed Bitsy's mind like a laser. She knew Riddlejax was manipulating her to get what he wanted, but she didn't care. She couldn't let them die.

She read the second line of the puzzle again: *Answer this, precise and true: what does the wheel mean to you?*

According to her mum's notes, this was a test of *conviction*. Bitsy was pretty sure that conviction meant belief. Her mum had written that Gilander Arkwright believed in using the gyrowheel to help others and that he wanted the device to be claimed by someone who felt the same.

She read the final line of the puzzle: *Make your choice and then stand fast. Your first guess shall be your last.* Bitsy looked at the empty easel beneath where the riddle was written and wondered...

Sweeping her torch around the room, she perused the various paintings on display. She jolted as her

293

beam glided over a landscape painting of Greenwich Observatory, in London, where Arkwright's Riddle had first been discovered. Browsing further, she found images of some of the other places where coordinates had been hidden – the Bodleian Library in Oxford and the Palace of Versailles.

"Tick tock," Riddlejax said, tapping his cane against the flagstones. "Time is running out if you want to save them."

Bitsy glanced at Kosh and Mateo, writhing in pain. The fungus was spreading. "I think the answer to the puzzle is a painting," she told Riddlejax. "You have to find it in this room and place it on the easel beneath where the puzzle is written."

"I'd worked that out myself," Riddlejax snapped, scanning the shadows. "Which painting?"

Mind whirring, Bitsy tried to pinpoint the correct answer. Each painting must represent a different reason for wanting the gyrowheel. She supposed the library might symbolize *knowledge* and the fortress in Ethiopia could represent *protection*. Thinking of all the gold in Versailles, it seemed likely that the palace denoted *wealth*. But what was the correct answer? What was Gilander Arkwright looking for?

And then it came to her.

She remembered overhearing a tour guide at the

Taj Mahal say that, since the seventeenth century, the mausoleum had widely been thought of as a symbol of *love*. Only someone with good intentions would want to use the gyrowheel for love.

Love had to be the answer.

"It's the Taj Mahal," Bitsy said. "That's the painting you need."

Riddlejax narrowed his eyes. "A building that symbolizes *death*? If you're tricking me, your friends will suffer greatly. I will make sure of it."

"It's not a trick!" Bitsy insisted, thinking that only someone with no love in their heart would look at the Taj Mahal and see death. "The Taj Mahal's the answer."

Riddlejax regarded her for a long moment, apparently agonizing over whether to trust her or not. Finally, he growled. "So be it."

Endymion trotted forward as Riddlejax scrambled into the shadows, knocking down easels as he searched for the correct painting. He found it in seconds and hurried to the wall, placing it carefully on the easel.

The words on the bricks vanished and the ground trembled. Bitsy spread her arms for balance as her bookcase wobbled. The force field around the gyrowheel flickered on and off and fizzled into thin air.

Riddlejax grinned. As he snatched the gyrowheel off the top of the podium, torches crackled to life around the room, flooding the place with light. An archway opened in the far corner of the chamber. Bitsy heard the lashing rain and howling wind outside.

"That'll be our exit," Riddlejax told Endymion.

The doomicorn snorted and turned towards the archway.

"Wait!" Bitsy cried, clambering down the bookcase. "You said that if I helped you solve the puzzle, you'd save my friends."

"I did, yes." Riddlejax waved a hand at Endymion and the doomicorn stomped his hooves. "But I lied."

A wave of hissing fungus came oozing straight towards Bitsy. She turned to run, but she was too slow. Pain splintered up her left heel as the fungus caught her shoe. She screamed and hobbled forward, feeling a cold stab to her chest as Pumpkin extinguished.

Riddlejax waved his cane in farewell as he and Endymion exited into the storm. The fungus carpet retreated towards the doomicorn, but the damage was done. They'd all been infected.

Bitsy winced and squeezed her knee as the fungus crept past her ankle. "I'm so sorry," she cried, shambling towards Kosh and Mateo. "It's all my fault."

She was a few metres from them when the air shimmered and Blue appeared, sitting in the middle of the floor. In the amber torchlight, Blue's iridescent coat glimmered violet and turquoise.

Blue peered worriedly up at Bitsy with their strange, glitching eyes. They lifted their bushy tail … and Bitsy gasped.

The gyrowheel was resting on the flagstones beneath. Blue nudged the device towards Bitsy's foot with their snout. The corners of Blue's mouth turned upwards, dazzling Bitsy with a strange, sabre-toothed grin. The vistis then closed their eyes and silently slipped into farthingdust.

22

"I don't believe it!" Bitsy's eyes watered as she reached down and collected the gyrowheel off the floor. Despite the device's age, it felt robust and sturdy. "Riddlejax doesn't have the gyrowheel. It's right here."

"How?" Kosh croaked, slumped against a wall. The fungus had spread past both his ankles and was now creeping up his jeans in furry green tendrils. There were large holes in the soles of his trainers where the mould had eaten away at the rubber.

"I think Blue might have been watching the third test to ensure that the right person claimed the gyrowheel," Bitsy answered, puzzling it all through. "The gyrowheel that Riddlejax took must have been an illusion."

Mateo grimaced as he shuffled closer, dragging his

infected leg behind him. "We've got to get it out of here. Once Riddlejax realizes what's happened, he'll return for the *real* gyrowheel."

"Maybe we can send it to safety using a pull-through?" Bitsy suggested. "Can you conjure Swift?"

Gripping the farthingstone beads on his right hand, Mateo took a deep breath and closed his eyes. A few floating particles of farthingdust twinkled above his fingers, glowing like embers. The muscles in Mateo's face tensed. His free hand curled into a trembling fist...

And then, as quietly as the particles had materialized, they disappeared into thin air. Mateo let out a gasping breath, opening his eyes. "It's no use. The fungus is sapping all my strength. I don't have enough energy to conjure anything."

Cold sweat dripped down the back of Bitsy's neck as she tried to suppress her panic. They weren't going to get very far moving the gyrowheel themselves. Even if they opened a doorway to the root-network, she doubted they'd be able to stumble more than a few paces inside. And the fungus was worsening by the second. She could feel it crawling up her leg, sucking the life out of her like a parasite. They probably had only ten minutes before it engulfed their bodies.

Kosh's jaw stiffened as a swathe of black mushrooms blistered through the sleeves of his hoodie. "We can't die here. If we do, Riddlejax will get the gyrowheel and everything we've done will have been for nothing."

"But there's no way to stop the fungus," Bitsy admitted tearfully. Pain tore through her thigh as the deadly mould climbed higher. Unable to balance, she dropped to the floor beside Kosh.

"Don't give up," Mateo rasped. "We've got to think and hope. There must be something we can do."

Hope…

Like a ripple on the surface of water, Bitsy had the stirrings of an idea. "Melasina wanted to use the gyrowheel to conjure an everwing: a magicore whose source emotion is hope. She said that an everwing's cocoon can cure all magicore-related ailments. So, what if we use the gyrowheel to conjure an everwing ourselves? If its cocoon can heal us, we can get the gyrowheel away from Riddlejax."

Mateo coughed as he sat up straighter. "We'll need to conjure it *together*, channelling what's left of our combined strength into the gyrowheel."

Bitsy scanned their surroundings thoughtfully. "Master Ollennu said that to activate the gyrowheel, you need to charge it with six different types of energy. We can hold it over a flaming torch to give it heat and light, but that's only two."

"I suppose shouting will produce sound energy," Kosh

wheezed. "And we can get chemical energy from one of the batteries in our torches. What other types are there? Electrical, gravitational, kinetic…"

"If we throw the gyrowheel up in the air, it will gain kinetic energy from the movement and gravitational energy from the height – that's all six!" Bitsy realized.

"At the rate the fungus is multiplying, we probably only have time to try this once, so we'd better give it everything we've got," Mateo said. "To conjure the everwing, we must each think of a hopeful memory. It's got to be something powerful."

Bitsy racked her brains. Hope made you feel uplifted and strong. It was the belief that, no matter how much the odds were stacked against you, there was a chance you would make it. It was the emotion people felt when they saw light in the darkness, land on the horizon or the sun in the morning sky. Hope was a new beginning.

Like meeting a member of your family that you never knew existed, Bitsy thought. She remembered talking to Melasina in the supply room earlier. They had only spoken briefly, but it had filled Bitsy with optimism. Until now, almost everything she knew about her mum she'd learned from her dad. But with Melasina, there would be more stories to share and more moments to discover. There would be a new relationship to build with someone whom her mum had loved very much. Bitsy got tingles even now, thinking about it. "I have a strong memory," she said confidently.

"Me too," Kosh declared. "It was the final game of the season three years ago. Oddingham FC were three–nil down until we got two back in the eighty-third minute. In the closing moments, I clung on to my scarf and hoped – *really* hoped – that we'd get another one and draw."

The corners of Mateo's mouth lifted. "I've decided on a memory too. It was the first time Esme and I used our proxicups to find each other. I'd been worrying I might never see her again, but then the proxicups worked and I realized that everything would be OK."

Getting into position, Mateo and Kosh hauled themselves a few paces towards the nearest torch, while Bitsy made her way opposite. She sucked air through her teeth as pain spiked in her left ankle. She could no longer feel anything in her foot. It was like lugging a sack of mouldy potatoes behind her.

"Let's do this," Kosh said, holding the gyrowheel in one hand and a torch battery in the other. He wedged the battery between two metal sections at the bottom of the gyrowheel, so the positive and negative points were in contact with the metal. Then he took a deep breath and shouted, "ODDINGHAM FC FOR EVER!" at the device. His mouth twitched as two of the rings started rotating, making a thrumming noise like a spinning tin can. He touched the farthingstone sphere at the centre of the gyrowheel and closed his eyes. No farthingdust materialized, but when Kosh opened his eyes a second later, it was as if the colour had faded from his skin. "Your turn," he croaked.

Creases formed on the bridge of Mateo's nose as a patch of white mould crackled over his hip. He took the gyrowheel from Kosh and held it over a flaming torch. Tiny facets of light circled the room as the fire reflected off the gyrowheel's metal rings. Another two of the wheels began to turn. Mateo pressed his fingers against the farthingstone ball and clenched his jaw, but still no farthingdust appeared. Mateo lifted the gyrowheel over his shoulder. "This is it, Bitsy. Catch!"

He tossed the gyrowheel to Bitsy. As it tumbled through the air, the final two rings started moving. Bitsy caught the gyrowheel in one hand and reached for the farthingstone in the centre. She felt it grow warm against her fingers as she summoned her hopeful memory as clearly as possible. She pictured her aunt sitting there – the crooked tilt of her mouth, the gloss of her raven-black hair. She evoked the pitch of her aunt's voice and the musty smell in the supply room. She brought to mind the tizzy feeling in her stomach as she thought about how her aunt would be there for the rest of her life…

The rings on the gyrowheel spun faster. Sparks

jumped from the device and into Bitsy's fingers, feeling like tiny electric shocks. She gasped as energy rushed out of her body and into the gyrowheel like sand through a net. Her skin turned cold as she felt her strength leave her. The gyrowheel fell from her fingers, and she collapsed to her knees.

Wind blustered around the undercroft, scattering paintbrushes and torn rags. Mateo and Kosh cowered before her, shielding themselves from the gale. Spinning above the gyrowheel was a giant whirlpool of farthingdust.

Bitsy squinted, trying to see a shape inside it. As she watched, her eyelids grew heavy. The pain in her body dulled. Her vision swam, and everything faded to black.

The insides of Bitsy's eyelids flashed orange. She opened them a fraction. She was lying with her cheek against the flagstones. What looked like a two-metre-high pineapple sat on the floor beside her. Its rough, golden skin was slightly translucent and Bitsy thought she saw shadows moving inside, before her eyelids flickered closed once more...

Liquid trickled down Bitsy's chin. The sweet taste of honeycomb and sharp tang of apple exploded on her tongue. She swallowed and lifted open her eyes.

This time, a face hovered over her: a long white snout,

pointed ears and blue eyes that sparkled like sunshine on water. Bitsy brought a hand to her mouth and found the flesh of some fruit hanging there. She wiped her chin clean and pushed herself onto her elbows.

The majestic magicore that stood before her was the size of a caravan. It resembled a dragon, with a winged body, four clawed feet and a swishy tail. Rather than scales, it was covered nose to wing in fluffy white feathers that glimmered with rainbow colours like an underwater pearl.

An everwing.

Even in Bitsy's delirious state, she knew what this meant. The gyrowheel had worked. This everwing was *theirs*.

She peered into the creature's dreamlike eyes, feeling its heartbeat inside her own. She could sense that the everwing identified as female and tried to think of a good name for her. "How about Brightbeam?" she whispered, inspired by the sunset she'd seen through Melasina's bedside window. She reached up to pat the everwing's snout. "Do you like that?"

Brightbeam tipped her head side to side like she was tossing the name around. Then a huge slobbery blue tongue poked out from between her lips and she licked Bitsy from navel to forehead with one stroke.

Bitsy smiled, wiping her face dry. "I'll take that as a yes."

Kosh and Mateo were both stirring. Squashed clumps of juicy yellow fruit were smothered around their mouths – the same flesh Bitsy had found on her lips. Brightbeam must have been feeding them the stuff. Bitsy picked a lump off the floor and gave it a sniff. It smelled like honey.

"Bitsy?" Kosh rasped, lifting his head. "What happened?"

As Bitsy reached for him, she noticed that the furry green fungus had stopped spreading up his jeans and was retreating back towards his ankles.

Mateo groaned as he pushed himself up. His entire right leg was plastered in flaky white mould, but some of it shook off as he moved. "An everwing!" he said, breathlessly. "We did it!"

"Her name's Brightbeam," Bitsy told them.

Brightbeam gazed at them all with a matronly look of concern. Bending her long neck, she reached over her shoulder and lifted forward the sticky remains of a golden, pineapple-shaped eggshell in her mouth. Bitsy had a hazy memory of seeing the pineapple earlier, but she must have been dipping in and out of consciousness. "Her cocoon – I think she's been feeding us it to heal us," she told the others, feeling grateful but slightly grossed out. "The effects of the fungus are reversing. Can either of you move your feet?"

Wincing, Kosh wiggled his toes. "Yeah, but it still hurts."

"Just about," Mateo said, brushing dead fungus off his leg.

Bitsy checked in with her own body. The soreness in her ankle had gone and she could feel pins and needles in her heel as her circulation returned. With a sickening dread, her mind turned to Riddlejax. "We've got to get up. Riddlejax could be back at any moment."

They staggered to their feet. Bitsy stowed the gyrowheel into her satchel, while Mateo collected as many pieces of Brightbeam's cocoon as he could fit into his rucksack. Brightbeam used her feathery tail to sweep away a heap of junk from the wall, clearing a space for Kosh to open a door to the root-network.

Still a little wobbly, Kosh steadied himself against Brightbeam's side as he plunged the root-key into the bricks. This time, the roots wove a doorframe wide enough for Brightbeam to fit through. The everwing honked in appreciation and set her tail sloping towards them like a boarding ramp.

"She wants to give us a ride," Kosh realized. "It'll be quicker. Everyone, get on."

Brightbeam's feathers were silky and strong. As Bitsy clambered onto her back, she felt the everwing's muscles shifting under her weight. Bitsy straddled Brightbeam's spine, settling herself in front of Kosh.

As Mateo mounted Brightbeam's tail, a foul smell went up Bitsy's nostrils. She heard the clatter of hooves and looked back the way they'd come.

Endymion was galloping towards them like a zombie racehorse, clouds of black spores puffing out of his nostrils. Jockeying atop, Riddlejax was bent low over Endymion's ears, his coat tails flapping wildly behind him. He thrust his cane towards them. "There they are! Get them!"

23

"Brightbeam, go!" Bitsy shouted, digging her heels into the everwing's side.

Brightbeam honked and flung Mateo onto her back with a flick of her tail. As Mateo grabbed Kosh's hoodie, Brightbeam raced into the shadows of the root-network.

The root pathways creaked under Brightbeam's weight. Splinters flew into the air as her claws tore into the wood. Wobbling around on Brightbeam's spine, Bitsy clung tightly to the everwing's feathers. She glanced over her shoulder. The opening to the undercroft was slowly knitting closed. *Hurry up,* she pleaded, *hurry up...*

She jumped as the tip of Riddlejax's cane burst through the roots. Green fungus started seeping through the wall like ink on tissue paper. But the roots fought back, lacing together as they tried to close the gap. All of a sudden, everything went dark.

"What happened?" Mateo said. "Did Riddlejax make it through?"

Bitsy was about to reach for her torch when light radiated beneath her. Brightbeam's feathers were glowing pure white like fresh morning snow.

"That's so bright!" Kosh exclaimed, shading his eyes.

Even the dense fog of the root-network was no match for Brightbeam's light. As the everwing shone brighter, the darkness washed away. Everything within a five-metre radius became visible, then everything within a twenty-metre radius. Pathways appeared out of the gloom, snaking above and below them.

Suddenly, Kosh screamed. "He's behind us!"

Twisting round, Bitsy saw Riddlejax clambering through a mould-infested hole in the wall. "Give me the gyrowheel!" he roared as Endymion rammed through the roots beside him.

Bitsy touched Brightbeam's cheek. "Fly off! We've got to lose them!"

Brightbeam opened her wings with a dull thud, expelling a honey-scented blast. She snorted like she might be saying, *Hang on!* and charged forward.

Bitsy squeezed her thighs as they juddered up and down, clinging to Brightbeam's feathers. The everwing reared on her hind legs, throwing the three of them backwards. Then with a mighty flap, she leaped into the air.

It felt like a hook yanked on Bitsy's stomach as they pitched upwards. Wind gusted into her face, making her eyes water. She flinched as roots swept close by on all sides, but Brightbeam was as nimble as a dragonfly, using her long tail to stay balanced as she weaved between the pathways.

"Let's GO!" Kosh yelled.

Mateo spread his arms. "Yes, Brightbeam!"

Stupidly, Bitsy looked down. Tangled roots zigzagged beneath them, getting smaller and smaller. She couldn't see the bottom. There would be no surviving a fall like that. Still, with the wind whipping through her hair, Bitsy had never felt so exhilarated. Brightbeam seemed to be enjoying it, too. She flicked her ears and hooted as they coasted into the vanishing darkness, heading deeper into the root-network.

"I don't believe it!" Kosh suddenly cried, twisting round. "They're chasing us!"

Bitsy looked over her shoulder and tensed. Endymion was galloping towards them in mid-air, Riddlejax riding on his back. At first, Bitsy couldn't understand how the doomicorn was airborne, but then she noticed giant umbrella-shaped toadstools spawning near his hooves. They appeared to float long enough to support the magicore's weight as he leaped between them like a champion show pony.

Pointing his cane at Brightbeam, Riddlejax shouted, "FIRE!"

A boulder of furry black mould launched towards them. Instinctively, Bitsy ducked.

"Brightbeam, evasive manoeuvres!" Mateo commanded.

The everwing kicked her legs and sped up, shooting through the shadows like an arrow. Bitsy's raincoat flapped under her armpits as tears flew off her cheeks. But Endymion kept pace, firing mould balls in all directions. Brightbeam looped up and around, dodging the blasts.

The air turned thick with the fuzzy brown detritus of decaying roots and the pervasive smell of garden compost. Bitsy coughed heavily as it settled in a thick layer on her clothes and hair. Brightbeam had to shake her feathers clean so her radiance wasn't dampened.

"We can't keep doing this!" Kosh said. "We've got to choose an exit and get the gyrowheel out of here."

"But which one?" Mateo called.

Bitsy racked her brains. Many of the exits led to highly populated places. If Riddlejax and Endymion followed them, they could harm thousands of innocent people. "We need to choose somewhere Riddlejax will be at a disadvantage. What about the European Conservatoire? There will be other conjurors there to help us get the gyrowheel to safety."

They all ducked as a mould ball went shooting over their heads. Brightbeam dived under another pathway and veered into the central chamber of the root-network, where glowing icons marked the various exits.

It was Mateo who spotted it first. "Brightbeam, over there!"

The symbol looked like an outline of the conservatoire atrium with its domed ceiling and multiple rotating balconies. Giving a honk in reply, Brightbeam swished her tail and soared higher, whizzing straight towards the door.

As they hurtled closer, Bitsy yelled, "Brace yourselves!"

Brightbeam lowered her head so that the thickest part of her skull hit the door first. The impact threw Bitsy and the others backwards. Pain spread between Bitsy's shoulders as her neck jerked, making her feel like a crash-test dummy. The root wall exploded as Brightbeam tore through it.

Although the lights were on in the conservatoire atrium, the place was empty, which made their arrival sound even more like a bomb going off. A booming thud echoed around the space, rattling the domed glass ceiling high above. Brightbeam's claws screeched against the marble floor as she went skidding forward, scrambling to a stop just before the Chancellor's desk.

Bitsy, Kosh and Mateo slid off her back, bending their knees as they landed on the ground. They all turned to face the wall they'd come through. Brightbeam's emergency exit had left a gaping hole, which was slowly starting to repair itself. Bitsy held her breath, expecting Riddlejax to burst through at any moment.

"Whoa..." Kosh muttered, swaying. "That was some ride."

A door slammed open, and a group of conjurors came rushing out. Bitsy recognized the moustachioed faces of Hasim and Lars, and the short, bald figure of Master Ollennu. They were joined by others in red, blue, green, white and yellow overalls. At the back of the bunch hurried Chancellor Hershel, Giverna and Bitsy's dad.

"Dad!" Bitsy cried, running towards him.

Chancellor Hershel stared at Brightbeam. "Everwing..." she mumbled, aghast. "You've conjured an everwing."

Eric gave Bitsy a tight squeeze. "What happened? Why aren't you with Melasina?"

"There's no time to explain." Bitsy fumbled with the buckles on her satchel. "We have Arkwright's Gyrowheel and Riddlejax is chasing us. He has a doomicorn with him."

"Then he really is alive..." one of the conjurors muttered.

Giverna looked like she might faint. "Good gracious!"

Eric paled as Bitsy pulled the gyrowheel out of her bag and handed it to him. His jaw went loose. "I…"

A rumble sounded from deep within the root-network. Everyone turned to look at the dark opening on the far side of the atrium.

Chancellor Hershel bristled and threw back her shoulders. "You heard her – we're about to be under attack." She pointed to the upper balconies. "Lars, Régine and Felix – get up high, defend from the air. Hasim and Giverna, you're with me on the ground. Eric – hide the gyrowheel. Make sure Riddlejax doesn't know which one of us has it. I'll lock down the exits. No matter what happens, that doomicorn does not leave this building."

As Lars and the other conjurors hurried to the stairs, Giverna pulled her chopstick out of her hair. "Right," she muttered, rubbing her hands together. "Time for something big and scary, I think."

Bitsy's dad arched an eyebrow. "Snowball?"

"Exactly." Giverna summoned a cloud of farthingdust out of the end of her chopstick, and it transformed into an enormous, owl-like magicore. The beast was as tall and wide as a wardrobe, with a round belly and two clawed feet. It was covered in gleaming, indigo-black feathers with a solitary white stripe down the middle of its breast. In the centre of its flat, heart-shaped face was a flint-grey beak and a pair of pupilless white eyes the size of portholes. Eric slid his fountain pen out of his top pocket and conjured Quasar. Electrical sparks pulsed along the waywurm's silver body as they whipped through the air.

"We can help!" Bitsy piped up. "Or at least, our everwing can."

Chancellor Hershel nodded. "Very well, but stay out of the fight yourselves. Find a place to hide."

As the Chancellor marched towards her desk, Mateo adjusted his rucksack. "I've got to get these cocoon pieces back to the Hunter Guild's barracks. Every second counts if I want to save my sister and the others."

Taking Melasina's root-key from Kosh, Mateo disappeared through one of the brass doors on the ground floor. As another rumble echoed around the atrium, Brightbeam whirled around to face the opening to the root-network. She flattened her ears and flared her nostrils, growling at the dark hole.

The musty stench of decay swept into the atrium, making them all cough. Eric stuffed the gyrowheel under his jacket and edged backwards. "Get out of here," he whispered to Bitsy and Kosh. "Go through a door and take shelter in one of the demonstration rooms. They're built to withstand blasts."

A menacing crackle sounded from deep within the root-network. Tiny black spores started seeping through the opening, increasing in number until they became dense fog.

Bitsy's chest tightened as Endymion's snout emerged through the haze, followed by his glacial-blue eyes.

"How nice of you to arrange a welcome party," Riddlejax remarked, appearing on Endymion's back. He stretched his arms behind his head like he was getting comfy. "It's so good to be back…"

24

The Chancellor stood with her hands hanging loose by her sides. Her jaw stiffened. "Riddlejax," she growled.

"Chancellor." Riddlejax grinned, flashing a set of pearly teeth. "Give me the gyrowheel and I'll be on my way."

"I don't think so." The Chancellor's fingers twitched. Quick as a flash, she reached up and tapped the frames of her glasses. A wisp of farthingdust swirled into the air and transformed into a glutinous yellow blob the size of an armchair. A pair of glowing amber eyes and a thin black mouth floated inside the magicore's body like they were suspended in jelly.

"Pity," Riddlejax sniffed. He pointed his cane at the Chancellor's desk. "Endymion, turn this place to ash."

A rancid sheet of fuzzy yellow fungus spread out of Endymion's hooves and slithered across the floor and walls of the atrium. The Chancellor's gungy magicore leaped into the air, hurling itself at Endymion's head. When it made contact, it wrapped itself around Endymion's muzzle. The doomicorn brayed and tossed his nose, throwing the magicore off.

Meanwhile, the fungus advanced. One by one, the portraits of former chancellors rotted and fell off the walls. The Chancellor's desk became a mound of green fur. On the upper floors of the atrium, the balcony railings rusted and began to decompose. Black mushrooms popped up along the handrails like crows on a telephone wire.

Giverna's giant owl lifted its wings, and a blizzard of snowflakes blasted out from under its armpits. Giverna pointed out areas of fungus to target and the owl directed the snow there, trying to freeze the mould solid. Other conjurors used weaver magicores to create walls that could slow the fungus's progress; some directed flying magicores to dive-bomb Endymion with balls of fire. Eric sent Quasar zooming into the fray, blasting fungus with lightning bolts.

"I told you both to get behind a door!" he shouted at Bitsy and Kosh, who were watching the chaos unfold with awe. *"Now!"*

But Bitsy had other ideas. She couldn't just hide

away while her dad and the others were out fighting. She grabbed Kosh's arm and pulled him towards Brightbeam. "Come on, we've got to help."

They clambered onto their everwing's back and, with a flap of her massive wings, Brightbeam generated enough downforce to lift them into the air. As they wheeled towards the ceiling, Bitsy tried to come up with a plan. Apart from glowing feathers and a healing cocoon, she wasn't sure what Brightbeam's gifts were. "We need to extinguish that doomicorn," she said, rubbing Brightbeam behind the ears. "I don't know what your powers are, but can you give it your best shot?"

Brightbeam honked and swished her tail. They circled the ceiling and then dropped into a dive. Brightbeam's ribcage vibrated, sending tremors through Bitsy's legs.

Kosh juddered up and down. "What's she doing?"

"No idea!" Bitsy cried.

A high-pitched whistle emanated from Brightbeam's throat. She opened her jaws…

There was a flash of light and a brilliant-white laser beam fired out of Brightbeam's mouth.

It shot in a straight line towards Riddlejax and Endymion. Bitsy watched as, almost in slow motion, Riddlejax sensed the threat and dug his heels into Endymion's ribs. Just in time, the doomicorn brayed and vaulted to safety. The area it had been standing on exploded into smithereens as the laser ripped through it.

"Melasina didn't mention that everwings can fire lasers!" Kosh said breathlessly.

Bitsy wondered if Brightbeam's gift allowed her to control and generate light. That would explain the glowing feathers *and* the lasers. "A near miss, but let's try again!" Bitsy called, thankful she'd told Brightbeam to give it her best shot. She clenched her thighs as Brightbeam swung around, preparing for another attack.

"Look out!" Kosh cried, yanking on Bitsy's hood.

Bitsy stooped as something sailed over their heads. When she looked up, she saw that Endymion had fired a barrage of red saucer-shaped mushrooms towards them. One of them hit Brightbeam's tail and she grunted in pain.

The everwing's chest rumbled. She opened her mouth and sent another laser blast at Endymion. This time, it made target. Endymion brayed and staggered back, a sticky black wound in his flank. Brightbeam followed with another strike to the fungus carpet under Endymion's hooves. The laser beam hummed as it penetrated the fungus, which started to pulse with light. A second later, it ruptured into a thousand ugly chunks, leaving an area of clear marble below.

"Way to go, Brightbeam!" Kosh hollered.

But the attack only seemed to infuriate Riddlejax and Endymion. Roaring wildly, Endymion reared on his hind legs. There was a ground-trembling *boom* as he landed back down, propelling a two-metre wave of hissing, wriggling fungus ahead of him.

The effects were devastating. Giverna's snowflake-blasting owl and Chancellor Hershel's gloopy yellow magicore turned to farthingdust instantly. Quasar managed to zip over the fungus wall, only to be struck by a flying toadstool, which extinguished him a second later.

The remaining magicores retaliated, but Endymion deflected their strikes by launching more saucer-shaped mushrooms. Riddlejax stood on the doomicorn's back, waving his cane and directing each shot like an evil ringmaster. Protecting the gyrowheel, Eric retreated to the farthest point in the atrium. Sweat shone on his brow as his eyes darted around frantically. Bitsy desperately wished she could help him but didn't know what to do.

Brightbeam came to a stop in mid-air, beating her wings to keep the three of them hovering over the battlefield. "How are we going to win?" Kosh asked hollowly. "Endymion's really powerful, and even with Brightbeam's lasers, it's as if Riddlejax can predict an attack before it happens."

Bitsy couldn't bear to admit it, but Kosh was right. Many of the alliance conjurors already looked exhausted and their magicores were continuously being extinguished. It felt like the chances of defeating Riddlejax were quickly slipping away. "There must be something we can do to even the odds. Just think."

As she tried to devise a plan, Riddlejax signalled to three conjurors attacking from a balcony and Endymion dispatched a boulder-sized puffball towards them. The mushroom exploded in mid-air, spraying the trio with black spores. Coughing and choking, they fell to the ground as fungus infected their bodies.

Shouts of dismay rang out from the other alliance conjurors. "No!" Eric roared.

Bitsy tensed as Riddlejax's gaze landed on her dad. His lips curled into a greedy smile. "Over there, Endymion! He has the gyrowheel!"

Before Bitsy could react, Endymion hurled a mammoth puffball at her dad. Bitsy's heart stopped as she watched it fly across the atrium. It soared over Giverna's head and past the Chancellor's desk, heading straight for Eric…

But it never exploded.

Out of nowhere, an enormous purple grobble came hurtling through the air with its jaws open and swallowed the puffball whole. The grobble's cheeks bulged as it landed on all fours on the ground below. Its lips wobbled, and for a moment, Bitsy thought it might be about to vomit the puffball back up, but then it grinned and waddled off.

"Where did *they* come from?" Kosh asked happily.

"*Magicalia* said that grobbles have strong constitutions, but that's taking it to the extreme!"

Relief washed through Bitsy's chest. "A grobble is a hunter-type species, so…" Her voice faded as she noticed a dark opening in the far corner of the atrium – another exit from the root-network.

Shadows stirred within the hole. Figures appeared, dressed in rugged clothes, heavy boots and baseball caps. Some of them carried equipment – ropes, grappling hooks and net launchers – and *all* of them had magicores.

Bitsy gasped as a tall, raven-haired woman at the front stepped into the light of the atrium.

It was Melasina. And she'd brought the Hunter Guild!

The hunters scattered quickly and silently. They all looked healthy – including Melasina, whose jagged red spikes had disappeared from around her knees. Some clambered up to the next level of the atrium, while others crept around the edges, moving from shadow to shadow with their magicores. A scrawny boy carrying a floppy rucksack appeared at the back of the group and Bitsy's spirits lifted. It was Mateo. Brightbeam's cocoon must have worked.

The hunters worked as a team, attacking Riddlejax and Endymion with terrifying efficiency. Flying magicores moved in professional-looking attack formations, while those on the ground discharged multicoloured missiles or blasts of energy in organized waves. Conjurors swung across the atrium on ropes, releasing chemical-filled water balloons that burned away the doomicorn's fungus and filled the room with green-tinged gas.

Kosh shook Bitsy's shoulder. "We need to attack Endymion now, while Riddlejax is distracted."

"You hear that, Brightbeam?" Bitsy said. "Now's our chance. Charge up your most powerful blast and let's vanquish that doomicorn once and for all!"

Brightbeam hooted and swooped lower. Her feathers trembled, glowing ice white. Bitsy shaded her eyes as Brightbeam opened her jaws to reveal a tiny sun hovering between her lips. There was a clap of thunder and then … *zap!* A searing beam shot out of Brightbeam's jaws and struck Endymion in the face.

The atrium shook with the sound of the blast. Thick, black smoke clouded the air. Bitsy coughed and wafted it out of her face, trying to get a better view. "Can you see anything? Did we get him?"

"Over there!" Kosh pointed to a swirling mass of farthingdust, appearing through the smoke right where Endymion had been standing. "We did it!"

Bitsy punched her fists above her head. "Yes!"

As the last of Endymion's farthingdust vanished, the fungus smothering the conservatoire walls began to break up. The mould on the floor fizzled away like hundreds of dying firecrackers. Down below, Bitsy spotted Mateo cheering and pointing at Brightbeam.

But as the everwing lowered her and Kosh to the ground, she sensed something was wrong. The radiance of Brightbeam's feathers had dulled and her tail was hanging between her legs. Brightbeam touched down gently and exhaled through her nostrils as Kosh and Bitsy slid off her back.

"Brightbeam?" Bitsy said softly.

Kosh stroked Brightbeam's ribs. "Are you OK, girl?"

"Brightbeam!" Mateo cried, running over. He rubbed her nose tenderly, examining her face. "I don't think she has any energy left."

Brightbeam nudged Bitsy's cheek with the end of her snout, her blue eyes sparkling. She gave Kosh and Mateo a slobbery lick. She didn't need to talk for Bitsy to understand what she was saying.

It was *goodbye*.

A lump formed in Bitsy's throat. Brightbeam was an omega-level species. Without the gyrowheel, it was unlikely she and the others would ever be able to conjure her again.

Still, Bitsy could always hope.

Brightbeam faded away gracefully, her farthingdust swirling up to the domed ceiling like a spiral of autumn leaves.

Turning her attention back to the atrium, Bitsy saw

Mateo's sister hurrying towards them. Now completely visible, Esme was as tall and lean as Mateo, with a marathon runner's physique. She was dressed in a tight black T-shirt and cargo trousers, with a coil of rope slung over one shoulder.

"Did you spot Riddlejax?" Esme asked worriedly. "Nobody knows where he is. By the time the smoke had cleared, he'd vanished."

Mateo frowned. "Maybe he got caught in Brightbeam's laser? Either way, he can't have escaped; the Chancellor said she was going to lock down the conservatoire exits and both holes to the root-network have now closed."

Scanning the faces of the remaining conjurors, Bitsy shivered. "In that case, he must have shapeshifted. Is there anyone here now who wasn't here to begin with?"

The group's gaze moved slowly around the atrium. Endymion's assault had destroyed much of the building. Three balconies had collapsed; there were jagged cracks in the walls and debris covering the floor. Pockets of foul-smelling gas hovered in the air, the residue of decayed furniture. Most conjurors were trying to free those trapped under the rubble, although some had slumped to the floor, exhausted. Bitsy could hear shocked voices whispering Riddlejax's name. She spotted Giverna tending to the wounds of a man in red conjuring overalls while her dad talked urgently with the Chancellor.

"I've tallied all the hunters," Esme said. "Everyone who's here came from the barracks."

"Then Riddlejax must be masquerading as one of the alliance conjurors," Kosh deduced. "But I can't think who was present when we arrived. It all happened so fast; my memory is a blur."

"Mine too," Bitsy said. "Until everyone is pulled from the wreckage, no one will know for sure. I need to warn my dad – he's still got the gyrowheel."

Hurdling the rubble, she and the others raced towards Eric, who had now gathered with a group that included Hasim, Lars and the Chancellor. They all looked like they'd just lost in a game of elemental paintball. There were scorches on their overalls, sticky green goo splattered over their skin and icicles melting in their hair. Eric's glasses had smashed, Hasim's moustache had turned a bizarre shade of blue, and the Chancellor's pinstripe shirt was slashed and torn.

"...keep your wits about you," Hasim told everyone as Bitsy drew closer. "He's here somewhere."

Bitsy skidded to a stop beside her dad, and noticed Giverna walking towards the group. "Riddlejax shapeshifted into an alliance conjuror," Bitsy warned. "You have to be careful."

"I thought I told you and Kosh to stay hidden," her dad scolded, although he sounded more relieved than angry. He tightened his arm around the gyrowheel, stowed under his jacket. "Are you sure about Riddlejax?"

"Esme's accounted for all the hunters," Bitsy exclaimed. "That's how we know he's disguised as an alliance conjuror."

"Riddlejax could *be* Esme," the Chancellor remarked, throwing Mateo's sister a dubious glance. "Right now, everyone is a suspect."

"It might be prudent to lock the gyrowheel away until we've unmasked Riddlejax," Giverna suggested, brushing dust off her white overalls. "There's a clairvoyant supply vault on the fourth floor. It has a magi-woven lock – impenetrable without the right combination." She tapped a finger against her temple. "I'm still the only one who knows it."

Eric gave a curt nod. "Better there than under my jacket. Show me the way."

Although Giverna's plan sounded sensible, Bitsy wasn't confident it would work. If Mateo had stolen a pair of proxicups from a supply vault, surely Riddlejax could loot one too. She was about to voice her concerns, when a thought stopped her in her tracks.

Proxicups...

There were still two questions she had yet to answer about the last few days: how had Riddlejax learned the truth about her mum's notebook, and how had he and his chaos-conjurors tracked her and Kosh across London, Agra and Versailles? Mateo had said that if people drink from the same set of proxicups, they can locate each other using a special map – maybe that's what Riddlejax had been using to find them? She leaned into Mateo's ear and hissed, "What do proxicups look like?"

A wiggly line appeared on his forehead. "Erm, each set is slightly different, but they're always made of glass. They're shaped like chalices with weird markings on the sides."

Recognizing the description, Bitsy reeled. She and Kosh had been drinking from vessels just like that: the glass mugs in Giverna's kitchen.

Her heart thumped faster as her brain raced to understand. Giverna had insisted on giving them tea the morning they'd first met her and again last night. Each time, they'd drunk from the same set of mugs – or proxicups. Giverna must have been using the cups to follow them; that was how she'd found them yesterday in the root-network…

The truth hit Bitsy like a puffball to the face. Riddlejax had told them he'd recently found out where her mum's notes were hidden. Someone must have told him. And apart from Melasina and Bitsy's dad, Giverna was the only one who knew that information.

It was *her*. She was a chaos-conjuror.

An elbow dug into Bitsy's ribs, throwing her from her thoughts.

"Everything all right?" Mateo whispered. "Why did you want to know about proxicups?"

"I, uh..." Bitsy wobbled, feeling dizzy. She couldn't believe that Giverna had been lying all along, manipulating them to help Riddlejax. Giverna was supposed to be her mum's friend, someone Matilda had trusted enough to give a root-key to. As Bitsy's focus switched back to reality, she saw Giverna leading her dad and the gyrowheel away. "Dad, wait! Giverna's a chaos-conjuror!"

Eric stopped dead. *"What?"*

Bitsy swallowed as Giverna turned around. She felt sick for ever trusting her. "Giverna tricked Kosh and me into drinking from the same proxicups as her," she explained hurriedly. "She was telling Riddlejax our location – that's how he's been able to follow us. She's been working for him this whole time."

Giverna blinked, flabbergasted. "Bitsy, I'm not sure why you..."

"She *wants* Riddlejax to have the gyrowheel," Bitsy persisted. "That's why she suggested you store it in her supply vault."

Eric backed away from Giverna, staring at her like she was a ghost.

"Giverna?" the Chancellor asked suspiciously.

331

"What's Bitsy talking about?"

Giverna's eyes bounced from face to face, searching for someone to defend her. When no one spoke up, her expression slowly changed. The softness left her cheeks, her brow wrinkled, and her mouth twisted into a sneer. "I've served cosmotypicals for over forty years – nursing them, healing them, risking my life to save theirs – and what do I have to show for it? An ungrateful community, a house that's falling apart, arthritis in both knees and empty pockets. Being cosmodynamic shouldn't mean we have to live such thankless lives." She lifted her chin. "Riddlejax is trying to bring about change. He wants us to *thrive*; to use our magicores to become more powerful and prosperous. He will lead us into a new future where we are respected and revered."

"You mean *feared*," Eric said, his tone wary. "Feared and obeyed. That's what Riddlejax desires: to dominate everyone on this planet."

Giverna shook her head. "He wants to make things better for us. Please, Eric, you have to understand."

"How can you say that?" Bitsy cried. "Riddlejax is a murderer! It wasn't Melasina who caused my mum's car accident; it was *him*, shapeshifting as her."

Surprise flickered across Giverna's face, but her tone held firm. "Change requires taking difficult actions, Bitsy. When you and Kosh arrived on my doorstep on Saturday,

332

I contacted Riddlejax after speaking to the Alliance. He instructed me to send you back home so you would find his ransom note and set out hunting for the gyrowheel yourselves. After your trip to Agra, his instructions changed: he wanted your notebook. I was planning to steal it from you, but you slept with it under your pillow and snuck out of my house before I could." She sighed and shook her head. "I never wanted to put you in danger. That's why I tried to convince you to abandon your search for the gyrowheel. If only Matilda had trusted me enough to let me read her notebook, there would have been no need for you to be involved at all."

Bitsy's jaw moved up and down, but no words left her lips. She couldn't believe what Giverna was saying. Her mum had died trying to protect the gyrowheel, and now Giverna had betrayed her with this!

"I've heard enough," the Chancellor said, flaring her nostrils. She signalled to Hasim and Lars. "Take her to a cell. She and Clyde Hess can stand trial together."

Before Giverna could do anything to stop him, Hasim pulled her farthingstone chopstick out of her hair, instantly disarming her. As her silver waves fell to her shoulders, Lars produced a pair of strange metal handcuffs and fastened them around Giverna's wrists. They had to be magi-woven because they glimmered with tiny lines of light.

Giverna grumbled under her breath, futilely trying to pull her hands apart. As Lars and Hasim gripped her shoulders and pulled her away, her gaze flicked across the atrium towards a conjuror dressed in red overalls. Bitsy had seen Giverna tending to his wounds earlier.

He stood alone from everyone else, holding something against a wall. It wasn't until the wall's texture started to change that Bitsy realized what the something was. "That's *him*!" she gasped, pointing. "That's Riddlejax!"

Even though the conservatoire exits were locked, there was still one way out of the building: the root-network. Giverna must have slipped Riddlejax her or Eric's confiscated root-key while treating his injuries.

"Stop that imposter!" the Chancellor yelled, her voice echoing to the ceiling.

All around the atrium, conjurors sprang into action. Magicores appeared out of puffs of farthingdust; net launchers were triggered, and desperate shots were fired.

But they were all too late.

As conjurors dashed towards him from all angles, Riddlejax disappeared into the darkness of the root-network and the opening closed behind him.

25

There was an uneasy atmosphere in the atrium and it was nothing to do with the noxious fumes in the air. As the adult conjurors regrouped, Bitsy, Kosh and Mateo found a bench to sit on beside the Chancellor's desk.

"Esme looks so much better," Kosh said, fist-bumping Mateo's knee.

Mateo smiled. "Yeah, thank goodness. The cocoon worked straight away, just like it did with us, only faster. And there's still loads left over to heal the hunters in the other barracks and everyone here. When I told Melasina what had happened, she rounded up a group of hunters to come here immediately. She wanted to help."

"The alliance conjurors don't seem that appreciative," Kosh said, nodding at the atrium floor.

In front of them, the hunters either stood or sat on one side, talking or nursing their wounds. The alliance conjurors were doing the same, opposite. Although both groups threw each other wary glances, the alliance conjurors seemed angry. There were red faces and heated discussions within their ranks. The only person that moved between the two sides was Bitsy's dad.

"The Alliance should be grateful," Bitsy said. "Without the Hunter Guild, Riddlejax would have won this fight and taken the gyrowheel."

"What's happening with the gyrowheel?" Mateo asked, scratching the back of his neck.

"I think it should be used as Gilander Arkwright originally intended," answered a solemn voice beside them. Chancellor Hershel stepped out from behind her desk, cleaning her glasses. Although her strawberry-blonde bob was tangled with slime and dirt, she still looked elegant. She peered up at the lamp holder hanging from a rusted chain above her desk. "As long as we have proper security guarding the device, there's no reason we can't use it for initiate training."

Bitsy frowned at the lamp holder, realizing it must be where the gyrowheel was originally kept. Reflecting on what she'd read in her mum's notes, she decided that Gilander Arkwright would probably approve.

"You're not welcome here," a voice hissed suddenly.

An alliance conjuror pointed at Melasina. His face was almost as red as his overalls.

"You know the rules," he continued. "It's forbidden for a member of the Hunter Guild to step foot inside a conservatoire."

Melasina folded her arms. "Yes, but in the circumstances…"

Master Ollennu gave her a stern look. "It will be safer for everyone if you leave. Gather your things and go."

"You can't be serious!" Melasina protested. She turned in a circle, blinking at them all. "We *saved* you. You bunch of arrogant, ungrateful…"

Bitsy cringed as Melasina's temper got the better of her and she yelled several magicore-related insults at the alliance conjurors. She snatched her root-key from under her T-shirt and marched towards the nearest wall, her long leather jacket flapping behind her. The other hunters scowled bitterly before picking up their equipment and following suit.

"Never wanted to come here anyway," one of them grumbled.

Another tossed her net launcher angrily over her shoulder. "Complete waste of time."

A couple of the hunters' magicores huffed tetchily or flicked their tails as they walked off. Looking crestfallen, Eric hurried towards Chancellor Hershel.

"It's not right," Kosh said, keeping his voice low. "To come here and fight after everything they've been through – they should be celebrated as heroes."

Mateo scowled. "Nothing's ever going to change. This is the way it's always been."

Something tugged at Bitsy's heart as Melasina stormed past. There were bruises on her aunt's jaw and a cut on her lip. Her stubborn expression reminded Bitsy of how her mum used to look whenever she was trying to finish a story…

An impulse took hold of Bitsy and she scrambled atop the Chancellor's desk. "Wait! You're making a terrible mistake."

Her voice echoed like a bouncing ball around the atrium. The hunters paused. Murmured conversations fell silent. Everyone on both sides turned to look at her.

Heat prickled in Bitsy's cheeks. She cleared her throat, searching for the right words. Her mum wouldn't let this happen; it was precisely the kind of injustice she had fought against. Perhaps Bitsy could be the same voice of reason.

"Riddlejax has been using your prejudices against you," she said. She turned to Master Ollennu. "The more suspicious you are of each other, the easier you are to manipulate. Riddlejax fooled us all into thinking the Hunter Guild had kidnapped my dad, when in fact they'd just asked him for help. If you banish the hunters again, you're just letting Riddlejax win."

Master Ollennu adjusted his waistcoat. "Those are all valid points, but the issue is not that simple. The Hunter Guild is an organization of soldiers, spies and thieves. They are treated like outlaws because they break our laws. That is why we cannot trust them."

"But that's—" Bitsy bit back her frustration. If she was going to win this argument, she had to take a different angle. "Whatever you think of the Hunter Guild, they came here tonight to *help* you, even after you'd refused to help them. Those are the actions of a group of heroes if you ask me."

"Well, I..." Master Ollennu shuffled his feet.

"Our rules have existed for hundreds of years," a conjuror in green overalls piped up, "and for hundreds of years they've kept us safe."

Bitsy clenched her fists. "Well, for hundreds of years, Riddlejax has given you all the slip! It's entirely *because* the hunters are trained in espionage that they've discovered some of what he's been up to." She offered her aunt a thin smile. "You have to listen to Melasina. She wants to work *with* the Alliance to defeat Riddlejax."

"The number of chaos-conjurors is growing," Melasina warned, her tone serious. "Finding the gyro-wheel is only one of Riddlejax's schemes. His ultimate goal is to seize power in the world by using magicores as weapons – and we're the only people standing in his way. We'll be stronger if we fight him together."

"She's right," Eric said, stepping forward. "Besides, we've treated the Hunter Guild as our enemies for so long that we have forgotten who they are. They are our family, our friends and our colleagues."

Chancellor Hershel, who had been carefully watching everything, lifted her voice. "Riddlejax is still out there, and he won't stop. Let us consider defeating an old enemy with a new solution. I propose a meeting with six chairs around a table. Melasina, if you are prepared to talk to us, we will listen."

"I'll tell you what that sounds like to me," Melasina snapped, her face like stone. But then the corners of her mouth lifted. "Progress."

26

"This is it," Kosh said, rubbing his hands together before pressing the launch button on the Star Wars pinball machine. "This is going to be a new highest score. I can feel it!"

The machine made a comedic *boing* noise as a ball bearing fired up the ball shooter lane and dropped into play on the table. Mateo bounced up and down by Kosh's shoulder, encouraging him: "Come on, come on…"

Since Bitsy had last visited the Hunter Guild's barracks, the recreation room had been cleaned and reopened. She nosed around inside a cupboard above the sink. Apart from a torn packet of raisins and a handful of nuts, it was empty. "Looks like you need to go shopping, Aunt Melasina."

"On the contrary, those cupboards were full this morning," her aunt said, sitting on the sofa, anxiously tapping the heel of her boot. Her raven-black hair was brushed into an impressive quiff and she had swapped her usual T-shirt and combat trousers for a smart grey suit. "Most hunters are greedy and ambitious by nature, Bitsy. I expect everyone has stolen a personal supply of snacks and stashed them somewhere in their quarters."

Bitsy couldn't tell by her aunt's tone whether she disapproved. She shook her head as she joined her on the sofa. Her aunt had some ... questionable morals, but there were qualities about her that Bitsy could admire: a defiant spirit, courage and loyalty. She was looking forward to getting to know her better. "Are you nervous about what the Chancellor is going to say?"

It had been three days since Riddlejax had attacked the European Conservatoire. Talks had started between the Alliance and the Hunter Guild, but negotiations were slow. Having reconnected with the Elemental Guild, Bitsy's dad had decided to act as a brokering agent between the Alliance and Melasina. The Chancellor was visiting the Hunter Guild barracks today to discuss the prospect of accepting a hunter as a tutor at the conservatoire next term.

"Me? Nervous?" Melasina uncrossed and recrossed her legs. "Of course not. I put forward a solid proposal and I'm sure your father will have fought my corner."

"It would be so cool to be taught by a hunter," Mateo called over from the pinball machine. "The other initiates would love it."

Melasina chuffed. "Fingers crossed."

The pinball machine whirred and rattled as Kosh's ball bounced off bumpers and flippers. "NO!" He slammed his hand on the glass as a wipe-out sound played through the machine speakers. "I was so close!"

"Better luck next time," Melasina said, smirking. "You'll beat my score one day."

Just then, the door opened. Melasina sprang up as Chancellor Hershel, Master Ollennu and Eric filed in.

"Well?" Melasina asked, impatiently.

Chancellor Hershel steepled her fingers. "If, as promised, the Hunter Guild ceases all anti-alliance activity, then the conservatoire will be proud to welcome one hunter as a tutor next term. Their workshops will need to be supervised for the time being."

Rising to her feet, Bitsy squeezed Melasina's arm. "That's great news!"

"It's a start," Melasina sniffed, although Bitsy could tell by the line of her jaw that she was pleased.

"It was a tough negotiation, but we got there in the end," Eric summarized, shaking Melasina's hand. He nudged Bitsy's shoulder. "What about you? Have you made any progress with your decision?"

Bitsy stepped aside so Master Ollennu could reach Kosh and Mateo at the back of the room. Given the changes of the last few days, the Chancellor had decided to reissue Bitsy's dad with an invitation for Bitsy to take an official cosmodynamics test ... and enrol at the European Conservatoire this summer.

"Training to be a conjuror can be dangerous sometimes," Eric acknowledged nervously, "but it can also be fun. And if you become an initiate, you'll get the opportunity to experience everything that your mum and I did when we were growing up."

Bitsy shuffled her feet. "Are you ... happy for me to become a conjuror? After everything that's happened? After Mum?" The truth was that Bitsy desperately wanted to accept, but she didn't want to upset her dad.

Eric repositioned his glasses. "I expect if your mum were here, she and Melasina would both be telling me off for refusing your first invitation. She wanted this for you more than anything. She believed in the good you would do."

"*Really?*" Kosh blurted from the back of the room. "You're serious?"

"This is awesome!" Mateo cheered.

"What is it?" Bitsy asked, walking towards them.

Kosh held up a letter written on European Conservatoire headed paper. "I've been invited to take an official cosmodynamics test too, Bitsy! I'm going to be an initiate!"

Bitsy's jaw dropped. "That's … amazing!"

"We need to research where Koshan's cosmodynamics gene comes from," Master Ollennu explained, his fingers clasped across his green overalls. "But I've got a feeling he'll make an excellent conjuror. In my workshop on Saturday, Koshan managed to conjure a hix within a few minutes. Remarkable considering it was the first time he had conjured at all. That's the sort of talent we need."

"Are you going to accept?" Bitsy asked.

"Of course I am! Are you?"

Bitsy glanced back at her dad, who was smiling. She thought of all the amazing things she'd witnessed in the last four days and her heart filled with light. "Yes. I can't wait."

— NARPHIN —

ACKNOWLEDGEMENTS

I would like to thank Denise Johnstone-Burt and Megan Middleton, whose brilliant editorial contributions have made this book possible. Thank you also to the talented and hardworking team at Walker Books UK, including Ben Norland, Rebecca J Hall, Kirsten Cozens, Jenny Collins, Jill Kidson, Josh Alliston, Helia Daryani, Marina Rodrigues, Daniel Purvis, Aaliyah Riaz, Peter Smith, Ruth Evans, Karen Coeman, Lara Armstrong, Luca Di Cristofaro Alfaro, Sarah Parker, David McMillan, Ellie Milward, Faith Leung and Meera Santiapillai. I am grateful to David Wyatt for illustrating such a beautiful cover and for bringing so many magicores to life. Finally, a personal thank you to my amazing mum, my inspiring sister and my patient friends, who are the best support network a writer could ask for.

When Arthur, Ren and Cecily investigate a mysterious
explosion, they find themselves trapped in the year 2473.
Lost in the Wonderscape, an epic in-reality adventure
game, they must call on the help of some unlikely historical
heroes to play their way home before time runs out.

Arthur, Ren and Cecily are stuck in Legendarium in the
year 2493, where the secretive villain Deadlock has discovered
dangerous time-travel technology. To save the universe, the
friends must enter the deadly Irontide Tournament, where legends
are real and one wrong move could cost them their lives...

— RUMBLEPLUME —